Black Fire

STEVE BROWN

Black Fire

CHICK SPRINGS PUBLISHING

TAYLORS, SOUTH CAROLINA

© 2000 Steve Brown
Cover design © 2000 Boulevard Productions

First published in the USA in 2000 by
Chick Springs Publishing
PO Box 1130, Taylors, SC 29687
e-mail: ChickSprgs@aol.com

Text design/composition by Mary Lou Nye
Cover design by Boulevard Productions
Printed in the United States by Baker Johnson

Library of Congress Catalog Card Number:
99-96202
Library of Congress Data Available

ISBN: 0-9670273-2-2

Dedication

For Margaret Olivia Ingram of Montgomery, Alabama, and Vernon Stevens Brown of Framingham, Massachusetts, who fought the War Between the States every day, thereby creating one hell of an interesting family to grow up in.

Acknowledgments

*T*his book was edited by Skye Alexander, was typeset by Mary Lou Nye, and the art work was produced by Matt McCoy. Mark Brown, Phil Bunch, and Bill Jenkins proofread the manuscript.

This author would like to also thank all those people, over the years, who have discussed with him the political, social, and economical aspects of the American South, and, of course, Mary Ella.

Tell me about the South.
What's it like there?
What do they do there?
Why do they live there?
Why do they live at all?

William Faulkner
ABSALOM, ABSALOM!

Chapter One

The night someone tried to burn down the Shiloh AME Church, Wheeler Adams was installing a new bay window that would overlook the yard behind the Big House. Through the new window Adams' housekeeper would be able to see the garden and barn and to make sure the chores were being done. Nell believed if she didn't keep an eye on Adams, he might slip off down to the river and go fishing. And he just might. Adams had a new eight-and-a-half-foot, five-weight, Winston graphite fly rod. Intent on her supervising, Nell didn't see the orange glow off in the night sky.

Nell was a skinny black woman with a streak of gray wandering through hair which she pulled back into a bun. She was small of frame and had a lantern jaw. Over forty years ago she'd been hired as the Adams' nanny. Outnumbered four to one by the

Adams' children, Nell favored a switch, something sorely lacking when it came to Adams' own daughter, a seventeen-year-old who was spending the Fourth of July weekend in the country with her father.

Savannah stood beside Nell, her arms crossed. She had her mother's dark blue eyes and auburn hair, and Adams' lanky frame. "Other parents let their kids out at night, Daddy."

Adams said nothing. He was well over six feet tall, deeply tanned, and in almost as good shape as he'd been when he'd played ball at Georgia; but he was no match for his daughter.

"I used to drive the pickup when I lived out here, even the tractor. Anyway, I just want to run into town and see what's going on." But the teenager was going nowhere. The last time she had taken the pickup out for a spin, Savannah had been caught drag racing by the Chick County sheriff.

"Savannah," Nell said, "it's after ten. Jest where were you planning on going at this hour?"

"Oh—to see someone."

"Who?"

"Really, Nell, it's none of your business."

"Yes, it is, girl, long as you're here at the Springs."

"Nell, I was talking to my father."

Adams picked up another screw and fastened it to the bit, forcing the screws into shims and through the rough opening. "Perhaps you should reconsider where you live, Savvy."

His daughter shook a finger at him. "Don't go there, Daddy! Whenever my friends ask me why you and Mother don't live together, I tell them you have to live out here to take care of the Springs." The teenager looked through the new window and beyond the gardener who stood on a ladder and assisted from the outside. Behind the elderly black man was a one-acre garden lit by an arc light. "Not that you do much of that."

Savannah was referring to the fact that ten thousand acres might make up Chick Springs Plantation, but her father and the few people who lived here did little more than subsistence farming. And the house in which the bay window was being installed was a fifteen-thousand-square-foot antebellum monster situated on a low hill overlooking acres and acres of South Georgia farmland. In theory, Adams was the master of all he surveyed; in practice it was quite another thing.

Nell raised her voice over the whine of the drill. "Girl, you are jest too judgmental for your own good."

Savannah sniffed. "I think for myself, Nell. My father taught me to do that." Then a change of tone for her father, "It's really the pits to be stuck out here if you can't go anywhere."

"Why, girl," Nell said, "you used to love living here. Your horse is still in the barn, though you ain't been riding him much."

Savannah tossed her head. "I'm more into cars these days, Nell, but I'll drive a pickup when I'm desperate." The drill stopped again, and what the teenager said next proved her father wasn't the only one using a sharply pointed instrument. "Mother sees other men when she's in town, Daddy."

Adams didn't appear to hear her, the key to survival for any Southern male.

"Mother says you're pigheaded about living out here. Nana thinks so, too."

Roosevelt, on the other side of the glass, looked away. The elderly black man wore a Braves baseball cap, overalls, and was amazed that windows came in boxes; he remembered when they'd been built from scratch.

"It's hard to explain," continued Savannah, "that your parents are married but don't live together."

"Mister Wheeler," said Roosevelt, "you better come out here and take a look at this."

"In a minute," said Adams, fitting another screw into the bit. "I don't want to lose this thing."

Roosevelt pointed in the direction of the county seat, leaving a hand and his face holding the window in place. Roosevelt didn't trust brackets. It wasn't natural for a window to be hung this way. "Look at that."

Adams was bent over inside the bay. Now he looked in the direction the gardener pointed.

"Ain't that the church?" asked Roosevelt.

Nell shouldered Adams out of the way and leaned into the convex shape. "Oh, Lordy, Wheeler, it is! There ain't nothing between here and Lee's Crossroads but the church."

"Roosevelt," said Adams, putting down the drill, "get the hose, ax, and fire extinguisher from the barn."

"Yes, sir." The elderly black man stepped down from the ladder. Immediately the bay sagged. So much for brackets.

On his way out of the house Adams stopped at the back door to activate the security alarm—which was on a three-minute delay to allow people to leave the

Springs. "Nell, bring the portable and call Bobbie Lee. Savannah, you stay here."

Adams went through the mud room, down the steps, and into the backyard. He climbed into the pickup, found the keys in the ignition, and cranked the engine. As he did his daughter ran around to the other side, opened the door, and climbed in.

"Savvy, I told you to stay here."

"Don't be silly, Daddy. That's my church, too."

Nell followed the teenager into the cab, shoving Savannah over and closing the door behind her. When Adams backed the pickup around to the mouth of the barn, Roosevelt threw a thick, black hose in the bed, followed by a fire extinguisher and an ax, then climbed in after them.

"Hurry, Wheeler," said Nell. "Hurry."

"Just make that call, Nell."

The truck jerked forward, causing Roosevelt to lose his balance and sit down in the remains of the last load—in this case, hay. Roosevelt was lucky this hadn't been the week to muck out the stables.

Inside the cab Nell fussed at the phone. "What's Bobbie Lee's number? I can'ts remember."

"Speed-dial one."

Nell punched in the number while Savannah held onto the dash. In the rear Roosevelt gripped the side of the bed as the pickup raced across the gravel turn-around in front of the Big House and down the dirt road between the cedars. As they approached the gate, Savannah touched a remote on the passenger-side visor and the metal gate swung open. And the girl had to punch at the remote several times to hit it. Her father was driving faster than she'd ever seen before and the road was seriously potholed. The potholes didn't bother her father. Adams didn't care much for visitors.

"Bobbie Lee's on the way," said Nell, turning off the phone. "Lelia Plummer done called her already."

At the county highway the pickup made a wide arc and the wheels ran off the road. This caused Roosevelt to lose his grip and slide across the bed, thumping into the cab along with the hose, ax, and fire extinguisher.

"Still with us, Roosevelt?"

"So far, Mister Wheeler."

A mile down the blacktop they turned onto the state highway and headed toward the county seat. Even with the windows down everyone began to sweat. It was August-hot, although this was only the first of July. The night was dark, thick with humidity, and in the distance they could see that yellow glow—a bright yellow light at the end of a tunnel giving scant hope.

"What if Bobbie Lee doesn't get there in time?"

Adams patted his daughter's knee. "She will, Savvy. She will." He glanced at his housekeeper. Nell didn't look so confident. Not only did the volunteers have to be rounded up, but the fire truck was housed on the other side of the county. Savannah bit a nail while Nell said a prayer. The pickup raced down the highway.

The Shiloh AME Church sat in the middle of a gravel horseshoe: a wood frame building with no windows at the front as the congregation had tired of panes being knocked out by vandals. A long row of windows on the sides, covered by shutters and locked from inside, plus a series of overhead fans cooled the interior. The new addition at the rear had been built with its roof lower than that of the original auditorium to allow for windows over the sanctuary. Morning services could be quite a sight with all that sunlight streaming in.

As the truck pulled into the parking lot, Roosevelt spoke through the sliding glass window in the rear of the cab. "I've got the hose ready, Mister Wheeler."

"Give it to Nell. She can hook it up while I'm using the extinguisher on the doors."

And Nell was raring to go—until the pickup slid to a stop in the parking lot. The sight of the vestibule doors in flames stunned her. And broke her heart. This wasn't just any church on fire here. This was the first place black people had felt free to speak their minds in Chick County. All the pennies, dimes, and dollars that had gone into keeping up this . . . shrine. That's what it was, a shrine to the Lord, and to their ancestors. At least to their ancestors' hard work.

"Nell, you've got to get moving."

The elderly black woman nodded, then fumbled her way out of the truck. Taking the hose from Roosevelt, Nell stumbled around the front of the pickup, unable to keep her eyes off the flames. She headed for a huge oak at the side of the church where parishioners almost came to blows over who'd park in its shade during the dog days of summer. Under the oak was a faucet. In the bed of the pickup Roosevelt stood up, looking for anyone lurking in the graveyard or running across the field on the far side of the road. He saw no one.

Extinguisher in hand, Adams headed for the fire.

"Stay in the truck, Savvy, and this time I mean it."

"Be careful, Daddy." The girl bit another nail and stared at the blaze. The whole building appeared to be on fire.

As her father strode over to the doors, the blaze ignited the hollies on either side and flames began crawling up the front of the building. Adams opened up with the extinguisher and it quickly foamed out, having little effect. He cursed, dropped the empty canister to the ground, and headed for the faucet.

More cars and pickups arrived; people piled out with buckets and hoses in their hands. All were from Creekside, the black community. Most were elderly, many wearing clothing over pajamas and gowns. Some used canes. One was even on a walker. Off in the distance a siren could be heard.

"Where's the preacher?" asked Nell as Adams took the hose from her.

No one knew.

"Where's Lelia and Minny?" asked Nell.

Everyone looked around, studying those next to them, then staring at the fire, first with a dazed look, then with growing horror.

"Oh, Lordy."

Nell gripped Adams' shoulder. The white man was bent over, connecting the hose to the faucet.

"Wheeler, there's people inside."

Adams straightened up and stared at the fire. The rapidity of the flames' climb told him an accelerant had been used. Flames were reaching for the roof and the cross mounted up there.

"It's Saturday night," explained Nell. "Lelia Plummer and Minny Jackson are pulling guard duty."

Behind them a black sports car slid to a stop and a teenager leaped out, leaving the door ajar. He was a caramel-colored young man wearing a tee shirt, jeans, and a backwards baseball cap. "Miss Nell, have you seen my grandmother?" It was Gary Plummer.

"Mister Wheeler, you might need this," said Roosevelt, holding out the ax. Adams snatched the ax out of the elderly man's hand and disappeared around the side of the building.

"Daddy!" Savannah flung open the door of the pickup and ran after him. So did Nell and Gary Plummer. At the rear of the church they found Adams going at a door with the ax.

Nell's hand rose to her throat. "The door's locked?"

Sweat ran down Adams' face and arms. He gripped the ax firmly so it wouldn't slip away from him. "Front door on fire . . . back door locked? Doesn't make . . . sense."

"Did you check the door?"

"I said it was locked, Nell!"

"Is there any heat? Remember what the volunteers taught us."

Adams stopped in mid-swing, then nodded. "You're right." He touched the door. "No heat."

"Thank God." The fire guards might still be alive, just overcome by smoke.

Gary Plummer was doing a jig, like a little boy who needed to pee. "Hurry, hurry!" he said. When the door splintered, he muttered, "Thank you, Jesus." As it fell to pieces he dashed inside but was driven back by the smoke. He staggered away, coughing. Others joined him.

Adams covered his nose and mouth and reached

inside, flipping the light switch. Amazingly, the lights came on, and when he stepped back to clear his throat, the others peered down the murky hallway. To the left were the rest rooms; to the right, a storage room, then a larger room where Sunday School was taught and the choir practiced Thursday nights. But with all the smoke you could see none of that.

"Minny!" yelled Nell. "Lelia—you in there?"

No answer from inside the building.

Nell coughed. "I don'ts know, Wheeler. Looks pretty bad in there."

Roosevelt joined them. He held a flashlight, a small can of fire extinguisher, and a bucket of water with a red bandanna floating inside. "I moved your truck, Mister Wheeler, or that pumper is gonna run over it for sure."

"Thank you."

Adams leaned the ax against the church, then fished the bandanna from the bucket and wrapped the cloth around the lower part of his face. The small extinguisher he hooked to his belt.

"I need something," said Plummer, referring to Adams' bandanna and light. "Get me something!" The boy was doing that jig again. The kid just couldn't stand still.

Adams said, "Gary, you'd better let me check this out first."

"Daddy, why can't you wait for Bobbie Lee?"

Her father gestured at the sky before taking the bucket from Roosevelt. In the distance you could hear the sound of the approaching siren. "Bobbie Lee's still a good five minutes away."

Adams held the bucket over his head, and after dousing himself with water, returned the bucket to Roosevelt. Flipping on the flashlight, he took a breath and plunged inside.

He glanced inside the rest rooms, then gave more attention to the storage room. In that room water ran into an over-sized sink; mops and brooms sat alongside a heavy steel bucket and shelves ran the length of the room. Those shelves were filled with detergent, toilet paper, and farther down, blankets.

Adams pushed on through the smoke and into the Sunday School room: a large room separated by dividers decorated with scenes from the New Testament. Fluorescent lights burned overhead, but they were of little help. Working his light around, Adams saw neither woman, but he could tell they had camped here. Soft drink cans and several baggies littered child-size chairs. On one chair lay a cell phone.

Plummer joined Adams, a wet blanket over his shoulders, a towel held to his face. "My grandmother?"

"Probably in the auditorium."

"I told her not to do this thing."

"Gary, the elders told the fire guards not to try to put out any fire."

But Plummer was gone, looking for a way into the auditorium. Chairs were knocked aside, dividers fell over, and the piano made an out-of-tune sound as the young man banged into it, unable to see in the smoke.

"Over here, Gary!" Adams stood at a small door leading into the sanctuary, the only access between the auditorium and the new addition.

With Adams going first the two men hustled up a

set of short steps that came out behind a staggered row of pews and a wrought-iron railing that separated the choir from the congregation. They could see where the flames had burned into the vestibule, then been channeled to the ceiling and its overhead beams. From those beams hung fans and the auditorium's lights: rectangular-shaped canisters crafted out of copper with small crosses on all four sides. Flames cast strange shadows across the pews and down an aisle running the length of the auditorium.

Adams thought he saw something at the end of the aisle and was moving toward it when he stumbled over . . . Lelia Plummer.

"Maw-Maw." Plummer shoved the white man out of the way. Next to the unconscious woman lay an empty bucket and a pool of water.

Plummer scooped up his grandmother and headed for the door. As he turned around, the blanket fell from his shoulders and he clunked the woman's head into a choir pew. Then he raced through the small door, down the stairs, and into the smoky darkness.

Outside, Gary ignored questions about his grandmother, along with those about Adams and Jackson. "I told her not to do this thing. I told her not to," he muttered to himself.

"Call EMS!" Nell hollered after the boy. "Minny might need it."

Savannah stepped toward the smoking door. "Daddy, please come out of there!"

"This ain't right," said Nell, shaking her head. "At the first sign of trouble, them guards was 'pose to call Bobbie Lee, then git out of there."

Roosevelt nodded. The phone call was to make the

guards stop and think—and remember that the arsonist might still be around, making sure his fire took. But the fire had been started at the front of the church. Why?

Inside the auditorium Adams picked up Plummer's blanket, threw it over his shoulder, and headed down the aisle. In light from the flames he saw the large form of Minny Jackson lying in front of the burning doors.

"Mrs. Jackson, get away from that door!"

The woman did not move or answer him. As Adams stumbled in her direction, one of the lamps lost its grip on an overhead beam and crashed into the pews. In the parking lot someone shouted how best to attack the fire. The volunteers had arrived and were going to shoot a stream of water through the vestibule. When they did, those doors would certainly collapse on Jackson.

Adams yelled for them to hold up and for his trouble got a mouthful of smoke. Smoke was everywhere, rolling off the ceiling, pushing down in black balls, looking for new victims. The front of the building was completely engulfed in flames. So were Jackson's feet.

Adams coughed, then put down his light, grasped the heavy woman under the arms, and pulled her out of the flames. From his belt he unsnapped the fire extinguisher and sprayed foam over Jackson's feet and lower legs. His head ached, tears blurred his vision, and for the life of him he could not stop coughing. And it was hot. The hair on his arms was gone, the skin dry enough to cook.

Tossing away the empty can, Adams threw the

blanket over the woman. He was brushing a piece of smoldering wood off when someone on the other side of the burning doors shouted "Ready!"

Adams started pulling Jackson down the aisle, but he wasn't quick enough. When the water hit the doors the people outside let out a cheer; inside the doors exploded down the aisle like Fourth of July fireworks.

Adams threw himself behind a pew, then quickly returned to the aisle where he jerked the blanket off Jackson, along with several pieces of burning wood. Her body lay in a puddle of water. Standing up and waving his hands overhead to catch the attention of the firemen, Adams was hit by a stream of water from the fire hose which knocked him to the floor. Stunned, he could only sit there and watch the flames engulf the roof as the hose was worked around the auditorium and the overhead lamps dropped to the floor. One landed where Jackson had once lain. That was enough to get Adams moving. He grasped Jackson under the arms again and started pulling the woman toward the sanctuary.

It was tough going. Adams' every move was labored and he couldn't stop coughing. The water soaked him but did nothing for the smoky buildup, perhaps even made it worse. Another lamp crashed into the pews. Left, right, ahead of them; at this point, Adams didn't know or care. For some reason the room was growing darker. Was that right? There were all these flames.

Trudging along, one step at a time, and struggling with Jackson's heavy body, Adams bumped into the steps leading to the sanctuary. He lost his hold on Jackson and sat down hard. He could see the volunteers on the other side of the flames, less than a hundred feet away. It would be so easy to just sit here and wait for them. Ludicrous, too.

Gripping the wrought iron railing, Adams pulled himself to his feet and teetered over Jackson. The woman lay at his feet somewhere, in the haze below. He was dragging the unconscious woman toward the door at the rear of the sanctuary when the water hit him again, knocking him back. Adams lost his grip on Jackson, slid down the stairs into the Sunday School room, and passed out.

Chapter Two

By the time the Volunteer Fire Department arrived the front of the church was completely engulfed in flames. The young woman driving the pumper threw open her door and climbed down. The heavy rubber boots she wore made that rather tricky. Bobbie Lee was already suited up. So was Ernie Ellis, who got down from the passenger seat and went around to uncoil the hose. The pumper carried 750 gallons and could put water on a blaze in less than a minute. That is, if the civilians didn't get in the way, and that's just what they did now. Several old women surrounded the white girl as she climbed down, preventing Lee from joining Ellis at the hose. When told there were people still inside the building, Lee turned and stared at the fire.

"You're shitting me."

The black women insisted they were telling the truth; one of them scolded Lee to watch her language, that this was a church on fire here.

Bobbie Lee was a tall, skinny woman, who, under her fire suit and coveralls, was covered from head to toe with freckles. Her red hair was pulled back into a ponytail. Her hands were greasy from running the local junkyard. Lee could fix just about anything and that's why the men let her ride along.

Her partner was at the rear of the truck, uncoiling the hose with another white guy who'd followed the pumper over in his pickup. Quickly, they and some of the male members of the congregation laid out the hose, hooked it up, and started the pump. And just as the volunteers bragged, less than a minute after they arrived, a stream of water blasted through the front doors. A cheer went up from the congregation.

Good luck, thought Ellis, gripping the hose that had come alive in his hands. These old wooden buildings were the worst. Finally, Bobbie Lee showed up.

"Where you been?" Ellis asked. If the gal wanted to drive the truck, the least she could do was help out.

Lee held a lamp, hatchet, and her breathing apparatus. "Wheeler's inside." She put down the lamp and hatchet to swing the tank up on her back. Nobody in his right mind ate smoke these days.

"You're kidding me," Ellis said. The guy who'd followed them over was busy suiting up and the hose was all Ernie's. Sweat ran down Ellis' face, soaking the clothing inside his yellow suit.

"I'm going around back," said Lee, fastening the harness across her chest. "They say there's a door back there."

"Wait. One of us will come with you."

Lee shook her head. "Let me make sure there's people in there first. None of the rest of the building's on fire. Looks like a smoke problem, if anything."

Lee picked up the hatchet and lamp and disappeared around the corner. As she made the turn she ran into one of the black kids who played on the Legion baseball team: that quick colored kid at shortstop. In his arms was an old woman, or a sack of clothing.

"Need any help there?"

All Lee heard was, "I told her not to do this thing. I told her." Then the young man hurried across the parking lot toward a black sports car.

"Miss Bobbie Lee?"

Lee turned around to face the gardener from Chick Springs.

"Mister Wheeler's still in there," Roosevelt said. "Minny Jackson, too."

Lee slapped the old man on the back and set him shuffling toward the front of the building. "Then get some people back here! Tell Ernie to shut down the hose if he has to."

"Yes, ma'am."

At the rear of the building Lee found Adams' daughter and his housekeeper.

Savannah wrung her hands. "Bobbie Lee, Daddy's in there." The girl pointed at the entrance where smoke poured out, causing anyone who ventured close enough to cough.

"He went in to get Minny," added Nell.

Lee fitted her mask over her face, turned on the

oxygen, and flicked on the lamp. The breathing apparatus, much like a miniature scuba tank, gave her up to thirty minutes of air, depending on how she used it. Then she stepped inside the doorway and made her way down the hall. After a glance in the utility room and bathrooms, she moved into the Sunday School room and worked her beam around.

Bobbie Lee wasn't all that familiar with the layout of this, or any other church for that matter, and smoke—well, there was plenty. Not like on TV where you could see the actors. In a real fire smoke was the enemy, sometimes the killer.

At the rear of the room she found the small door and where Adams lay, after sprawling through it. Just inside the sanctuary was the dark form of an old, fat, colored woman. Putting down her lamp and hatchet, Lee grabbed Adams under the arms and dragged him out of the doorway. As she did she knocked over a partition with a poster featuring Jesus walking on water.

"Sorry, Wheeler," she said, though the man was unconscious, "the one who's been in here the longest has to be first one out."

Lee took a pillow from the seat of the piano and left it under Adams' head and focused the lamp on him. After that she returned to Minny Jackson, got her hands under the heavy woman, and started dragging her across the floor.

And she were a load! Children's chairs were bumped aside; a partition fell over. Slowly but surely, Lee moved toward the hallway leading out of the building.

"Let me give you a hand there," said a voice behind her, a voice like James Earl Jones'. A huge fellow, the preacher towered over Lee with nothing over his face. That was nuts. Maybe the fool was expecting divine intervention.

"Get Wheeler!" Lee shouted through her mask. As the preacher started away, she called after him, "Look for the light! Near the door going into the . . ." The what? What was the front part of a church called? It couldn't all be sanctuary. Oh, well, the preacher knew where he was going. After all, it were his church.

At the back door Roosevelt took an arm of the unconscious woman and helped drag Jackson through the grass, over among the picnic tables.

Savannah was wide-eyed, gulping air, and close to hyperventilating. "My . . . my daddy?"

Lee ripped off her mask and turned off the oxygen. "The preacher's got him. EMS?" She looked up at the black faces.

"Dr. Nance is on his way," said Nell.

Lee nodded. "Roosevelt, there's blankets on the truck. Would you . . . ?"

But the elderly man had plunged back into the building. Another dumb move. The preacher had Wheeler.

"How's Minny?" asked Nell, kneeling down beside the unconscious woman.

"Still with us," said Lee, touching the unconscious woman's throat.

Gripping Jackson's hand, Nell said, "Thank the Lord."

Roosevelt was coughing as he stumbled out of the building. He handed a blanket to Bobbie Lee and bent over, trying to clear his lungs.

Lee covered the woman with the blanket. There

wasn't much light and the woman's skin was dark, but Lee had the distinct feeling Jackson's feet had suffered third degree burns. She could smell the charred flesh. Lee unhooked the radio at her hip and radioed EMS. She told the driver where they were, the condition of those still here, and that one victim was en route to the hospital.

The preacher was coughing and dragging Adams across the Sunday School room when Ernie Ellis appeared out of the darkness. Ellis wore the same yellow suit and breathing apparatus as Bobbie Lee. Together, the two men hauled Adams out of the church and among the picnic tables where a small crowd had gathered. Like Roosevelt, the preacher stumbled off, coughing and gasping for air.

The moment the men stepped back from Adams, Savannah threw herself across his body. "Daddy!" When she didn't get the response she wanted, she looked up. "Do something, Bobbie Lee! He's not breathing."

Lee touched Adams' throat. "He is, too, Savannah. Now calm down."

"Then why won't he wake up?"

"Savannah, he's just fine. The smoke got to him, that's all."

"Then wake him up!"

Lee frowned, then fitted her mask over Adams' face. She didn't want a fight with this brat. There were more important things to be done.

It felt like someone was smothering him . . . biting into the sides of his face. Adams fought with whatever had him by the face and with those who held him down. His head hurt, his lungs burned, and when he opened his eyes he was looking through a plastic shield. People leaned over him, peering down at him. He recognized the one holding the mask to his face: Bobbie Lee.

Adams pushed the mask away, then coughed. "Mrs. Jackson . . . ?"

Lee stuck the mask over his face again. "Shut up, Wheeler, and take some more air. Nell's on her way to the hospital with Jackson. She took Savannah. Had to. Girl was driving me nuts."

Again Adams pushed away the mask. "The Plummers . . . ?"

"Who? Oh, the shortstop. Threw his grandma in his car and took off with her—is what I heard."

"Are they going to be all right?"

"Ask this fellow here." Lee gestured at the black man standing over them. It was Edward Nance, the doctor for the black community.

"Can't say, Wheeler," answered the doctor. "I really need to get into Lee's Crossroads and make sure both women are properly cared for. I just stayed behind to make sure you didn't need to make the same trip. Promised Savannah I would."

The white man slapped the black one on the leg. "Then go! Go!" Adams knew as well as Nance that many a black person had died waiting for treatment in some white man's emergency room.

"I'd like to see you at the ER, Wheeler."

"Okay . . . " He coughed. "Just go!"

As he walked away, a couple of young black men took the doctor by the arm, offering to run interference for him. "Just take it easy with your driving, boys," Nance said. "We don't need to be stopped by any cracker cops tonight."

With Lee's help Adams sat up and looked around. Down the side of the church he could see the parking lot was full—so many vehicles you couldn't see the far side of the highway. More of the congregation had arrived: oldest first, then middle-aged, but few young people. Young people generally dated outside Chick County to avoid being hassled by any number of law enforcement types. They would probably show up a good bit later.

Adams used a picnic bench to help him stand, then leaned on Lee as they made their way toward the front of the church.

"You know, Wheeler, you're getting heavier and heavier in your old age."

"Has anyone . . . ?" He coughed. "Has anyone called the sheriff?"

He could see the answer to that on the faces of the black people standing under the oak tree. Nobody thought anyone was going to investigate the burning of any black congregation's church, certainly not in Chick County.

The volunteers were soaking the remains of the church. The altar, pulpit, and choir pews had been spared. On the altar stood a gold cross sheltered by the shell created by the remaining roof and the jagged walls on each side. Rafters, roofing, and beams lay in a jumble across pews, along with copper lamps and metal ceiling fans. One or two fans had landed so their blades, seen over the pews, seemed to be signaling for help. When the water hit the altar, the cross was knocked back, then to one side, and finally washed off the altar.

A sigh passed among the people under the oak. Women clutched each other. Men put arms around their women and held them, then wiped tears away with the backs of their hands. Moaning turned into singing. Many joined in.

Bobbie Lee said, "We got here as soon as we could, Wheeler."

Adams put an arm around the skinny woman and gave her a sideways hug as they walked over to the pumper. "I don't think anyone can fault you."

Glancing at the people under the tree, she said, "I would—if I were them."

"Bobbie Lee, it's hard to save these old wooden structures. The original church, the front half, has been here over a century."

"We should've done better."

"It was the civilians," said Ernie Ellis, putting away equipment at the rear of the pumper. The young man's mask hung down from his neck and sweat ran down his face, streaking places where smoke had stained it. "We had to get the civilians out first."

"And thank you for that, Ernie."

"Just doing my job, Wheeler."

Seeing Ellis reminded Adams that he was sweating again. And it was good to be able to breathe, without coughing. "Bobbie Lee, how'd I get out of the building?"

The skinny woman gestured at a large black man sitting on the tailgate of Adams' truck. "The preacher done it, Wheeler. Now, if you don't mind, I need to tend to my volunteers."

As she left him, Adams joined the preacher at the rear of the pickup, its tailgate pointed at the ruins of the church. Charley Morton was a middle-aged man with a neatly trimmed beard, most of that beard gone gray. There was very little neck between his square head and the massive shoulders Morton had used to move defensive linemen out of the way before someone had fallen across his left leg, snapping it at the knee. Now the preacher walked with a limp. Tonight he wore jeans over pajama bottoms, the tops of pj's, and a pair of running shoes. A shovel lay at his feet.

Morton was a proponent of "cumulative voting" where voters can split their votes among candidates of the local school board, or county council, or give all their votes to one candidate. If a black man wanted to hold office in places like Chick County it was the only solution, because black people were scattered all over the place and there was no way demographers could draw up an all black seat. Cumulative voting, however, wasn't what they talked about behind the preacher's back. It was the other baggage Charley Morton had brought to Chick County.

"Thanks for pulling me out of the fire, Charley."

"Just evening up the ledger some."

The white man took a seat beside one of the few men who made him appear small and the two of them sat there, staring at the smoldering remains. The air was thick with humidity, the sound of equipment being stowed away, and men more chatty than usual. The volunteers were pleased that none of their unit had been injured or overcome by smoke, not to mention the heat of a July night.

"Where did we go wrong?" asked Morton.

"Those women shouldn't have been allowed to be fire guards."

"Yeah—right," grunted Morton. "We tried to tell them that. It didn't take." The preacher continued to stare at what was left of his church. "I wonder if we'll ever know who did it."

"The GBI will be called in."

"White men."

"You could request the FBI."

"More white men." Morton shifted his heavy bulk off the tailgate and the rear of the truck rose a couple of inches. "Might make people feel better if they knew what we were going to do tomorrow." He left, limping over to his congregation.

Bobbie Lee rejoined Adams, handing him a tube of salve. Adams lifted the cuffs of his pants and applied the ointment, getting a good bit of the gooey stuff on a pair of jeans which were soiled and burned. Lee gestured with her head toward the highway.

"Look what the cat drug in."

Parked on the other side of the highway was a line of vehicles with men and boys leaning against them. Pickups had rifles hung across rear windows, and if you looked closely, you could see barrels of shotguns against the inside of doors, sticking out of open windows.

Lee said, "If Junior Bennefield isn't among that group, I don't know who is."

"Heard Junior got thirty days for brawling."

"Not if the judge had anything to say about it." Junior Bennefield's father ran Chick County.

"This was down Wallace County way."

The freckled-faced woman grinned. "Well, down there somebody just might have a chance of holding the bastard the full thirty." She looked in the direction of the county seat. "The sheriff should be here by now . . . ."

But Adams had sprung off the tailgate, forced the tube of salve into Lee's hands, and headed for Charley Morton who was limping toward the blacktop. As the preacher approached the line of vehicles, long guns and shotguns were drawn out, scraping across open windows.

Adams cut him off at the yellow line. "Charley, you don't want to go over there."

From the other side of the road someone said, "You cross that centerline, nigger, and I'll shoot you down like a dog."

Adams put a forearm across Morton's chest to hold his ground. It wasn't easy. The preacher outweighed him by fifty pounds.

"I'm not going to let those crackers stand over there and gloat."

Morton's breath was so minty strong Adams didn't think he'd have to gargle for several days. "You go over there and you'll only make things worse."

The pressure eased up on Adams' forearm as Morton uttered a sick little laugh. "How could things be any worse? I've lost my church. What kind of preacher does that?"

"A dead one if you cross that centerline. Let me talk to them. You get shot and you'll give the sheriff reason to forget all about investigating the fire."

Morton glanced down the highway. "Where is the son of a bitch? He oughta be here by now."

"It's a big county, Charley."

"Not that big." The preacher looked at the men across the highway, many holding weapons at the ready. "Maybe if I'm killed someone will have to look into all these fires."

Adams inclined his head in the direction of the oak tree. "And your people? What about them? They lose their preacher and their church, all in one night. That can't be much different from you losing your wife and church."

"And child!" Morton's son had been run down in Atlanta, making Morton look for a calling in the country. There his wife had died of cancer. Hence the drinking. And the mouthwash.

"Charley, give me a chance to move them along. Besides, like you said, you need to get organized for tomorrow."

"Wheeler, there's nothing to plan, no sermon to give, no nothing." He glared at the white men, their sons, their weapons. "All in all I think I'd rather cross that centerline."

"You can hold services in the Big House."

Now Morton looked at him. "Yeah, right. Those crackers would burn the Big House to the ground."

"Least we'd know they were coming. Now, are you going to give me a chance to move them along?"

The preacher let out a long sigh, then glanced at the oak. "Okay, okay. I'll work my side of the highway, Wheeler, you work yours."

Adams nodded, then when he was sure Morton

was going to rejoin his flock, he faced the men and their sons. Most wore tee shirts, jeans, and running shoes. Here and there he saw a pair of cowboy boots. A couple—there appeared to be about a dozen men—wore hats, baseball or cowboy. As usual the kids wore their caps backwards. Some of the men were broad-shouldered and had pot guts but several were rather skinny; most had weather-beaten faces. All held weapons, even teenagers had their own twenty-twos.

Heywood Chick would be their leader, a distant relative of Adams, and one he did not claim. Heywood Chick was the local den leader for the Ku Klux Klan. Heywood saw his relation cross the highway and slipped the rifle through the window of his station wagon. Beside Heywood stood his son, Jody, wearing his cap backwards, baggy shorts drooping around his waist, and a tee shirt from Hard Rock Café in Atlanta. On the other side of Heywood stood a wiry man who wore a cowboy hat and smoked a cigarette. Ozzie Tucker. Seeing Heywood put away his weapon, Tucker slid his rifle through another window of the station wagon.

Adams stopped at the edge of the blacktop. "What brings you out tonight, Heywood?"

"Saw the fire and come to have a look. It's still a free country, ain't it?" Heywood Chick was a larger edition of G. Gordon Liddy with the bald pate and thick brush under his nose. Heywood worked rebuilding engines and had the muscles to prove it.

"You wouldn't have any idea how this got started, would you?"

His cousin rolled off the station wagon where he

had been leaning. "You saying I had something to do with this?"

"No, but the GBI will have some questions."

"And why would they question me? Maybe your colored friends were having a barbecue and it got out of hand."

Up and down the blacktop men chuckled. No way Heywood Chick was going to take any shit off Adams. Any man who drove and shot as well as his relative, even if he owned a damn plantation, was considered the squire's equal. Truly, an egalitarian society existed in the South—for white men. The remaining weapons were put away and the men grouped around the two cousins.

"Why didn't you and your friends pitch in and give us a hand?" asked Adams.

"The fire was under control when we got here. Not much we could do."

"Not much we wanted to do," said the man wearing the cowboy hat. Ozzie Tucker dropped his cigarette to the ground and snubbed it out. He had black hair, a narrow face, and stubble for a beard. Under the brim of his hat, Tucker was sunburned. Tucker didn't farm, so maybe he'd been fishing—after slipping over the fence at Chick Springs. There were plenty of ways to reach the river, but Tucker preferred crossing Adams' property.

"We woulda helped if we coulda," Jody Chick said.

Heywood froze his son with a look. Jody jammed his hands down deep in the pockets of his already drooping shorts and stared at the roadbed.

Ozzie Tucker grinned. "Don't know about these

boys, Adams, but I come to see how good a job they done."

Adams turned on the man. "Who done, Ozzie? You know who did this thing?"

"He don't know nothing, Wheeler. Let him be."

"Aw, Heywood, you never know what I might know."

"Ozzie, the FBI will want to talk with you."

"Wheeler, for God's sake, don't get him started—"

Tucker stuck out his stubbled chin. "They got nothing on me."

"They talked to you about the Centennial Park bombing and that abortion clinic in Alabama." Turning to his cousin, Adams added, "Heywood, you better be ready for questions, too."

"We'll tell them nothing!" said Tucker.

Facing the shorter man again, Adams said, "Then you'd better be in tight with your friends, Ozzie."

Tucker glanced at the congregation gathered under the oak tree. "Hell, Adams, at least I'm not known as a nigger-lover."

Adams looked Tucker over, starting with the soiled hat all the way down to a pair of mud-caked boots. "You actually worry what people think about you?"

Tucker got in his face. "Now you listen to me, Adams. I ain't one of them thinks you're hot shit. You'd better not cross me here."

Again the taller man faced his cousin. "Heywood, if some of your people know—"

Tucker put a hand on Adams' shoulder. "I'm talking to you."

Adams looked at the hand. "Take your hand off me, Ozzie."

Glancing at the crowd, Tucker said, "Strong talk for a man who's outnumbered."

"And the usual from a coward."

"Wheeler," said Heywood, "now don't be . . . ."

The hand came off Adams' shoulder and Tucker drew back to swing. "Why you, sumbitch . . . ."

Adams stepped inside the blow and planted a fist of his own deep in the skinny man's stomach. Tucker gasped, bent over, and stumbled back. His cowboy hat fell off and he lost his balance and bumped into a fat man behind him. The fat man tried to catch him, but Tucker stepped on one of his feet. Both men went down and the fat man clipped his head on a bumper and let out a howl.

That's when all hell broke loose.

Chapter Three

Someone clubbed Adams over his shoulders and he went to his knees where he was quickly surrounded. No one touched him—until he tried to get to his feet; then everyone let loose, kicking and hitting him. Some even spat on him. Across the highway Charley Morton saw his friend go down and hobbled across the blacktop where he threw himself at the crowd. Morton was followed by a couple of the church elders, but Roosevelt grabbed their arms and pulled them back.

"No, you ain't going over there."

"But Wheeler and the preacher—"

The elderly black man glanced at the fracas across the highway. "Let them git it out of their systems. It's what they want."

And the three black men stood on the far side of

the highway and watched as the preacher slammed into the white men, sending bodies flying.

Suddenly men were falling all over Adams or slamming into the side of his cousin's station wagon. Adams panicked and the momentary panic caused him to throw back both elbows; one hit flesh, the other hit bone. Men screamed as Adams lunged to his feet and came face-to-face with the fellow Ozzie Tucker had knocked back into the station wagon. In the fat man's hands was a rifle. When the fat man realized Adams wasn't armed, he handed the rifle to his son and threw himself at Adams.

Adams didn't want to wrestle, didn't want anything to do with being on the ground again, so he sidestepped the fat man, then kicked him in the butt as he went lumbering by. The fat man went sprawling, sliding across the blacktop and losing a couple of layers of skin in the process. When Adams looked at the man's son, the boy was pointing the rifle at him.

"I jest might have to shoot you for that, Mr. Adams."

"Just check with your daddy before you do."

The teenager looked to his father, who sat in the middle of the highway examining his arms. The fat man shook his head and the boy lowered the rifle, then Ozzie Tucker snatched the weapon out of the boy's hands.

"Now, Adams, it's just you and me."

Tucker tried to bring up the barrel. Before he could, someone slammed into Adams, knocking Adams into Tucker, Tucker into the pickup behind him. The rifle was caught between the two men and for a moment they faced each other, close enough to share each other's sweat. Then the man who had hit Adams from behind slipped off Adams and fell to the ground. His assailant had put his shoulder into Adams' back, his head into the fender over the tire well. The man collapsed in a heap and the rifle fell to the ground between Adams and Tucker.

Holding his back, Adams sat down on the blacktop, and as he did, kicked the rifle under the truck. The blow had knocked the breath out of Tucker, and when Ozzie eased himself down on the roadbed, Adams punched him in the face, thumping Tucker's head against the side of the pickup and collapsing the scrawny man to the roadbed. Before he got to his feet, Adams checked for a pulse on the idiot who had rammed his head into the side of the truck, and finding one, grabbed the side of the pickup to hoist himself to his feet.

"Yeah, Wheeler, get to your feet," said Heywood Chick. "I haven't kicked your butt in a long time."

Adams wasn't in the mood to tangle. His back felt like it'd just been adjusted by an army of chiropractors; so coming off the roadbed, he brought up his fist and delivered an uppercut to Heywood's chin that lifted his cousin off his feet. Heywood staggered back, then took his own seat on the blacktop. Eyes dazed, hands limp at his sides, Heywood looked at Adams but didn't seem to know what zip code he was in.

From the other side of the station wagon Heywood's son gaped at his dad, as did many of the teens. Unlike their fathers, these boys had paid a price for hassling black people; most of them had been expelled from school at one time or another. The boys were waiting to see how this thing shook out. Not to mention the nigger-lover and his friend were heavily outnumbered. The preacher had three on him and they rode Morton to the ground, flinging off blood, sweat, and tears.

A hand clamped on Adams' shoulder, and Adams let himself be turned around. As he did he raised his elbow and thrust back, planting the sharp edge of his arm in the man's face. It was Sammie Burns, a local pool hustler. Burns' nose exploded in blood and the pool hustler grabbed it, screaming, as Adams went to pull men off Charley Morton.

It wasn't easy. After years of pent-up rage and frustration, all four were enjoying this rare opportunity to kick each other's butts. Still, Morton was holding his own, throwing off one fellow, knocking another to the ground—until a skinny guy came up from behind and slammed the butt of a shotgun into Morton's upper back, knocking the preacher to the ground.

Adams grabbed the barrel of the shotgun and pulled the skinny man over to him. It was Pokey Furman who lived in a mobile home on the other side of town and who had been one of the first to be let go when the Big Mill shut down. Adams jerked up the barrel, connecting with Furman's jaw and snapping it shut. Furman yelped and stumbled back, then stopped to examine his mouth. He'd bitten all the way through his lip.

Adams used the butt of the shotgun on the men pummeling Morton, giving them both kidney punches.

Both men grabbed their backs as they fell off the preacher. That left "Silent Al" clinging to Morton, a guy who hung around the barbershop but never voiced an opinion. Using the barrel of the long gun across Al's throat, Adams forced the silent man off Morton, but lost him when Al's sweaty body twisted around and slipped out of his grasp. Adams shoved Al away with the length of the weapon. Al lost his footing where the asphalt ended and went down against one of the trucks, and it was an awfully long time before he got back up.

Adams flung the shotgun into the field behind the row of vehicles, then reached down to give Morton a hand to his feet. "Charley, you've got to get back across the highway!"

"To hell with that!"

And Morton threw a punch over Adams' shoulder connecting with Heywood Chick's jaw. Heywood staggered back until he found himself beside a pickup. He grabbed the door handle to stay on his feet.

"Charley," said Adams, gripping the preacher's arms, "get back across the highway where you belong."

"Where I belong, did you say? Know my place, Wheeler, is that what you're saying?"

"Charley, I didn't mean—"

Heywood Chick was back for more and this time he had brought along a friend. Without ceremony the two men rammed into Adams and Morton, knocking both to the ground. Pain raced up Adams' spine, the preacher said a dirty word, and while they were rolling across the asphalt, a car slid to a stop several feet away. Five young black men piled out, a couple pulling Morton to his feet. Another helped Adams, then drew back to hit the white man.

"No!" shouted one of the boys. "That's Mr. Adams."

The young man looked at Adams, recognized him, and dropped Adams where he stood. He joined the other four boys clashing with the white kids who had leaped into the fray. Someone stepped over Adams as he tried to get to his feet; another kicked him in the hip, rolling him off the blacktop. Heywood Chick had done that, and while Heywood stood over him, holding a shotgun and gloating, one of the young black men slammed into Adams' cousin, hitting Heywood low and hard. The shotgun fell from Heywood's hands and landed close enough for Adams to slap it to the far side of the pickup. That drew the attention of Jody Chick, hiding on the other side of the truck.

Adams saw the teenager reaching for the shotgun. "Leave it be, Jody." Adams grabbed the pickup's bumper and pulled himself to his feet.

As he came up, his cousin hit him in the face and Adams slid down the bed. Behind Heywood lay the black kid who had slammed into him. The boy lay on his back and did not move. When Heywood stepped in to finish off Adams, who clutched the side of the truck, Adams raised a foot and placed it in his cousin's stomach. The blow forced Heywood back and bent him over.

That was too much for Jody Chick. He had to do something, but when he ran around the truck it was into the fists of one of the black boys. Jody yelped, grabbed his face, and retreated behind the pickup.

The black kid didn't follow. A white man, Garland Kelly, who had slipped out of his car after using his CB, came up behind the boy, locked his hands, and clubbed the teenager over the back of the shoulders. The kid fell to the ground, and while he was down, Kelly kicked him.

Adams staggered over and pushed Kelly off. "Hey, guys, this is getting out of hand."

No one heard him or paid him any mind. And when the solid-built Kelly came at him, that was enough to keep Adams busy. He dodged a well-telegraphed blow and planted one of his own deep in Kelly's stomach, reaching for the man's spine. Kelly doubled over, backed up, and put a hand out to ease himself down to the blacktop. When Adams stepped toward him, Kelly shook his head; then, clutching his stomach, leaned over and vomited onto the roadbed beside the unconscious kid whom Adams recognized as Patrick Kaiser. Adams was checking on the boy when he noticed the preacher go down, several guys on Morton once again. The clump of men rolled across the highway, huffing, puffing, and beating the hell out of each other.

"Hey," said Adams, moving to where the four tussled, "let's stop this." One of the white men was thrown off the pile and rolled into Adams' feet, almost taking him down. Adams helped the man to his feet, someone Adams didn't recognize. "Come on, guys. Enough is enough."

The man came up, dripping sweat. "To hell with you, Adams. We've had enough of you and your niggers!"

Uh-huh. Well, thank you very much. And Adams hit the man on the sweet point of his very damp chin. The stranger's eyes rolled back in his head and he went down for the count.

In the distance came the sound of sirens; across the road a woman screamed for the black kids to get out of there. One of the boys yelled back that his mother should stay out of this. That didn't go over well with his mother or several of the other women. They threatened to cross the centerline and kick some butt themselves. All in all it wasn't long before the young men piled into their sports car. As the car raced away, the sheriff and his deputies arrived from the opposite direction, their headlights lighting up the fight scene.

Men and boys lay along the asphalt, some whimpering, some moaning, many out cold. One boy cried for his mama. A man rolled around holding his gut, and as Adams and Morton tried to get to their feet, Heywood Chick stuck a shotgun in their faces. Blood ran down the side of the Klan leader's face and sweat dripped from his chin. His shirt was wet and spotted with blood.

"You sons of bitches, I'll blow your damned heads off!"

The two men froze, so quiet they could hear their sweat plop on the blacktop.

"Put down the shotgun, Heywood," said Bobbie Lee. The freckled girl was out of her fire suit and dressed in a pair of coveralls now.

Morton and Adams did not move. Both barrels of Heywood Chick's shotgun were pointed at them. One little twitch and . . . .

Heywood glanced over his shoulder. "Bobbie Lee, you got no right—"

"Put it down, I said!"

"Bobbie Lee, you siding with the colored now?"

"You've kicked their asses, Heywood, now put down the shotgun."

"Bobbie Lee, you want to continue doing business in this county?"

"Yeah, right, I'm supposed to score points with customers by letting you blow off these folks' heads. Put down the shotgun, Heywood, or I'm gonna have to take your legs out from under you." The young woman lowered her own shotgun.

The men on their knees watched all this with great interest. Sweat ran down their faces and not all of it from the brawl. The lights of the patrol cars could be seen now and their sirens were louder.

Heywood glanced at the two men, then again at Lee, and finally uncocked the shotgun and lay the weapon on the blacktop. As he did the Klan leader got a quick look under the pickup where his son hid.

"Jody, get your ass out here!"

The teenager did, shyly slipping around the front of the truck. There wasn't a mark on the boy and that seemed to enrage his father even more.

"I don't know what I'm going to do with you, boy. You shame our family."

"Shut up, Heywood," said Adams, pulling the preacher to his feet. Morton's bad knee made it difficult for him to get up and down.

Heywood glared at Adams but kept his counsel. After all, Bobbie Lee still held the shotgun.

With the flashing lights approaching everyone tried to sit or stand. Many had to hold onto the side of a car or a truck or the hand of a friend.

They'll need a paddy wagon to take us all in, thought Adams. In that he was wrong. Only Adams was handcuffed and stashed in a patrol car. The sheriff said, "I know who incites the colored to riot around these parts."

Tall, blond, and with a year-round tan, Dale Posey could've been a poster boy for Sheriff of the New South, despite what folks said behind his back, that Dale Posey had the brains that went with being a natural blond. The sheriff, however, had one thing going for him: He had married Judge Bennefield's spinster sister, and for getting that woman out of his house, the judge would do just about anything for the sheriff. And the people of Chick County knew it.

Bobbie Lee tried to intercede on Adams' behalf but got nowhere. She couldn't even tell the sheriff who'd started the fight, but she was damn sure it wasn't Adams.

"Bobbie Lee," Posey said, "we all know you're sweet on Wheeler. Now get back across the highway and finish your job. I saw some flames when I arrived."

"And you'd seen a damn sight more if'n you got here sooner," snapped the freckled girl. "Where've you been, Sheriff?"

"Just move it back across the street, Bobbie Lee."

Lee said something that proved she was no lady, then stomped across the blacktop where volunteers and members of the congregation stared at the scene being played out on the state highway.

"Listen, Sheriff—" started Charley Morton.

"Preacher, it's best you don't get involved."

Blood and sweat ran down the black man's face and dripped onto his pajama top. His arms were nicked and scraped and the tops of his pj's torn in several places.

The sheriff jerked a thumb toward the other side of the highway. "You have more on your plate than you can handle. If you're able."

A deputy snickered at the reference to Morton's drinking. The preacher glared at the deputy, then limped away. He'd been in the Chick County jail before and still wore the scar; still, before he reached the other side of the blacktop, the raging impotence most black men feel from living in a white man's world surfaced and Morton couldn't help but turn around and head back toward the patrol car where Adams sat.

Bobbie Lee was there this time and she took his arm. "No, you don't, Preacher." In the young woman's other hand was a towel.

Morton looked down at her. "Why you making this your business, Bobbie Lee?"

"Wheeler's my business, not you, Preacher. Now, if you don't mind I'll handle this."

Morton stood there for a moment, then shook his head and rejoined his congregation under the oak tree while Lee went over to the cruiser and opened the door. After giving Adams the towel, she returned to where the volunteers were loading the pumper.

"Ernie, you finish up here. I've got business in town."

"Over here, Miss Bobbie Lee." Roosevelt stood near Adams' pickup, holding out the keys.

Lee took the keys, and when the white girl wouldn't let him get the door for her, he climbed in the other side. In seconds they'd cleared the crowd and were racing down the road toward the county seat.

Morton's flock was angry and frustrated. They demanded to know what was going to be done about the burning of their church.

"The FBI will be called in," said the preacher. "I imagine they'll arrive in the morning."

"I'll stand guard until they git here," Norwood Sibley said. "But I gots to run home and git a few things."

Dean Meckler shouted after him. "Don't forget your shotgun." Meckler sold industrial life insurance and collected weekly premiums.

"I don't know about that, Dean."

"Preacher, nobody's gonna stay out here without no gun. I'll go get mine and stay with Norwood."

Meckler's wife went after him. "Dean Meckler, I'm not gonna let you do this. Better the whole church burn down than another person be hurt."

"Woman, I'm not hearing you."

"You'll be hearing me when I put that shotgun of yours up side your head."

"My great-grandparents helped build this church," said a woman who had been a seamstress for as long as anyone could remember. "They were some of the first colored folks born free in Chick County."

"Colored folks ain't never been free in Chick

County," said Tad Browning, who owned a recapping business, "and I'm thinking of moving down to King County." King County lay to the south of Chick County and was so thoroughly black, it didn't make sense to mention the few white families living there.

"Now let's not be hasty, people."

Meckler was back again. "Preacher, maybe you don't know what we lost here. My family's been going to this church for as long as I can remember. I've been an elder."

Congregation members murmured in agreement.

"All right, people, all right," said Morton, looking around, "but the rest of us need to go home and get a good night's sleep. Tomorrow's going to be a busy day."

"Where you gonna preach tomorrow?" asked one of the elder's wives, Selma Reynolds.

"I'll call the preacher at the First Baptist Church. The elders will get the word around."

"I don'ts want to go to church with no white people," said Dean Meckler, gesturing at the highway. The EMS had finally arrived and the injured white men and boys were being loaded into a van. "Some of the same people who done this will be there tomorrow."

"We don't know that, Dean." Morton glanced at the shell of his church. "I can't believe another Christian could've done this."

"Only one who thinks he can git away with it."

"Do we need to set up a schedule to watch the church?" asked Selma Reynolds.

"Not more than one or two people," said the sheriff, walking up behind the preacher. "I don't want another riot here tonight."

"We wouldn't've had the first one, Sheriff, if you'd been here sooner."

"Dean Meckler, either shut your mouth or mosey on over to that patrol car and climb inside with Adams."

Meckler chose to shut his mouth.

"You'll be responsible for our church?" asked Mrs. Reynolds.

"I'll be responsible for running in anyone who's still here after the pumper leaves."

Everyone glanced at the volunteers locking down the pumper.

"This ain't right," muttered several members of the congregation and it was said with considerable heat.

Dale Posey only shrugged. "Hey, y'all want to go to jail, just be here after the pumper leaves."

The Chick County hospital was a four-story brick building built after the world war. The First World War, that is. Inside the waiting room Bobbie Lee reported to Adams' housekeeper what had happened out on the state highway.

Savannah gripped the elderly black woman's arm. "Nell, we can't let them keep Daddy in jail. Last time they almost killed him."

But Nell wanted to make sure she was hearing what this white girl was saying. "There was a fight between white and black folks on the state highway?"

"More like Wheeler and the preacher against the Klan," explained Bobbie Lee.

"Some kids showed up later," said Roosevelt, "but

they were long gone before the sheriff got there."

Nell glanced down a hallway leading to the treatment rooms. "So that's why Patrick Kaiser was brung in."

"Was he hurt bad?" asked Roosevelt.

"They done already took him upstairs to intensive care along with Lelia. They didn't arrest the preacher, did they?"

"The sheriff said he was to take care of the church," said Roosevelt. "He and the elders were meeting under the tree when we left."

"How many those white men they arrest?" asked Nell.

Roosevelt shook his head.

"Oh, God, Nell," asked Savannah, gripping the elderly woman's arm, "what are we going to do?"

Nell set her lantern jaw. "I'll call Mister Knox. He'll know what to do." Knox Tate was Adams' attorney.

Savannah followed Nell over to a pay phone as those from the fight began to drift in and demand attention at the desk. Several arrived on stretchers.

Unfortunately, Knox Tate was out of town for the Fourth of July, and when Savannah became hysterical, Nell clamped her hands on the teenager's shoulders and got in her face.

"Hush!"

People in the waiting room turned and stared.

"But Nell—"

"Girl, when I tells you to hush, I means it. I gots to think."

Savannah chewed on her lip. Bobbie Lee surveyed the waiting room. There weren't many colored folks in here and she stood with the few that were here. That just might not be such a smart idea.

The sheriff released the town drunk and sent him home. The other prisoners were a couple of white girls who'd been hooking and he turned them loose, too. Now Adams was the only prisoner.

The Chick County jail didn't have separate cells. The whole cell block served as one large holding pen and it was split down the middle by a row of floor-to-ceiling bars. During segregation one side had held blacks, the other side whites. Now one side was for women, the other for men. In the center was a holding cage where the really wild ones could be penned. And the not-so-wild ones had been known to hassle the wilder prisoners, never allowing the drug-crazed or drunk-out-of-their-mind prisoners to calm down.

The Chick County jail had been sued by the Americus, Georgia-based Prison and Jail Project. According to the Project, the county hadn't lived up to an agreement to improve conditions at the facility. The Prison and Jail Project wanted a new jail built and had the weight of the U.S. Justice Department behind it. So, until a new jail was built, Chick County farmed out all their long-term prisoners. That was fine with Judge Bennefield; he didn't want prisoners in Chick County anyway. Still, the prisoners' families bitched about having to drive all the way over to Macon to see their loved ones. That didn't bother the judge either. Most crime was committed by criminal families and not the sort seen in *The Godfather.*

A deputy stepped into the cell block through an over-sized door. Johnny Temple was a string bean of a man who picked up extra money as a member of a multi-jurisdictional task force working across county lines with other law enforcement agencies. The extra money was how Temple's family made ends meet. Otherwise they'd be long gone from Chick County.

"Sorry, Wheeler, but I've got to return to patrol. It's Saturday night and we're shorthanded." Temple was referring to a deputy who had accidentally shot himself in the foot, then blamed it on a black man no one seemed to be able to find.

"Don't worry, Johnny. I'll be okay."

"Want me to park out in the alley a while?"

"I don't think that's going to win you any points with the sheriff. Besides, if they come for me tonight, it'll be through the front door. Is Posey still on duty?"

Temple shook his head. "Went home complaining he'd lost enough sleep on your account. Wheeler, this time I think you crossed the line. It's one thing to side with the colored working the Springs—"

"Johnny, that's Nell's church that was burned."

"Well, Wheeler, all I can say is where the rubber meets the road, white is always white and black always sides with black."

Chapter Four

An hour later Adams heard Robbie Simpson telling someone they couldn't go back there. The deputy raised his voice so it carried through the oversized-door and into the cell block. Adams opened his eyes. He lay on a bunk and when he turned his head, the movement brought tears to his eyes. Involuntarily, he coughed.

The door opened and a slender, almost frail-looking, elderly man pushed his way through. From behind the man, a voice said, "Mr. President, I don't think you should go back there."

A young man with a short haircut, who wore a business suit and what looked like a hearing aid, joined Jimmy Carter in the cell block. The young man's eyes scanned the cell block, then focused on Adams who was getting to his feet. Robbie Simpson followed the former president and the Secret Service agent to the entrance, stopping in the doorway and filling the opening with his enormous bulk. Pieces of cheese stuck to the front of the deputy's blouse, his gut hung over his belt.

The former president stepped over to the bars. "You okay, Wheeler?"

Forcing a smile, Adams said, "Never thought seeing a politician could make me feel so good, Jimmy."

Carter looked him over. Adams had cuts on both arms, scrapes on his elbows, and a knot on his head. His shirt was stained with blood and there were holes in his jeans that weren't any fashion statement. As far as Carter was concerned the Chick County jail was a disgrace. Two cells with bunks with worn and soiled mattresses were hooked to the walls. At the rear, sheet metal had been fashioned into a privy.

Turning to the deputy who hung on the jamb, Carter said, "It's obvious Wheeler needs to see a doctor. Would you let him out of there, Robbie?"

"Couldn't if'n I wanted to, Jimmy. Sheriff's the only one with a key."

Carter stared at the fat man for a moment, then said to the Secret Service agent, "Stanley, would you go into the office and find the sheriff's number? When you contact Dale, make sure he knows if he's not down here in ten minutes, I'll call someone to open this cell."

The agent nodded, and when Robbie Simpson didn't move fast enough, he pushed the fat man through the door ahead of him.

Carter and Adams shook hands through the bars.

"Another church is what I heard."

"Nell's."

"Anyone injured?"

"Lelia Plummer and Minny Jackson. I think Lelia was overcome by smoke, and Minny, well, frankly, Jimmy, I'm worried about her feet."

The former president shook his head. "Lelia Plummer worked to help me carry Chick County the first time I ran for governor. What were they doing there at that hour of the night?"

"Guarding the church."

"Guarding the church? They had weapons?"

Adams shook his head. "Just a cell phone. They were supposed to call the volunteers if a fire started."

"But who allowed such a thing? Charley Morton?"

"The elders."

"That's irresponsible. I don't know Ms. Jackson, but Lelia Plummer has to be seventy, if she's a day."

"I think they wanted to be proactive."

"Then be proactive about turning out the vote, but old women guarding a church—that's outrageous, not to mention dangerous."

The Secret Service agent returned, sliding his cell phone into a pocket. "The sheriff is on his way, sir."

"Thank you, Stanley. Stanley, I don't think you've met Wheeler. He owns ten thousand acres here in Chick County. Wheeler Adams, Stanley Jenkins."

After saying "good to meet you" and gripping Adams' hand through the bars, the agent studied Adams. How did someone who owned ten thousand acres end up in jail? He didn't look drunk, but he did look like he'd taken quite a beating.

"Wheeler leases his land to black people,"

explained the former president. "Most folks aren't as color-blind. Robbie says you're being held for inciting a riot." The former president scanned the cell block. "If so, why's no one else in here?"

Adams only smiled.

"Why wasn't anyone else charged?" Carter asked Robbie Simpson, who had returned to his position at the door.

"You'll have to take that up with the sheriff, Jimmy."

Adams touched his head where he'd been kicked and felt a knot. When had that happened?

Carter saw this. "Robbie, you got any ice—something for Wheeler's head?"

"I'm not supposed to have anything to do with the prisoners."

"Did you even feed him? Give him any water?"

"There's water in the spigot." Simpson gestured at a metal basin which emptied into a hole in the concrete floor.

Carter shook his head. "They ought to close this place down."

"I think that's been tried," Adams said. "How'd you hear about me being in here?"

"Nell called. Knox Tate is out of town for the Fourth."

"I appreciate you coming over."

"It's no trouble . . . " Carter saw his Secret Service agent move toward the door. Startled, Simpson had stepped back, out of the doorway, to make way for the sheriff.

"Evening, Dale."

"Evening, Jimmy." The blond man came through

the door, glancing at the Secret Service agent, then Adams in his cell. "What brings you here?"

"Come to see Wheeler. Think you might let him out?"

"Seems like you're doing just fine where you are."

"I understand Wheeler's in for inciting a riot?"

"That, along with disturbing the peace."

Carter gestured at the cells. "Then where are the others?"

"Others?" Posey looked genuinely puzzled.

"It takes more than one to cause a riot."

Posey shook his head. "It was Adams."

"All by himself?"

"One man shouts fire in a movie theater, you know how it works, Jimmy."

"You've had Wheeler in here before on that same charge, haven't you?"

"And I can't make it stick because of people like you sticking their noses in where they don't belong."

"Am I doing that?"

"You know you are, Jimmy."

"Don't you think it'd be prudent to have Wheeler examined by a physician so Chick County doesn't face another lawsuit, a suit Judge Bennefield will figure was completely avoidable?"

Posey considered the idea, then took a set of keys from his belt, unlocked the cell, and stood back, opening the door. After Adams walked out, Posey said, "You'd better get Robert Nance to check him out. I don't think there's a white man in all Chick County who wants to be called out in the middle of the night on Adams' account."

❖   ❖   ❖

During the winter of 1732, Stafford Chick and his family were evicted from their farm in the English Lowlands. Stafford had worked diligently to retire the debt left by his father-in-law, but several poor harvests dashed all his efforts. Overconfident to a fault, Stafford thought he could breathe life into his father-in-law's farm—which had been the burning desire his wife had seen in her suitor's eyes: to own land. Now the Chicks faced years of imprisonment; the father-in-law was dead. For the baby, a girl, not yet a year old and sickly, imprisonment was a death sentence. Filled with despair, Stafford's wife took the baby to church where she began to pray. Not long after that James Oglethorpe entered their lives.

After undergoing an examination to weed out the debtors and convicts, Stafford and his family were considered members of the "worthy poor." If Stafford Chick and his family were willing to forsake their homeland, the Oglethorpe trustees would provide passage to the colony of Georgia. There the Chicks could earn, by the sweat of their brows, fifty acres of the most hospitable land a farmer ever put a plow to. And as a condition of ownership the trustees required Stafford's family to grow a number of mulberry trees to feed the silkworms which would make each and every Georgian rich. But absolutely no slaves. Slavery could only lead hardy yeomen into becoming members of the idle rich, and all you had to do was look across the river at South Carolina to see how decadent a colony could become when slavery was introduced. In Georgia the air was temperate; it was never too hot or too cold, and the soil so rich there was no need to add manure. Stafford could not believe his good fortune. Not only did he become a regular church-goer, but he kept a journal of what he learned in Georgia. So did many of his descendants.

> *Chick Sprgs. Ga.*
>
> *8 May 1867—It has been a long time since I have fulfilled my responsibilities for a Journal, but once again, I turn my hand to what is required by tradition of me & others responsible for Chick Sprgs. However, whatever my descendants might learn from the tornado that blew through Ga. during the recent War & how it could benefit posterity continues to elude me.*
>
> *To-day I was working on the accts. when my overseer asked to see me. Belle brought James into the study, a room becoming filled with more & more books as Maggie has taken to educating the children. I finally had to ask the family to leave so as to finish my Work. But I have to admit it makes me feel more confident about the future to have Numbers to figure again. Truth is, I did not think we would make it through the Winter, but Maggie, James & Belle did not share my concerns. Sometimes I forget they lived here during the War, in conditions much like Great-Grandfather's. Probably why James*

had to remind me—I think the War has
affected my mind; at least the faculties
responsible for remembering—that an eclipse
of the moon had taken place before I
returned to the Sprgs. & that practically
guaranteed an extraordinary harvest.

James is certainly a bright negro & could
have run away on more than one occasion.
But James told me—it is strange to have a
negro as a confidant, but we two are alone
at the Sprgs. James told me he expects little
from Life—after being sold into Slavery in
Africa. People selling their own Kind into
Slavery! It made you stop & think! James
considered running away while I was at
War, but it was a long & difficult trip north &
he did not think Belle strong enough to make
the journey. And the ship that had brought
him from Africa had been from Boston; its
captain from Philadelphia, so what was he
to expect from Those People? Perhaps all this
Conversation about freeing slaves was so
much Talk. However, after becoming a freedman, James just had to try his hand in
Atlanta. Another disappointment. Too many
freedmen bidding for too few Jobs. But that
is the History of Atlanta & always shall be.

James was at the door of my study when I
looked up from the accts. There was no hat
in his hand. When James belonged to me, he
came into the Big House rarely, but always
hat in hand. Now he left his hat in one of the

chairs on the veranda. For some reason that was important to him. I told James he had contributed to the numbers I was figuring. I meant the Profits but did not elaborate. He thanked me kindly & added I did not have to rehire him when he returned from Atlanta.

Re-hire him! My God, but I wanted to rescind the Compliment. I never hired this negro in the 1st place. He had been my Slave. It was enough to drive any White Man to distraction, the things negroes said these days. You would think they were never taught Civility when we were their Masters.

But that was not why James was in my study. He asked to speak to me about his people. The manner in which he stated the question surprised me & I sat back in my chair & regarded him. There were only James & Belle at the Sprgs. All the other negroes had left for Atlanta, despite offers of Forty Acres of My property—given by the Yankees!—to the freedmen to settle at the Sprgs! But a handful of Gold from me & the so-called opportunities in Atlanta were enough to rid Me of these newfound Neighbors. As I had told Mrs. C. upon my return from the War—with that wagon load of gold I drove—we would operate the Sprgs. on our own terms, not those dictated by any Yankee.

James wished to speak about an education for his people. He said they needed a school where the children could be taught how to read & write. Of course, this would be after the crops were gathered in the fall— he stated his Cause very well for a negro— he did not want his children to grow up igno- rant, as he had. In the past I had never allowed any slave to read & write—until Mrs. C. asked if she could teach one of the slaves to read the Bible so they could learn the virtues of a Christian Life. After all, said Mrs. C, the White Man was put on this earth to care for the Colored Races. Now, because James lived at Chick Sprgs., the former slaves in the nearby countryside became his concern.

That came as no surprise. People were always coming to me to determine one dis- pute or the other, without involving Lawyers. The Law might be the correct way to handle things, but it is an awfully expensive Right at a time when few have any money. But a school? I did not know if I wanted to be responsible for any number of educated freedmen roaming around South Georgia.

Tho' this was not the objection I made. I asked James, that with all the work he did for my family & his, did he think he had the time to run a school? James said there were White People from up North who would come South & do the teaching. Now that rec'd a good deal of my attention. I told this former slave of mine that it would be a cold day in

Hell before another Yankee would set foot on the Sprgs. again. Only the Gold I had "appropriated" at the War's End kept the Tax Collector, Carpetbaggers & all the Scalawags at bay. No. You would not see any Yankees on my property anytime soon & I had had my Will changed for that Reason. No one who lived north of the Mason-Dixon Line would ever own Chick Sprgs.

Still, as strongly as I objected, James could have knocked me over with a feather with what he said next: that a woman would be doing the teaching. Examining him closer, James revealed a White Woman would be teaching the freedmen & their children. I told James I would think about it & after he left I opened my bottle & took a long pull. No wonder the Yankees had bested us on the Field of Battle. There appeared to be no limit to the Depths to which those people would stoop.

Chapter Five

Minny Jackson lay in a hospital bed with her feet higher than her head. She was unconscious and an IV fed into her arm. Orange and red stains had already bled through the sheet from her bandaged feet. Nell sat in a large hospital chair with Savannah lying across her lap, chest, and shoulder. The teenager was asleep; Roosevelt sat in another chair, and the elderly black man got to his feet as Carter, Adams, and the Secret Service agent entered the room.

"Good to see you, Mister Carter."

"Hello, Roosevelt."

They shook hands.

The Secret Service agent scanned the room as Carter stepped over to the bed, then stared down at the unconscious woman. "How is she, Nell?"

"They don't know, Jimmy, about her feet."

Savannah stirred in Nell's lap. "I 'preciate you gitting my boy out of jail."

"It was no trouble at all."

"I called Minny's people, but her son's no count and her brother's out drinking. I don't know when they might show up, and it don't have to be Saturday night for O'Neal to be out drinking."

The former president introduced the Secret Service agent to Nell, then Adams' daughter, who said "Hi, Daddy" without opening her eyes. When Adams reached for his daughter, his housekeeper brushed his hand away.

"She's jest fine where she is, Wheeler."

Adams stepped back.

"Have you seen the preacher?" asked Nell.

"Probably setting up guard duty."

Nell looked stricken. "Not with the young men?"

"I think Charley's smarter than that."

"Wheeler, what's this I hear 'bout you gitting in another fight—after Savannah and I left?"

Carter looked at Adams. The Secret Service agent stepped closer to his charge.

"Can we talk about it later?"

"We shore will." Nell shifted around in her chair under the load of the teenager. "The preacher from First Baptist Church were here. He'd heard of the fire and come to tell us we could use his church for services. We can join right in with the white folks or hold our own service after them. He's already called the preacher's house but didn't get no answer. I told him I'd make sure word got to the elders." Nell was a steward in the church, the good right hand of any preacher, but no elder was a woman.

"Well," Adams said, excusing himself, "if you don't need me, I'll be down in the ER."

Before he could leave Roosevelt passed along a paper sack from the Piggly Wiggly. "Here's some clothes for you, Mister Wheeler. Folks in Creekside rounded them up. They thought you might be needing them."

"That I do." Adams peered into the sack. Everything was there, including a pair of used sneakers. "Thank you, Roosevelt."

"I told folks you'd probably have your clothes cut off." Nell gestured at the unconscious woman in the bed. "It happened to Minny and Lelia—they cut the clothes right off them."

Adams and Carter shook hands. "Thank you again, Jimmy."

"Take care," said Carter, not letting go of Adams' hand, "and let the authorities handle this one."

"I'll do my best."

"Wheeler, I'm serious," said Carter, finally letting go of Adams' hand. "Nightriding's the FBI's business, not yours."

Adams was about to step off the elevator into the lobby when a red-white-and-blue tornado hit him. The tornado used both hands to shove Adams back into the elevator, then brace him against the wall. Rose Mary Bingham was an auburn-haired, middle-aged woman who'd lost few of her curves. She stood five ten, her legs were excellent, and she still had a very good chest. But it was her eyes that gripped you: dark blue and challenging, staring at you from a tanned face. Bingham was the type of woman that men died for—literally, and over a hundred years ago her type could've been seen on the porch waving a handkerchief as her cavalier rode off to defend the honor of the State of Georgia. Nowadays, those same belles can be found at football games and are easily recognized by the vigor with which they call for blood—from either team.

It was the second marriage for both—to each other. While Adams had trained for Vietnam in New Jersey, his new bride had attended Princeton, intent on finishing her education. Instead she took up with peaceniks. The result was the dissolution of their marriage as Adams refused to move to Canada. Then, during an emotional reunion years later, Rose Mary became pregnant. When faced with The Choice, Rose Mary found she couldn't go through with an abortion, and you didn't raise bastards in the Deep South, no, not someone who had debuted at the Piedmont Driving Club. But this time she would keep her maiden name. And when Rose wanted to climb the corporate ladder and her husband wanted to drop out, Adams took their daughter to Chick Springs where Nell raised her as Nell had Adams' siblings.

"Where's my daughter?" Tonight Rose Mary wore a white sleeveless blouse, jeans, and sneakers. Her hands kept Adams pinned to the rear of the elevator.

Tears formed in Adams' eyes. Some of the places his wife was bracing stung, not to mention his headache had returned with a vengeance. "And how are you tonight, Rose?"

"Don't give me any lip, Wheeler. I heard about the fire. Someone at the paper called. I got here as fast as I could. Where's Savannah?"

"Upstairs. Would you like me to show you the way?"

"Just tell me the damn room number." Rose Mary released her hold on her husband and gave him the once-over. "I don't need any help from someone who's evidently been brawling."

Adams gave her the number of Jackson's room as his wife punched the elevator button. When the doors opened, she said, "Get out!"

"Rose, you can throw me out of your house, even your bed, but not out of a public elevator."

Rose Mary took Adams by the arm, looping hers around his, and swung him and herself around, then flung him out the door. When the two of them came to a stop, Adams outside the elevator, his wife inside, she said, "I'm taking Savannah back to Atlanta and don't you try to stop me."

"And miss the judge's party?"

As the doors closed Rose Mary shot him a bird.

Adams shook his head, then turned away.

Going down the hall, the security guard called out, "See your wife, Mr. Adams?"

"Couldn't miss her, Orlando."

Rose Mary found Savannah sleeping across her husband's housekeeper. In the hospital bed was a big, black woman, her feet leaking through the sheet. Evidently a victim of the fire. Roosevelt dozed in another chair.

In a low voice Rose Mary said, "I'm here for Savannah, Nell."

"She's no bother, Rose Mary."

The white woman looked at her daughter snuggled

into this old black woman's lap like she never snuggled with her. "I'll be the judge of that."

Nell sighed, then lifted up the teenager. "Savannah, your mama's here."

Savannah opened her eyes and sat up. When Nell twisted around from the girl's sudden shift of weight, Savannah got to her feet. Across the room Roosevelt's eyes popped open. He saw Rose Mary and stood up.

"Evening, Miss Rose."

"Evening, Roosevelt."

"Mother, what are you doing here?"

"I've come to take you home."

"But I don't want to go." Savannah brushed down her blouse, then tossed her hair.

"You're going with me, young lady, and right now."

"Mother, I'm supposed to be at Annabelle's tomorrow."

"It's already tomorrow, but you're going home with me."

"You can't tell me what to do. I'm in the country now."

Rose Mary glanced from one black person to the other, then gritted her teeth. Roosevelt was staring at the floor, evidently remembering the old African proverb: When elephants tangle, it's the ants who suffer.

"We'll discuss this out in the hall, young lady."

"Mrs. Plummer—you remember her. She taught me in Sunday School. She was almost killed tonight."

"And that's why I want you in Atlanta. It's not safe out here."

"Don't be silly, Mother. It's always safe for white

people in Chick County."

Rose Mary flushed and Roosevelt headed for the door. Nell's face resembled the Sphinx.

"Savannah, are you disobeying me?"

"I'm not disobeying you. We have a deal—you and me and Daddy. If I want to leave, I can leave. Anytime I want. I don't understand why you're so upset. You're the one who came up with the idea."

"Savannah—"

"I don't want to leave. I want to go to the party tomorrow—I mean, today."

Her mother's mouth became a tight line across her face. Before Roosevelt could get away, Rose Mary asked, "Roosevelt?"

The old man stopped. "What can I do for you, Miss Rose Mary?" He could hear those elephants again.

Rose Mary put a hand to the gardener's back and guided him out the door. "Help me find Wheeler."

"Yes, ma'am."

Savannah trailed them to the door. "I don't care what either of you say, I'm not going back to Atlanta."

On the way down in the elevator Rose Mary grilled Roosevelt about the fire. "But Wheeler looks like he's been in a fight, not a fire."

"Well, Miss Rose, there was kind of a fight."

"What do you mean 'kind of a fight'?"

"The preacher and Mister Wheeler got into it with the Klan out on the state highway."

"The Klan burned down the church?" asked Rose Mary. "Do they know that for a fact?"

The doors opened and Roosevelt kept his finger on

the button until the white woman stepped off. "Mister Wheeler's in the emergency room. Want me to show you where that is, Miss Rose?"

"Roosevelt, with all the scraps Wheeler gets into, I certainly know where the emergency room is. Besides, I want to know for sure if the Klan did this."

"Yes, ma'am. Just let me walk you down there."

Rose Mary felt a hollowness in her chest. "There's more?"

"It's okay, Miss Rose. Jimmy Carter came over from Plains and got him out."

"Got him out? From where?"

"The jail."

The waiting room was empty. How could that be, wondered Rose Mary, with all the shit that was supposed to've gone down and two old women upstairs, one hovering near death. One of those women was someone who'd taught Savannah the Ten Commandments. Evidently there was no commandment against torching black churches in Chick County.

Rose Mary felt her way along the row of chairs, finally taking a seat. Roosevelt followed, pulling a flask from his hip pocket and handing it to her. One swallow and Rose Mary coughed. The liquid burned going down. Her eyes watered.

She held out the flask and looked at it. "What's this?"

"Uncle Ingram's."

"Well . . . I always knew there was good reason . . . not to drink his stuff." After another swallow, she added, "Except tonight." She returned the flask.

Roosevelt wiped off the lip and took a sip of his own. It'd been a long night and it might not be over. A black man with a green thumb, Roosevelt had planned, planted, and perfected the grounds of the Adams' city house in Buckhead. Roosevelt had also been the first to realize he wasn't cut out for city life, beating a hasty retreat to the Springs, until one by one, Nell and her family, then this woman's husband had joined him.

"I need to find Wheeler," said that woman, after clearing her throat.

"Why don't you jest sit here a while, Miss Rose." He gestured at the doors leading back to the treatment rooms. "Mister Wheeler ain't going nowheres."

"I don't know . . . Maybe you're right. Got anymore of that . . . liquor?"

Roosevelt passed along the flask and looked at the doors again. Wheeler Adams might be a right smart fellow, but he was country stupid when he thought he'd been wronged. It were a wonder the man had lived as long as he had. You wouldn't see any black man going out of his way to find trouble—not with white people. But Mister Wheeler—he always had to keep ahold of his honor. No wonder his wife couldn't live with him. At least not in the country.

After a final swig Rose Mary returned the liquor—what was left of it, then stood up and moved on unsteady legs toward the doors.

Roosevelt came after her. "Sure you're all right, Miss Rose?"

She waved him off. "I'm fine."

And that's where Roosevelt left her, going through

the swinging doors and heading for the treatment rooms.

He returned to Minny Jackson's room and found the preacher by the bed, staring down at the woman. No one else was there. Nell was in intensive care. Savannah had gone with her. Had the preacher seen Jimmy Carter? No, Morton said. Didn't know he was here. After a moment the preacher smiled and asked Roosevelt if he had any of that corn liquor on him.

Since Chick County didn't have the funding for doctors to work weekends, the Medical College in Augusta sent over a resident who bunked in and dreamed of setting up practice in Atlanta. The resident's nurse was Jean Chick and she had come on duty as her husband and his friends began to arrive to be patched up. Jean was short, stocky, with nimble fingers. There was no wasted motion as she cleaned up Adams.

"I patched up my husband over an hour ago, Wheeler. What took you so long?"

"I was held up."

"He was in jail," Rose Mary chimed in from the door.

Adams glanced at his wife, surprised to see her standing there. He also noticed her knuckles were white from gripping the sides of the door.

Jean stopped applying salve to Adams' calves. "It takes two to make a fight. They should've put someone in jail with you. Maybe my husband. Are you going to tell me where this happened? Heywood wouldn't tell me. Was it the Lonesome Pine? You and

Heywood have trashed that place before."

"Wheeler," said his wife, still at the door but no longer gripping the jambs, "the Lonesome Pine's a honky-tonk."

"That's right, Rose. It hasn't changed since I last took you there."

His wife made a face at him.

Jean Chick recapped the salve. "I hope Jody wasn't with him. That boy picks up the strangest ideas hanging around his father's friends."

"What kind of ideas?" asked Rose Mary, stepping into the treatment room.

Mrs. Chick went to work using tape and gauze to protect the more serious burns on Adams' lower legs. Amazingly, his hands had not been burned. Still, he ached all over and had an awful headache. There was a knot on the side of his head that would take a couple of days to go down, ribs that might be cracked, and his lower back—he didn't even want to think about it. It'd be good to get home tonight, and to bed.

Jean Chick was talking. " . . . foolishness about black people, how it's not meant for us to get along."

"You believe we should . . . get along, Mrs. Chick?"

"Oh, I don't hold with taking them in like Wheeler does, Mrs. Adams, it just encourages—"

"'Bingham.' I kept my maiden name."

Jean stopped what she was doing and stared at the woman. From that moment on Rose Mary could've said the moon was made of green cheese and Jean would've agreed. That's how you handled folks who were obviously unbalanced. You humored them. "Well, Mrs. Bingham . . . er—what do I call you?"

"How about 'Rose Mary'?"

With a nod, Jean said, "And as the tag says, I'm Jean. Somewhere along the line Heywood and Wheeler are related. Pleased to meet you." She returned to her work. "I've told Heywood before, if the Negroes aren't returning to Africa, then we have to learn to get along. At least, that's what the Good Book tells us." She tapped Adams on the knee. "You're done, Wheeler, but only sponge baths for the next several days. Rose Mary, you might help with that."

"I'm returning to Atlanta tonight."

"Thanks, Jean," said Adams, sliding off the table.

Jean was staring at his wife again. "You're . . . you're welcome, Wheeler." She pulled off her gloves and tossed them in a trash can before heading for the door. "Er—nice to meet you, Rose Mary."

"You, too, Jean."

Adams reached for a sack on a stainless steel table. Rose Mary saw her husband grimace and snatched up the sack. Pulling out the clothes, she asked, "Where'd these come from?"

"Donations."

Adams' other clothes lay in pieces on the floor on top of his running shoes. And the bottom of his shoes had melted in the fire, causing Adams to walk unevenly. Rose Mary helped her husband slip into the shirt, then the pants and shoes. As he was buttoning up the shirt a blonde appeared in the doorway of the treatment room.

The young woman paused to catch her breath. "Mr. Adams, security says you need to come to the lobby."

"Uncle Ingram?" he asked.

The woman nodded. "Yes. And he's got a gun."

"Ingram always carries a gun," said Rose Mary. "His interpretation of his Second Amendment rights is off the chart."

She followed her husband out of the room and down the hall where Jean Chick and the resident from the Medical College of Georgia were catching up on their chart work.

"Wheeler, have your doctor check you Monday," Jean said, looking up from a chart. "Who is your doctor anyway?"

"Edward Nance."

The woman nodded as if that was to be expected.

"May I use the phone?" asked Adams.

Jean nodded.

The doctor, a young white man with blond hair, looked up from the chart he was working on. "Can't be long distance." He wore greens. A stethoscope hung around his neck.

Adams nodded, then dialed the home of Thomas Traylor. Traylor said he was on his way over to the hospital to pick up Roosevelt and take him out to the Springs. Thomas Traylor was one of the black families that farmed the Springs.

"Thank you, Thomas." Adams hung up, thanked Jean Chick again, and escorted his wife out of the ER.

The resident looked up again. "Where's he going? I didn't release him."

"Louise says one of Wheeler's relatives is trying to get into the hospital. He has a gun."

"A gun?" The young man watched the Adamses go

through the swinging doors. To Jean Chick, he asked, "Have you heard anything about a fire? Someone tried to burn down another colored church."

On their way to the lobby, Rose Mary said, "I want you to tell Savannah she's to return to Atlanta with me."

Her husband glanced at her. "And why's that?"

"Don't play dumb, Wheeler. Any place my paper's going to send an army of reporters isn't a place where I want my daughter to be."

"She'll be safe at the Springs, Rose."

"Wheeler, I'm not going to argue with you about this. Besides, if Ingram's here, who's watching the Springs?"

They found Uncle Ingram, along with Orlando Hanks, the security guard, at the front door. Ingram was highly agitated and the guard's patience was wearing thin.

"Wheeler, this fellow won't let me in."

"And I won't," Hanks said, hitching up his Sam Browne belt, "unless he gets rid of the gun."

Ingram was a good-sized fellow with a weather-beaten face under uncombed gray hair over which he wore a John Deere baseball cap. His jacket covered a long-sleeved pullover, actually the top half of dirty long johns and the old man wore jeans. Dirt caked the heels of his work boots and he smelled of smoke. The odor came from brewing moonshine. Folks paid Ingram up to $100 a gallon for his moonshine which they turned around and sold to shot houses up north, mostly around Philadelphia and New York.

"Who's watching the Springs?" asked Adams.

"The Springs are just fine." Ingram looked his nephew over. "You know I don't truck with you riding around without a weapon." He brushed back the jacket, revealing the pistol jammed down in his jeans.

The security guard put his hand on his weapon.

"I appreciate your concern, Ingram, but you can head on home. Everything's under control."

"Don't you need people to stay with anyone?"

"Yes, but it's an inside job."

"An inside job?"

"Staying overnight in the hospital."

The old man drew himself up and the pistol slipped farther down into his pants. "I can do that."

"I'm sure you can, but we already have a guard."

Orlando Hanks nodded. "That's my job, Uncle Ingram. That's what I was trying to tell you."

Ingram glanced at the pistol jammed down into his belt. "Well, I guess I'd better get rid of this."

"Why don't you?" said Adams. "We'll wait for you."

"I'll be right back." And the old man shuffled across the lobby and out the glass doors.

"Thanks, Wheeler," Hanks said.

"No problem, Orlando."

Rose Mary watched the old man go. To the security guard, she said, "I'm surprised he didn't accuse you of being part of the conspiracy to disarm America."

"Oh," Hanks said with a laugh, "there's plenty of time for that. I just came on."

Savannah was asleep when they returned to Jackson's room, and Jimmy Carter's Secret Service agent eyed Uncle Ingram as he trailed Rose Mary and

Wheeler into the room. Jackson's condition had not changed. A nurse had told them as much, as she went about checking the IV, something about the Rules of Nine as it applied to burns. The long and short of it was that Jackson would live; Plummer's fate was still in doubt. Nell was in intensive care with her. The preacher sat in one chair, Carter in the other. The teenager slept in Morton's lap with her head on his shoulder.

Carter got to his feet as the Adamses entered the room. "Guess we'd best be getting back to Plains."

Ingram crossed the room to shake his hand. "Didn't know you were here, Jimmy."

Rose Mary introduced Ingram to the Secret Service agent and appeared to enjoy doing it, then pulled her daughter off the preacher. When Savannah came to her feet, she stood there wavering, eyes closed.

"Jimmy, you and Agent Jenkins are welcome to stay at the Springs if you like. I'm going to be there tonight."

Adams glanced at his wife but said nothing.

"Thank you, Rose, but we have several of the grandchildren with us for the Fourth and that's quite a chore for Rosalynn all by herself."

"What's your opinion on this new series of church burnings, Jimmy?"

"I didn't know there was a new series."

"There've been two up in Carolina and one over in Alabama."

"I think they're deplorable, but the fire in Alabama wasn't racially motivated. It was a prank by kids who were black and they did it on a dare."

"That still leaves the two in South Carolina."

"A black congregation was burned out up north last month," injected her husband.

His wife ignored him. "Your thoughts, Jimmy?"

"Rose, really, it's late. Can we discuss this at another time? Rosalynn's waiting." To the preacher he said, "Charley, there are people from the FBI who'll want to talk with you. I called the district office."

"Thank you, Jimmy."

Carter clapped the black man on one of his wide shoulders. "If you need anything, anything at all, just let me know."

"I will, Jimmy. I will."

Uncle Ingram wasn't going to let this opportunity pass without mentioning the business of registering firearms and how a man couldn't defend himself if he didn't have plenty of *pistoles*.

Rose Mary said, "I suppose you think Jackson and Plummer would've been safer if they'd had guns?"

"It couldn't hurt, Rose. I remember the time—"

"Yes, yes, Ingram, I think we've heard that story— whichever one it is."

"Don't know if Jimmy's heard it or not—about the time somebody tried to burn down the Big House."

"That was one of Wheeler's friends, Ingram."

Jean Chick was waiting for them when the Adamses stepped off the elevator into the lobby. "Wheeler, I was just coming upstairs to talk to you."

"Really, Jean, this isn't a good time." He steered his daughter off the elevator, eyes closed, as if she were sleepwalking. There was no one in the lobby but

Orlando Hanks and the security guard was at the front doors peering through the glass.

"What do you need to see my husband for, Jean?"

"It's about the fire, Ms. Bingham."

"I have the number of someone at the Georgia Bureau of Investigation, if you know something."

"No, no, I don't know who set the fire."

"But I thought—"

"Miss Bingham, do you mind if I speak with your husband. In private."

"If you insist."

Rose Mary took the keys to the pickup, then her daughter from her husband. Rose had left the keys to her car with Uncle Ingram so he'd have a way home. Ingram no longer held a driver's license, one less way the government could track his movements.

Jean watched the two women stagger down the hall where the guard opened the door for them, then accompanied them into the parking lot. She returned her attention to Adams. "Wheeler, you don't think my husband had anything to do with this, do you?"

"I have no idea, Jean."

"Wheeler, you know Heywood better than that— you're related."

"Umpteen times removed."

"But you can't honestly believe Heywood would have anything to do with burning a church. He's a deacon."

"Like I said, Jean, I have no idea what goes through your husband's mind."

She bit her lip. "Are you going to talk to the sheriff about this?"

"I already have and that's why I was put in jail."

"What do you mean? Dale thinks you had something to do with the fire?"

"No, that wasn't it at all."

She regarded him. "Maybe you were slandering my husband and the sheriff wouldn't put up with it?"

"Jean, you know me better than that."

"Wheeler, that's why I'm talking with you. We knew you at one time; none of us knows you now. You're as strange to us as we might appear to you—since you've moved back into the Big House. You live there with all those—"

"People."

"Yes—black people."

"To tell you the truth, there haven't been many white folks who've asked to sharecrop the Springs."

"Because of what people will say."

"Such as your husband?"

"Wheeler, Heywood knows I won't have that kind of talk in the house and I won't have you talking about my husband when he's not here to defend himself."

"Jean, have you forgotten your husband is the leader of the Klan in South Georgia?"

"Wheeler, that's something else you don't understand—if Heywood wasn't in charge, those boys would be in trouble every Saturday night."

"All I know is that one of the first people the FBI will want to talk to is your husband."

She snorted. "The FBI? Them again?"

"Torching churches is a violation of people's civil rights, not to mention—"

"A violation of the coloreds' rights? What about our

rights—the rights of white people?" She shook her head. "We pay taxes and what do we get? Handouts to the lazy and all that corruption in Washington."

"Jean, the FBI's not interested in your political opinions unless they have something to do with destroying black churches."

"Wheeler, I can tell you Heywood never would've had anything to do with something like that."

"I'm glad you're so confident, Jean, because I'm not sure this can't be laid at your family's doorstep, one way or another."

Chapter Six

As Adams returned with his family to Chick Springs, his wife said, "So it's Chick against Chick, is it?"

"Don't be so melodramatic, Rose."

She laughed. "Another black church is torched, a race riot breaks out, a former president is called in to have you released from jail, and I'm the one being melodramatic?"

"No bickering," said their daughter, who sat between them with her eyes closed.

"There are just too many Chicks in this county for you not to clash with one of them sooner or later."

"Heywood and I aren't going to clash, Rose."

"Yeah, right, and members of the Klan didn't do this thing."

"Nowadays they call themselves a 'militia.'"

"Same faces, same racists."

His wife stared into the darkness illuminated by the truck's headlights. Chick County was one hell of a lot darker than she'd remembered. "Anyway, Savannah has a life of her own in Atlanta."

"First, it was *you* who had a life in Atlanta. Now it's our daughter."

"Nobody with half a brain can live out here with these people."

"I said no bickering!" Savannah sat up and opened her eyes, then she leaned forward and peered through the windshield. They were approaching the scene of the fire. As they did, her father slowed down and pulled into a parking lot surrounded by crime scene tape. Here the night smelled like a recently doused campfire and the pickup's headlights made odd-looking shapes out of the gravestones on the far side of the parking lot. Jody Chick walked out from under the darkness of the oak tree. In the teenager's hands was a .22 rifle.

"Oh, hey, Mr. Adams. Didn't know it was you." His smile broadened as he saw who sat alongside Adams. "Hello, Savannah."

The girl brushed back her hair. "Hi, Jody. Were you here for the fire?"

A stricken look crossed the boy's face. "Of course not! I'd never done something like this."

"I didn't mean you done it, Jody. I wondered if you saw the fire."

"No—no!" said the young man, shaking his head. "Daddy and I got here after it started."

"Done it?" muttered Rose Mary in a voice only those in the pickup could hear.

Savannah glanced at her mother as Norwood Sibley skirted the crime-scene tape and walked around the corner of the half-burned building. Sibley was a wiry, energy-filled black man who owned a laundry and dry cleaning service in Lee's Crossroads. Norwood carried on with his customers and the white people loved it. That way they could say they *did* have friends in the black community.

A shotgun lay in the crook of Sibley's arm. "Everything's quiet for now, Wheeler. Hello, Rose Mary." He looked closely at the girl between the two of them. "Savannah, when you gonna bring that little black dress that you were talking about?"

"I will," said the teenager, looking into her lap.

"What little black dress?" demanded her mother. "Not the one I spent over two hundred dollars on? My God, Savannah, I can't believe you've ruined it."

The girl's head snapped up. "It's not ruined, Mother. I just spilled something on it."

"What?"

"None of your business, Mother."

"It will be when I get to the Springs and go through your closet."

"Mother, you can't do that."

"I certainly will . . ." She saw her husband staring at her. "We'll discuss this at the house."

Sibley cleared his throat. "Er—what you hear about Mrs. Plummer and Minny Jackson?"

Adams leaned on the sill of the window. "Minny's feet were burned pretty severely. Mrs. Plummer may not make it."

Jody Chick gasped and almost dropped his rifle.

"But that's Gary's grandma."

"Yes, and Gary's taking it pretty hard."

"But it weren't supposed to happen that way."

Everyone looked at the young man.

"What you mean, Jody?" asked Sibley. "You tole me you didn't know nuthing about this fire."

"But—but I don't."

"Come on, Jody," asked Adams, leaning out the window, "did someone you know have something to do with the fire?"

"No! No! No!" The boy gripped his rifle and stepped back.

"Then what'd you mean by 'it wasn't supposed to happen like this'?"

"Daddy," said Adams' daughter from behind him, "don't cross-examine him. You're not a lawyer anymore."

Jody looked from one adult to the other. "I know the plan. Everybody knows the plan. There's always somebody inside the church on weekends."

His audience stared at him.

Once again Jody looked from one to the other. "They were 'posed to get out! That's what Gary tole me. At the first sign of trouble they were 'posed to get out." He nodded rapidly. "Gary tole me!"

"Calm down, Jody," Adams said. "Nobody's accusing you of anything."

"But you think—"

"Jody, your father is the den leader. The FBI will want to talk to him. That makes sense, doesn't it?"

The boy shook his head. "But it's not right. He didn't do nuthing."

"Do you know who done it?" asked Sibley.

"No, no!" said Jody, stepping away even farther. "I don't know nuthing."

"Relax, Jody. Are you going to be here all night with Mr. Sibley?"

"Yes, yes, I told the preacher I would."

"Where did you see the preacher?" asked Adams.

"At—at the hospital. While—while waiting for daddy to be fixed up."

Rose Mary leaned across her daughter. "Jody, does your father know you're out here?"

"He's at a meeting." The teenager stepped toward the truck and peered into the cab. "I don't reckon you'd let Savannah stay, would you?"

"Absolutely not!"

"Mother!"

While the two women bickered, Adams reached out the window and shook the teenager's hand. "Thanks for doing this, Jody. I know this has to be difficult for you, but I'm sure the congregation appreciates the gesture." He inclined his head toward the man with the shotgun and said with a smile, "And Mr. Sibley makes good company, least that's what all his customers say."

Sibley nodded. "And I brought along some soft drinks and sandwiches. Why don't we have them right now. Wheeler, we'll see you in the morning. 'Night, Rose Mary. Savannah."

As Adams let his foot off the clutch, his daughter said, "Daddy, I want to stay with Jody. And Mr. Sibley."

"That's not going to happen," said her mother.

Sibley pulled out a cell phone. "We'll be fine, Savannah. Don't you worry none."

"I still want to stay!"

Adams put his foot on the brake and leaned out the window again. "What's the story on the sheriff's department?"

"A deputy comes by from time to time."

"Well, I guess that's about all that can be expected on a Saturday night."

"I wouldn't be surprised if the sheriff weren't at the meeting with Jody's . . ." started Sibley. He clapped the teenager on the shoulder. "Jody, how about let's chow down?" And the two men waved to the Adamses as the pickup pulled out of the parking lot.

"I've had a nap, Daddy. If you take me home I'm not going to bed. I promise I won't."

"Savannah," said her mother, "no daughter of mine is going to stay out all night with some boy. Especially in this county."

"Mother, I used to live here. I went to school with Jody."

"And that's what worries me."

"Now what does that mean? Jody's always been square with me."

"Savannah, if I've told you once, I've told you a thousand times, I don't want you talking like that."

The teenager sat back and crossed her arms. "You can't make me go to bed. You can't. Daddy, I'm not going to bed so you might as well turn around and take me back there."

Her father glanced at her. "Savannah, are you really serious about spending the night at a crime scene?"

"Two crime scenes," injected her mother, "if what I heard about a riot after the fire is true. Savannah, we've talked about this before. A young lady does not stay out all night with a young man."

"Mother, that was back in the Dark Ages. Things have changed since then."

"It wasn't that long ago."

"You stayed out all night with Daddy."

"I'm sorry, my dear, but your father and I weren't dating when I was your age."

"But you used to live together."

"I don't know where you get that idea—after we were married, we did."

"Mother—"

"Savannah, this discussion is over. Wheeler, you think it's safe for Jody to be there?"

"I don't think Jody subscribes to his father's beliefs. He has too many black friends on the baseball team."

His wife glanced through the sliding glass window in the rear of the cab. "Well, I guess it's better than a bunch of black people hanging around and waiting for the Klan to take potshots at them."

As they approached the Springs they saw a patrol car parked near the gate. Savannah opened the gate with the remote as her father pulled to a stop and leaned out the window.

"Evening, Johnny."

"Wheeler, this is a surprise. Next time I saw you, I thought you'd be on somebody's spit."

"Will you be patrolling the state highway tonight?"

Temple turned over his engine. "Off and on."

"Would you mind keeping an eye on the church?"

"Don't have to be told that." The string bean man touched a finger to his trooper hat. "Night, Ms. Bingham. Savannah."

The teenager watched him drive away. "I don't like that man."

"I don't want to hear about it, Savannah."

"But, Daddy, you don't understand—"

"I said I don't want to hear about it."

As they approached the Big House they saw a figure on the veranda. By the time they crossed the gravel turnaround, Roosevelt was walking down the side of the house, paralleling the pickup. In his hands was a double-barreled shotgun. At the barn Adams turned the pickup around and stepped down from the cab. When the elderly black man reached the barn, everyone could see he was not pleased.

"Nell and Ingram are staying at the hospital," explained Adams. "Nell asked if Aurelia could put together some clothes for her, and since everyone's in for the night, I'm going to set the alarm."

Roosevelt nodded.

Savannah slid out of the cab behind her father. "Really, Daddy, I'm not the least bit sleepy, and I'm not saying that just because . . ." The teenager saw her mother coming out of the cab behind her. "Oh, all right! I don't have a chance against the two of you." And she stalked off toward the Big House.

"Good night, Roosevelt," Rose Mary said.

"Good night, Miss Rose."

"And thanks for being there for me tonight."

"It were nothing, Miss Rose. I was happy to do it."
He watched the woman follow her daughter into the
house. After she was gone, the black man turned to
Adams. "Mister Wheeler, we gots a problem."

"I'll speak with Ingram in the morning."

"I'd 'preciate that," said the gardener, setting his
jaw. "If our cabins get burned down, Ingram can still
keep on living in his place down along the river, but
we'll have no place to go."

Roosevelt was referring to the Yuppie log homes in
which he and Nell's family lived. They stood between
the family garden and the wood line behind the Big
House. The two cabins had replaced a set of mobile
homes; before that a couple of forty-foot dogtrot cabins housed many of the slaves who had lived at Chick
Springs. The log homes fitted in with the look of an
antebellum plantation but were completely modern-
ized, down to having their own satellite dish. Roosevelt
had one cabin to himself; Nell's family consisted of a
grown daughter by the name of Aurelia and her grand-
daughter, Rebekah. Rebekah was off at SAT camp and
most days Aurelia could be found along the river helping Ingram brew 'shine. This disturbed Nell, but
Aurelia didn't appear to be sampling the wares and
there were few decent-paying jobs in Chick County.

"Good night, Roosevelt."

"Good night, Mister Wheeler."

After following the women into the house, Adams
set the alarm, then crossed through the kitchen where
everyone shared meals, then a dining room used for
public relations.

Whenever Nell thought they needed to schmooze

someone, the long table was set with china that had been in the family since the turn of the century and silverware buried when Sherman's Army marched through Georgia. A corner hutch and sideboard held even more silver, china, and crockery. On those special nights Nell pressed Roosevelt into service, having the gardener wait on the dinner table, pour drinks, and offer cigars after the meal. Nell only appeared once—for the guests to congratulate her on the meal. So when the guests left it appeared that the master was in his place, the servants in theirs. However, once the last guest was gone, it was Adams who cleared the table and washed the dishes. Silverware and china this special couldn't be run through a dishwasher— which might be one reason why Adams didn't care much for company.

Ten thousand acres is one hell of a lot of land to secure, so Adams didn't even try. He employed sensors along the road, more forming a grid around the Big House and the homes of Nell and Roosevelt, the garage and barn. Adams checked the double doors at the front entrance, then climbed the circular stairs to the master bedroom where his wife waited.

As he walked into the bedroom she handed him a bourbon and water. Rose Mary was already in a pair of long-sleeved, green silk pajamas; nipples already hard, but that could've been from the air conditioning.

"Get out of those clothes, Wheeler. You're stinking up the house."

"I need to say good night to Savannah."

"You're too late. The moment her head hit the pillow she was asleep. She didn't even take off her clothes. So much for being able to stay up all night."

The bedroom was furnished with antiques, but the bed had been extended to accommodate Adam's six-foot plus frame. As her husband eased down on the chaise lounge, Rose Mary asked, "You think Jody knows something about the fire?"

Adams nodded, then grimaced as he unbuttoned the shirt. When his wife saw the difficulty he was having getting out of his clothes, she put down her drink and helped him off with the shirt. At the sight of all the bruises, she shuddered. "Wheeler, you're too old for this shit."

"You may be right."

"You know, one day you're going to get yourself killed. Think of what that'll do to Savannah."

Adams didn't think there was an adequate response to that and reached for his shoes. When he did the pain left him gasping.

His wife bent down and pulled off one shoe, then the other. "What are you going to do about Jody?"

Leaning on the arm of the chaise lounge, Adams lifted his rump and his wife pulled off his pants. "I'll talk with him again tomorrow."

"I want to be there when you do."

"Don't push it, Rose."

Adams ignored the hand offered by his wife and fumbled his way off the chaise lounge. Taking his drink along, he tottered into the adjoining room which had once been a parlor. Now the former parlor had a tile floor, a modern tub, shower, and wash basin with plenty of light.

Rose Mary followed him into the bathroom.

"Wheeler, I may work in the editorial room, but I'm still a reporter."

Adams opened the cabinet and found a codeine tablet, which he downed with the last of his bourbon.

"Jody may have set the fire, Wheeler. Kids set fires outside buildings and run away, at least that's what all the studies show."

Adams turned on the water in the tub and checked its temperature. Jean Chick had said he was to take sponge baths, but he was really nasty and his wife was right. He stunk.

"Gary Plummer's the shortstop on the same team as Jody Chick. Jody could've learned the congregation's plans—for protecting the church."

"And picked a night when he was sure there would be fire guards there?" Adams handed his empty glass to his wife. "May I have another drink?"

When she returned Adams was naked and trying to figure how he'd wash himself without getting his bandages wet or soaking the floor. Rose Mary handed him the drink, knelt down, and tested the water.

"I'm not sure I can get in there, Rose."

Rose Mary took one of the good towels from a wooden rack and lay it on the floor beneath him. "Straddle the side by putting your hands in the water. I'll take care of the rest."

She did, saving his groin for last.

August 8, 1867—The schoolteacher arrived
& this Yankee Woman is just as difficult as I
had imagined. She is Katherine Sherwood
from Boston, Massachusetts & is an old

maid of 27 who will never find a suitable mate. Actually, that is not quite fair as there are quite a few women, on either side of the Mason-Dixon Line, who shall never have husbands. The War killed thousands, some say Georgia lost over 40,000 & I have little reason to doubt that figure. Many men I knew did not return & I helped dig many a mass grave for Yankees. The first Argument we had was over when the children would be available for Schooling. The conversation took place in my Study with me trying to keep a civil tongue in my mouth.

Katherine Sherwood is a large woman. She is not fat, but is big, bony & favors my wife in that regard—able to get chores done without a great deal of help from those need-ed in the fields. Miss Sherwood stands almost as tall as me, has brown hair worn in a kerchief & a severe look about her. And she shows considerable disdain for our Way of Life. When she said she was here to edu-cate the freedmen, I told her I for one, did not see the benefit of educating the former slaves. The woman astonished me by saying there were schools being built in Atlanta just for that Purpose.

I told her I had been to Atlanta & there was little left since General Sherman had passed through. What I wished to know was, is the Union Army building schools for the freedmen before putting up housing for

*White People? She said they were. I could
not believe what she said & told her so. She
replied there were negroes who did not have
a place to live. I said that was not the White
Man's concern. My slaves had chosen to
leave me, not the other way around. The
woman got on her high horse & told me she
would not debate the War with me, that we
Rebs would have to accommodate ourselves
to a new way of life. She went on to add we
better pay attention to what the Bureau
said. The woman meant the Freedman's
Bureau & there wasn't a more evil arm of
government ever created by the mind of
man. Now, I will grant you the Bureau did
good work when its goal was to care for the
former slaves, but when the Bureau tried
raising the freedmen up to the position of
White People, it lost all support in Ga.*

*I told Miss Sherwood that she would have
to change a lot of minds & she said that was
not her Business, but the Business of the
Army. She said Force was all we Rebs
understood & it was no more than the way
we treated our slaves before Mr. Lincoln.*

*The initial meeting came to an abrupt end
when Miss Sherwood said I could not pull
the wool over her eyes, that she had read
Uncle Tom's Cabin & was well aware of us
Simon Legree types. To my wife's credit, she
hurried the Fool out of my Study & kept her
away from Me the remainder of the day. And*

Me? I am proud to say I did not strike the Woman. Fiction or not, Simon Legree had been a Yankee.

Chapter Seven

The Klan met in the rear of Albert Lockaby's Garage, the Honorable Heywood Chick presiding. Those able to sit upright sat in the rear, licking their wounds; those who had missed the fight sat toward the front, spoiling for another.

Imagine! Going toe to toe with the niggers, and from what they'd heard, bested the lot of them, even when reinforcements had arrived. Must've been close to fifty of them baboons out there and their Den had stood their ground against them!

A lectern was flanked by the two most popular symbols of the Klan: the traditional blood drop which looked like a "t" within a circle. That drop represented the blood of Christ which had been shed for the Aryan race; Jesus Christ being the most popular Jew within the Klan. The second symbol was the crosswheel, popularized during the 1970s and appeared to be a cross within a circle, surrounded by a square tilted on one corner. It made the new members dizzy just looking at it, and you could always pick out the new guys, heads canted to one side, trying to make out the thing.

Heywood wore a bandage over his right eye; the side of his bald head had a scrape running the length of it and he had several cracked ribs, but as he told his wife, he didn't have time for x-rays. Leaning on the lectern now, he wagged a finger at the men in the folding chairs in front of him. There were about twenty between the ages of sixteen and sixty, but the fellow nearing sixty would have to be going home soon. His wife didn't like him staying out all hours and there was church tomorrow.

"Now listen up!" said Heywood, wagging his finger at his charges. "If you know something about this thing I don't want to hear about it." His gaze fell on each and every man in the room. An air conditioner worked overtime to reduce the heat and stink of too many bodies in need of a good bath. "And I don't want you bragging about it outside the Den."

Ozzie Tucker, who had both a sore jaw and a sore stomach from where Wheeler Adams had hit him, spoke up. Moments ago Tucker had been boasting to the latecomers about his prowess out on the state highway. "Now, Heywood, don't be that way. Maybe somebody has some bragging to do."

Garland Kelly sat alongside Tucker. Kelly was the one who'd used his CB to call for the reinforcements that had never arrived. It was later determined most of those reinforcements had been at the Lonesome Pine and deep in their cups.

"It ain't gonna happen here, Ozzie."

"Heywood—"

"Ozzie, you want to run this Den, then run for office next time it comes up."

"That wasn't what I was saying."

"Then shut your damn mouth!"

Tucker sat back in his chair, crossed his legs at the ankles, and stared at his boots. Garland Kelly looked from Tucker to Heywood and back again. Not only did Kelly have the same sore stomach as Tucker, but he'd left a good meal on the side of the road when Adams had hit him. Now he asked, "Heywood?"

But the Klan leader had turned to the sergeant at arms, the only member allowed to wear a sidearm during meetings. "Jerry, let the sheriff in."

That didn't set all that well with the sergeant at arms. He'd missed the fight and any chance at bragging rights. "Now wait a minute, Heywood," said the sergeant at arms from the door.

The Den leader lurched off the lectern. "Jerry, you want me to do your job for you?"

Tucker unfolded his legs and sat up again. "Heywood, maybe we're not through talking this out."

"And I said we were."

"Ozzie's got a point," Garland Kelly said. "Why can't we talk this out?"

Heywood gritted his teeth and told the sergeant at arms to inform the sheriff it'd be a few minutes before Dale Posey could speak to the Den. Actually it was a lot longer than that.

When the sheriff arrived home later that night he found his wife still up. That was odd. Their boy was a handful and his wife usually fell asleep in front of the TV waiting for him to come home.

Charlene Posey was as tall as her husband, with gangly curves, a flat chest, and a rather large nose. Behind her back folks said her son favored her husband with his good looks. To Charlene they said the boy favored his mother—with his intelligence.

"The judge said for you to call him." Though Charlene was Bennefield's sister, she still called her brother the judge. It kept peace in the family.

Posey glanced at his watch. Almost midnight. First, it had been Adams riling up the Negroes again, then Jimmy Carter sticking his nose where it didn't belong, and he had to go over and calm down the Klan after they finished crawling out of the emergency room. And he had to wait to speak to them. Would've fallen asleep if it hadn't been for all the screaming and hollering coming from their meeting room. And those people think they can keep a secret. He would've said to heck with them all, but the judge always wanted to know what the Klan was up to. And the dadgum soda machine had been out of Cokes. Oh sure, they had the diet ones, but who could drink that stuff? All he'd wanted was to hit the sack until the barbecue tomorrow, but that wasn't going to happen anytime soon.

"What'd the judge want?" he asked.

His wife shook her head.

"He didn't say nothing?"

"He didn't say nothing, Dale."

"Nothing?"

"That's right. Nothing. Just for you to call."

Posey stood there, then went over and plopped down in the recliner in front of a big screen TV. A nice-looking model bought at the Super Wal-Mart over in Macon. But what's the use of making payments on your MasterCard if you couldn't enjoy your purchase? Posey raised the recliner's footrest rather violently and loosened his string tie before picking up the portable phone.

"Why you still standing there, Charlene? Ain't I been gone long enough to rate at least a sandwich and a cold beer?"

His wife nodded. Charlene Posey didn't like it when her husband drank, but as long as he never missed a day of work and turned his paycheck over to her, who was she to complain?

After the woman disappeared into the kitchen, Posey touched "one" on the speed dial. The phone at the other end was picked up after the first ring. It always startled the sheriff that the judge knew who was calling. Fact was, Bennefield wouldn't answer the phone if he didn't see a name on the caller ID so all those out-of-area calls were left to his wife. If she was interested, and what woman wasn't.

"Dale, I am getting a lot of phone calls and it's not about tomorrow's party. What's the story?"

Posey laid out everything for the judge, including the fire and the riot on the state highway. It wasn't smart to keep anything from the judge. Bennefield had more than one person reporting to him. Posey added that he'd even locked up Wheeler Adams.

"You've still got him there?"

"No, sir." Posey explained why.

"Carter again—huh?"

"Yes, sir."

"Who you reckon called him?"

Sitting in the recliner, Posey shrugged, but that wasn't anything the judge could hear, so he said, "I suppose it was one of his colored friends."

More silence, then Bennefield asked, "What makes a white man hang out with those people? Adams played football in college, not basketball."

Posey said nothing.

"What you think he's up to out there, Dale?"

"What you mean, Judge?"

"Adams has got all the money he needs. Why'd he move back here? Was it just to get my goat?"

The sheriff didn't have an opinion on the subject, but he wouldn't have ventured one even if he had.

"You know that high yellow lives at the Springs—what's that gal's name, one about Adams' age?"

"The one he sleeps with? That's Aurelia."

Bennefield made a derisive sound from deep in his throat. "Yeah, right. There's those who say that high yellow's an Adams."

"You're shitting me." Now Posey thumped the recliner into the sitting position.

"Watch your language, Dale. You have a child in the house now. You know, it wasn't long after that gal was born the Adams moved into Atlanta. Where is he now—Adams' old man?"

"Heard he moved back to Boston."

"Uh-huh. My daddy always said Florence Adams was one of the best-looking women in all Chick

County. Did Jimmy Carter stay in town?"

"If he did it'd have to be at the Springs." Lee's Crossroads didn't have a decent hotel and wasn't likely to get one anytime soon.

"I don't like that answer, Dale."

"Judge, all my deputies are out patrolling. They would've seen Carter if—"

"With all your deputies patrolling, did they happen to see who tried to burn my son out tonight?"

Posey waved off his wife who had returned with his sandwich and beer. It was just like the judge to sandbag him. "Junior? What happened?"

"When the colored couldn't get to me because of all the goings-on here—we've got the pigs on the spit and Red and his people are staying up all night cooking it—the damn niggers went down the road and threw something at my boy's house. 'Bout scared Lizzie to death. She's here with us now and one of Red's men is guarding the house."

"What about the house?" Posey held his breath.

"Burned the carport, that's all."

"The cars?"

"One car's in Lockaby's Garage, the other's in Wallace County with Junior. You know, Dale, those people down in Wallace County best never be caught up here. A man should be home with his family on the Fourth, not in some jail for carousing."

The sheriff didn't know what to say to that. The judge had put many a Chick County carouser in jail.

"I don't want any more trouble tonight. You got that, Dale, no more problems."

"I got it, Judge."

The line went dead.

Posey put down the phone and sat there lost in thought, then took the sandwich and the beer from his wife. He ate one, drank the other, and left the house again. As he headed out the door, his wife asked, "Any idea when you'll be back?"

"Nope. I'll catch a nap before the party, but I'll miss church for sure."

"I was thinking of taking the baby over to the judge's for the rest of the night, you know, stay in the guest room."

Posey considered that. "Might not be a bad idea."

At the half-burned out church a cell phone buzzed. Norwood Sibley slipped the instrument off his hip and read the screen, then hustled toward his car. "Jody!"

The white boy stumbled out from behind the oak. He was zipping his fly. "Yes—yes, sir?"

Sibley stuck his shotgun in his 4x4 and climbed in behind it. "Somebody's breaking into my place." The black man cranked the engine, then wheeled around to leave the parking lot. "At least I hope that's all they're doing. You watch yourself, boy." Sibley slipped the vehicle into gear and was gone.

Jody ducked. "Yes . . . sir." Sibley's tires spit gravel. The teenager looked around. Now where had he put his rifle? Mr. Sibley had taken the light and he'd forgotten to bring one along.

On the way into town Sibley punched in some numbers on his cell phone. When the sleepy voice of Dean Meckler answered, Sibley explained his predicament.

"You say Jody Chick is guarding our church?" asked Meckler.

"That's right."

"Norwood, are you crazy?"

"What was I supposed to do—run him off?"

"You're damn right, and that's the first thing I'm gonna do when I get there."

At the hospital Charley Morton and Uncle Ingram left by the emergency room exit. In the parking lot they found Morton's tires slashed. The old Grand Prix sat like a defeated warrior, parked between a minivan and a pickup truck.

Morton sighed. "I guess I'll be walking home."

"No, you won't." Ingram fished a set of keys out of his jeans. "Take Rose Mary's. It's over there." He pointed at a lime green Z-car under a light.

"I don't know about that, Ingram. I heard Rose Mary doesn't like anyone driving her car."

Ingram snorted. "You pay attention to what that woman says and you'll be one of the few." He motioned Morton around to the front of the building. "Let me show you something."

At the front of the building were several camellia bushes and behind one of the bushes a water pipe ran up the side of the hospital. Stuck behind the pipe was a revolver in a bandanna. Ingram glanced at the front doors, then rolled the weapon out of the cloth and handed it to the preacher.

Morton raised his hands. "Ingram, I can't carry that. I don't have a permit."

"Charley, you've got to be prepared to defend yourself. Look what they done to your tires."

"Ingram, I don't think a pistol's going to solve my problems."

"You gonna let people push you around?"

Morton laughed. "That's the least of my worries."

"Charley, I don't think it's your knee giving you as much trouble as your spine."

Well, that did it. After having his church practically burned down, his tires slashed, and enduring a frosty reception by the church elders, Morton would not let this white man stand here and tell him he didn't have the *cojones* to carry a pistol.

Morton took the revolver and rolled the chamber, finding it empty. "But there's no bullets in here."

"Damn right." Ingram dug around in his pockets. "Some kid could've found that gun."

So the preacher took the borrowed pistol and the borrowed car and went home to the house lent to him by his congregation. When he arrived, he saw something he'd seen several times before: his dead wife waiting for him. Well, it had been that kind of a day. So he broke the seal on a new bottle, found a relatively clean glass, and brought the woman up to date on all the goings-on.

Wheeler Adams was in a deep sleep when the phone woke him up. He rolled over, trying to figure why he ached all over. Then he remembered the fire and the fight out on the state highway.

From the other side of the bed, his wife said, "If that's the paper, tell them I burned my hands and can't help with the rewrite."

"You called in a story?" Adams fumbled for the receiver as the phone rang again.

"A church burning—wouldn't you?"

Adams found the phone in the light from a clock with hands and Roman numerals. It was after 4 AM. Who'd be calling at this hour?

His daughter.

"I'll wring her damn neck," said Rose Mary as she bounded out of bed naked, then thumped across the hardwood floor to the chaise lounge where her robe lay. She slipped into the robe, jerked open the door of the bedroom, and stalked down the hall.

Adams' head felt like it was stuffed with cotton and Savannah sounded a long ways off. Well, at least his legs didn't sting. Maybe they did, just off in the distance somewhere. "Pumpkin, what's wrong? Are you having a bad dream?" Turned out it was Chick County having the nightmare.

Adams hung up and made a call of his own. He was hanging up when his wife rushed back into the bedroom.

"Savannah's not in her room! Not in the bathroom. Not anywhere."

"She's at the church. It's on fire again. I just called Bobbie Lee."

His wife's mouth fell open. "What in the world is she doing there?"

"She went to help Jody Chick guard the church."

Rose Mary stripped off her robe and tossed it on the chaise lounge. "When I get my hands on that young lady . . ." She jerked open a drawer of an antique highboy. Facing her husband after she had hooked her brassiere, she asked, "But how did she get out of the house without the alarm going off?"

Across the room Adams was struggling into his pants. "That's . . . the first question . . . I'm going to ask her . . . when we get there."

Chapter Eight

*T*he second fire wasn't anything like the first. This time, what remained of the building was in flames by the time Adams and his wife arrived. Dean Meckler was there, screaming and hollering and waving a shotgun. When the Adamses pulled into the parking lot he swung his weapon around on them.

"Easy, Dean," said Adams, climbing down from the pickup. "It's Wheeler." The black man stood in front of the burned-out vestibule and auditorium. Behind him the rest of the building was aflame.

"Come to see the fire, Wheeler?" Meckler's eyes were wide with rage or despair, Adams didn't know which. Spittle drooled from the corner of his mouth. "That why you're here?"

From behind the door on the other side of the cab, Rose Mary asked, "Where's my daughter?"

The shotgun in Meckler's hands swung around. It

was an older model with a single barrel and its ham-mer pulled back. "Your daughter? Why would your daughter be here?"

"She called us from here."

"What are you doing here, Dean?" asked Adams.

Meckler returned his attention to Adams and as he did, the shotgun swung in the white man's direction. "Me? I come to guard the church."

"Where's Norwood?"

"Had a break-in at his place." He shrugged and lowered the shotgun. "I took his place."

"Where's Jody Chick?"

"Haven't seen him." Meckler glanced behind him. "Guess he left after setting the fire."

Rose Mary came around her door, leaving it open. "I don't give a damn about any of this! I want to know what you've done with my daughter."

The shotgun swung in her direction. "I haven't done anything to your daughter."

"Put down the shotgun, Dean." Adams joined his wife at the front of the truck.

Meckler glanced at the weapon as if seeing it for the first time, then threw it to the ground. When the shotgun hit, it discharged across the parking lot. Everyone jumped. Adams looked from where the shot-gun lay and saw his wife running for the far side of the building and shouting their daughter's name. Adams picked up the shotgun, broke the barrel, and expend-ed the empty shell.

Meckler stood there, shoulders slumped, staring at the ground. "I'm—I'm sorry . . . I didn't mean for that to happen."

Adams took Meckler's arm and steered him over to his Cadillac parked under the oak tree. "Why don't you sit here, Dale. The volunteers will be here any minute."

In the distance they could hear the siren.

Adams sat Meckler on the edge of the seat, then took the keys from the ignition. He saw a box of shells scattered across the backseat and scooped them up and locked them in the trunk with the shotgun. Tossing the keys on the floorboard of the backseat, Adams left Meckler sitting on the side of the front seat, shoulders slumped, staring at the ground. By now the sanctuary was completely gone and the fire had chewed its way into the choir room. Behind the church Adams found his wife and the two teenagers.

Savannah sat with her back against the bench of one of the concrete picnic tables. She held Jody Chick's head in her lap, a folded handkerchief under his head. Her mountain bike leaned against one of the tables; on her back was a pack, and she wore the clothes she'd supposedly fallen asleep in. Her mother sat on the bench with a helpless look on her face.

Suddenly a patrol car whipped into the parking lot and slid to a stop in the gravel. Johnny Temple stepped out and shone his spotlight, first on Adams' pickup, then Dean Meckler in his Cadillac. Not finding what he was looking for, Temple slid into his patrol car and pulled around the church to check out the rear of the building.

Smoke billowed out the door Adams had knocked down earlier; down the hall you could see a flickering light. But the best light came from the spotlight

Temple left on to stride into the picnic area. The string bean man couldn't help looking at the fire.

"I don't understand. I was just here. Damn CNN was just here." He stared at Jody Chick lying with his head in Savannah's lap. "What happened?"

Savannah looked up. "Somebody hit Jody over the back of the head, Mr. Temple."

"See who done it?" asked the deputy.

Jody shook his head, winced and stopped. Tears ran down his cheeks. "Daddy ain't gonna be happy. He always says a good soldier is . . . is never caught unawares."

"They hit him from behind, Mr. Temple. How could he see anything?"

"Savannah, watch your tone," cautioned her mother.

"What did you see?" asked her father.

"When I got here the church was already on fire. I called you from the rise." She gestured at the field behind them, but all they could see beyond the picnic tables was darkness, and the occasional weird shadow cast by the flames advancing under the eaves.

"Who's that in the Cadillac?" asked Temple.

"Dean Meckler," Adams said.

"He was in the front? The boy was in the back?"

"It's more complicated than that."

Temple shook his head. "This don't make no damn sense at all." He returned to the cruiser and turned off the engine and made a couple of calls. One of them was patched through to the sheriff, the other to Heywood Chick.

Adams asked, "Have your cell phone handy, Savannah?"

"Yes, Daddy."

Rose Mary replaced her daughter, holding the handkerchief to the back of Jody's head as her daughter wiggled out from under the lanky teenager. Savannah dug the phone out of her backpack and handed it to her father. Adams powered up the instrument and called Bobbie Lee. On the other end he heard the pumper and its siren.

"There's no hurry, Bobbie Lee. This time it's a total loss."

"We've still got a fire to put out. What the hell happened? We soaked everything in sight."

"The rear of the building, too?"

For a moment there was only the sound of the siren and the roar of the engine, then Lee said, "We soaked the roof and the sides and the rear, but there weren't no fire in the choir room. I went inside and checked. I can guarantee that fire was out, and it didn't make no sense to water down the rest of the church and ruin everything. Those folks had already lost enough."

"The arsonist probably entered through the back door and started the fire there."

"Weren't the sheriff guarding it?"

"Johnny Temple was making his rounds."

The deputy heard this as he returned to the picnic area. "All I was told to do was ride by as often as possible. Saturday nights we don't have enough people to pull guard duty anywheres."

"What about the congregation?" shouted Lee over the noise at her end. "Didn't they have anybody there?"

"Norwood Sibley."

"He had to go into town," said Jody, sitting up and holding the handkerchief to the back of his head. "Somebody broke in his place."

"I didn't hear about that," Temple said.

Rose Mary flashed a look of incredulity.

"Mrs. Adams, I'm telling you I didn't get any call. Now whether you believe me or not ain't my problem."

"My name is 'Bingham,' Deputy."

"Do we have to get into that?" asked her husband.

Jody twisted around, looking for something. "Where's my rifle?"

Adams patted the boy's shoulder. "Don't worry. We'll find it. Just sit there and rest."

"My daddy gave me that rifle for Christmas. He'll whip my butt but good if'n I've lost it."

"I don't think your father's going to be anything but proud of you for what you've . . ." Rose Mary saw everyone staring at her and stopped. She shrugged.

The siren wound down as the pumper pulled into the parking lot and Bobbie Lee climbed down from her side, Ernie Ellis from the other. Following the pumper was a sedan. The car stopped beside the Cadillac and a middle-aged black man got out. It was Tad Browning. Glancing at the fire, he opened his trunk and pulled out a garden hose, then hurried over to the faucet. Tears ran down the black man's face as he hooked the hose to the faucet, then quickly uncoiled it down the side of the church. In seconds he was spraying the side of the burning building.

As Bobbie Lee and Ernie Ellis laid out the fire hose, more black people arrived. Most were teenagers and

Bobbie Lee could see they were hotter than any fire. By the time the sheriff arrived the young men had clumped together, not giving the volunteers any assistance, just standing there, glaring. Following them into the rapidly filling parking lot was Heywood Chick's station wagon. Oh my, thought Bobbie Lee, but this is going to get interesting and in a real hurry.

"Around here, Sheriff," shouted Johnny Temple, who stood near his cruiser parked on the other side of the crime scene tape beside the burning building.

Heywood Chick followed Dale Posey toward the rear. They in turn were followed by the young black men.

As the sheriff passed by, Temple asked, "Want me to call for backup?"

Posey stopped. "And why would you do that?"

Temple gestured at the clump of young men. Even Edward Nance was there, heading toward the people gathered around the picnic benches.

"That might be a good idea," said Posey, seeing the young men. "CNN still around?"

Temple shook his head. "Took their pictures and left. Said they'd be back at first light."

"On the Fourth? I doubt it."

"Thanks for the call, Johnny," said Heywood Chick before following the sheriff around to the rear of the church.

There they found Jody Chick on a bench and Edward Nance examining the back of the teenager's head with a penlight. Savannah Adams sat across from Jody, her parents stood behind her.

"Adams, what are you doing here?" asked the sheriff.

"What are you doing here, Jody?" asked the boy's father.

"I—I was . . . I was—"

"He was guarding the church," Savannah said.

"But why?" asked Heywood. "They've got plenty of niggers for that."

Nance looked up from Jody's head. "Heywood, you want your son to bleed to death?"

The Klan leader stepped over, took his son's head in his hands, and looked for himself. "That ain't nothing but a scratch. He'll be just fine."

"If you can get him out of here." Nance inclined his head toward the group of young black men between them and the police cruiser.

Heywood nodded. "Guess it's best you do what you can do . . . Doctor."

Nance pressed the handkerchief against the boy's head again. "Jody, I need to stitch this up."

"Adams," said the sheriff, "this is the second time I've found you at a crime scene."

"Savannah called and said the church was on fire."

"And what were you doing here, young lady?"

"Coming to help Jody guard the church."

"In the middle of the night? No daughter of mine would be out at this hour. It's not right."

"She certainly didn't have our permission," said her mother.

"You oughta tan her hide."

"I'm almost eighteen, Mr. Posey," said Savannah, standing. "Much too old for whippings."

"Maybe in your house, young lady, but the kids I find out after midnight are the ones I usually have to put in jail when they grow up."

"You won't have to put me in jail. I can guarantee you that. I'm an honor student."

"Can we get back on track here?" asked Adams. "You should be worried about who set this second fire."

"And who hit Jody over the head," added Savannah.

"Jody," said his father, "when I left you at home I told you to stay there."

"I—I just wanted to help out . . . ."

"This ain't none of your business, son."

Adams said, "It's all of our business, Heywood."

"Don't tell me how to raise my kid, Wheeler. You ain't doing such a good job yourself."

"Shut up, you two!"

The roof of the addition collapsed, landing in one piece and shooting flames from under it. Those standing too close yelped and jumped back. Many coughed. But none of the young men moved. Those in the picnic area could feel the spray from the water being put on the fire by the volunteers. Rose Mary took her daughter by the hand and led her away.

"Mrs. Adams, I may have more questions for her."

Rose Mary stopped and sighed, then pointed at the darkness behind the picnic area. "When Savannah topped that rise she saw the fire and called us, then came down here and found Jody behind the building. He was unconscious. That's all she knows, Mr. Posey."

"That may not be—"

"Sheriff, if you wish to interrogate any members of this family please call ahead so we can have our attorney present. Wheeler, would you bring along Savannah's bike?" And the two women left, skirting the fire and the crime scene tape by going through the church graveyard.

Nance stood up. "Let's take your boy out to my car, Heywood. I'll stitch him up there."

"If it's all the same to you, I'll take him to the hospital and have his mother do it."

Nance let out a sigh. "Heywood, do you ever think before you open your damn mouth?"

The white man bristled, leaned forward, and jutted out his jaw. "Now what makes you say something like that?"

"Nance," Posey said, "you got no right talking to him like that."

The doctor gestured at the black kids huddled between them and the cruiser where Johnny Temple was on the radio. "Got a pretty good crowd here, Heywood. Wouldn't it be smarter for me to stitch up your boy where they can see you and me working together, not fighting among ourselves?"

As Adams rolled his daughter's bike past them, he said, "You'd better listen to what Nance has to say. Someone firebombed Junior Bennefield's house tonight."

The doctor was plainly shocked. The Klan leader looked surprised.

"Adams," asked Posey, "how do you know that?"

"My gardener told me before I left the Springs."

"I may want to speak with your gardener."

"Like my wife said, if you want to interrogate any member of our family, give us a call before you drop by."

"And you, Adams, don't be in such a hurry to leave."

"Just running the bike out to the truck, Sheriff. But I'd be quick with your questions. Sooner or later my wife's going to remember *she* wants to question you about where you were when this fire broke out."

"At a meeting with me," volunteered Heywood Chick.

"A Klan meeting."

"Hell, Adams, figure it out," Posey said. "When the GBI arrives the first question they'll ask is if I've talked with the Klan."

"Still won't look good in my wife's paper," said Adams as he rolled the bike away.

"That family thinks they own this damn county," Posey muttered after him.

"Well, they do, don't they?" Nance slapped the Klan leader on the shoulder. "Come on, Heywood, let's get your boy sewn up."

Jody looked at his father. "The colored guy is going to stitch me up?"

Nance had started away. Now he returned. "Yes, Jody, I'm a colored guy. But what color?"

The boy glanced at his father. "Er—black."

"Yes, and what color are you?"

Jody glanced at his father again. "White?"

"Yes, Jody. We're all colored people, aren't we?"

And Nance took the teenager by the arm and walked him through the clump of young men who made way for them.

Adams wheeled the bike toward his pickup parked at the front of the church. He had left the keys in the ignition and someone had moved his pickup again, but the crime scene tape had been trampled underfoot. Savannah sat on the edge of the seat in the cab, staring at the ground and taking a tongue-lashing.

"She disabled the alarm, Wheeler."

Adams lifted the bike into the bed of the pickup. "How'd you do it, Savvy?"

"Wheeler, how many times have I told you I don't like you calling her that. It makes her sound like some kind of wild animal."

"Well, Pumpkin?"

His daughter looked up. "I wrote a new program."

"I beg your pardon?"

"Savannah, where in the world did you learn how to write computer programs?"

"A guy at school taught me."

"What does the program do?" asked her father.

"At the top and the bottom of the hour, the sensors shut down for one minute, but only for a minute."

"Savannah, that computer belongs to your father."

"He lets me use it. Sometimes I write papers on it."

"Don't give me that. You don't surf the Web, you chat with your friends."

The girl shrugged.

Her father was studying his daughter. "That's why you always set your watch by the computer, isn't it?"

She stared at the ground. "Yes, sir."

"Do you understand what you did that was wrong?"

Her mother jumped in with, "You didn't ask permission to use your father's computer, you disobeyed us when we distinctly told you not to go out again, and you put yourself in danger." Rose Mary glanced at the ruins being soaked by the volunteers. "Did you ever think what might've happened if you'd been here when Jody Chick was attacked?"

Savannah slid off the seat. "Nothing would've happened, Mother."

"Nothing would've happened? What do you mean nothing would've happen? You don't have any idea what could've happened. Seventeen years old and you think you know everything." A finger was waved in the girl's face. "You're grounded, young lady. You hear me? You're not to leave the house until I say so."

"Mother, you can't do that."

"What are you talking about? I certainly can. I'm your mother. Wheeler, are you going to help me here?"

"Maybe you should back off a bit, Rose."

His wife shot him a look, then reaching past her daughter, she snatched a pack of cigarettes and a lighter off the dashboard. "She's all yours. And while you're at it, do something about that attitude."

"Hers or mine?"

"Both!"

Savannah opened her mouth to say something, but her father silenced her with an upraised hand. He was watching the people following Edward Nance and Jody Chick to the doctor's Buick. Behind them came the boy's father, the sheriff, and a group of angry young black men.

At his car Nance opened his medical bag on the hood, then worked on Jody Chick while his father held the light. Johnny Temple remained at his cruiser where he had unlocked the shotgun from the dash and had the weapon within arm's reach. Tad Browning leaned against the side of his car, garden hose in his hand, water still spraying the side of the building. Someone turned off the faucet. Still, Browning didn't move. Tears ran down the black man's cheeks as he stared at what was left of his church.

"What's Jody Chick doing here?" asked someone beside Edward Nance's Buick.

Heywood glanced in the direction of the voice. When he did Nance complained. "Heywood, keep that light steady. I'm opening a suture here. To answer your question: Jody was guarding the church."

"Maybe he torched it after Norwood Sibley left."

"And hit himself over the back of the head?" asked the sheriff. "Are you people stupid? Heywood didn't know his boy was here, didn't want him to be here."

The Klan leader cleared his throat. "That's right."

"People," said Edward Nance, "please go home. We've got a long day ahead of us and it just got a lot longer."

"Yeah," said one of the young men, "and we know who's responsible for that."

The sheriff tried to say something, but Nance cut him off. "Where's the preacher?"

"I went by his house and hammered on his door," said Dean Meckler, "but he didn't answer."

"He's in there," said someone in a derisive tone. "He just can't make it to the door."

"Listen up, folks," said the sheriff. "We've all got problems. Now, I'm giving you two minutes to clear this lot, then my deputies are going to—"

"Do what?" demanded Dean Meckler, stepping forward.

A hush fell across the crowd. All you could hear was the sound of the hoses dousing the ruins of the church.

"Dean," said Nance as he stitched up Jody Chick, "if you remember I was the one replaced you on the board of elders."

"I know that, Edward."

Nance stopped his stitching. "Well, you don't act like you remember why."

Meckler started to say something; instead he chewed on his lip.

"Dean," said Nance, returning to his work, "you being a former elder, why don't you tell these good folks they need to go on home now."

Meckler cleared his throat. "Let's turn in, folks. We've got a busy day ahead of us."

The crowd shifted around, muttered among themselves. No one moved. This crowd was different than the one earlier in the night. There were plenty of young men here and absolutely no women.

Nance glanced at the sheriff. Posey stood with his hand on his pistol. It wasn't that these boys were bad kids, but they had been insulted and they weren't old enough to let it go. Nance returned to his work. "You doing okay, Jody?"

"Yes—yes, sir." The boy gritted his teeth.

"Good for you. Most kids can't take the pain. I'll bet you're a lot tougher than most people think." His remark got everyone's attention. Jody Chick was the whiniest member of the baseball team. Nance went on to add, "And I can understand your father's concern— about the advances black people have made."

"You—you can?" Jody tried to turn his head, but Nance wouldn't let him.

"Stay still. Yes, Jody, things are not looking good for the white race."

"I don't need any help raising my son, Nance."

"That's right," Posey said, "it's not your place to tell a father how to raise his boy."

So the doctor shut his mouth.

That wouldn't do for Jody. All his life he'd heard how the colored race was inferior, and still, every year when baseball season rolled around, he was assigned to right field, the first to be subbed for when a critical hit was needed. "Why . . . why'd you say you understand why my daddy's so upset with . . . black people?"

"Jody, would you shut your mouth?"

"I want to hear what the colored . . . what the doctor has to say, Daddy."

Evidently the crowd did, too. They pressed in from all around. From his cruiser Johnny Temple leaned forward.

"Just think about it, Jody. Who are the folks most looked up to in our country these days?"

The white boy thought about this. "I—I don't know. Who?"

"Well, I think you'd have to agree the most admired people are Michael Jordan, Oprah Winfrey, and Colin Powell."

There was a split second of silence, then the young men stepped back from the Buick, convulsed with laughter. They slapped each other on the back, some breaking into horse laughs. The sheriff unsnapped his weapon, and at his cruiser, Johnny Temple pulled out the shotgun. But what could they take a shot at? All the boys were doing was laughing and giving each other high fives. It didn't look too threatening.

When the noise died down the doctor asked, "Now you think you boys could find your way on home?"

Lots of nods, more laughter as the young men piled into their cars and left. One or two actually waved good-bye to the Klan leader. Johnny Temple drifted over with his shotgun, watching them go.

Dale Posey said, "You know, Doc, I might need to talk to those boys about the firebombing of Junior Bennefield's house."

"Tomorrow will be soon enough," Nance said.

Posey saw a black sports car leaving the parking lot. "Johnny, you follow that car and make sure those boys go home."

The deputy nodded and returned to his cruiser, relocking the shotgun to the dash; then he pulled out of the parking lot and followed the sports car toward the county seat.

Nance returned to his stitching, Heywood to holding the light, and Wheeler Adams to his original question for his daughter.

"Do you understand the danger of shutting down the alarm around the Big House, even for a minute?"

The teenager stared at the ground. "Yes, sir. When the alarm is off, even for a minute, the Springs is unprotected."

"That's right and we have—"

"People depending on us."

"Not that those people would like—"

"Us to know they depend on us, but they expect us to have better sense than to leave them unprotected."

Her father smiled. "I take it you've heard this lecture before."

"Umpteen times, Daddy. Umpteen times. That's why Roosevelt was so mad when we got home, isn't it?"

"Right, Pumpkin, but I don't think your mother would like to hear you use that word. 'Umpteen' might sound country."

"I am country. I was raised here. Why can't I be from both the country and the city?"

"As far as I'm concerned, you can." He gave his daughter a hug. "Just don't let your mother hear it." Placing her on the seat of the cab, he asked, "Savannah, tell me what you know about what happened before your mother and I arrived."

The girl glanced at the ruins, then suddenly she was crying, leaning into her father. Rose Mary saw this and started toward the pickup. Adams shook his head as he held an arm around the girl.

"They could've killed him, Daddy."

"Yes, Pumpkin, but did you see anything the sheriff needs to know?"

She pulled back, wiping tears away. "You want me to talk to him?"

"If you know something."

"But I thought you didn't like him."

"We want whoever did this caught, don't we?"

"I thought the FBI was coming in the morning."

"Savannah, don't try to be clever. What do you know about this?"

"Like I told Mama, the fire was already going when I got here. After I called you, I pedaled down the rise as fast as I could and found Jody lying on the ground behind the church. I almost ran over him, Daddy. I called for Mr. Sibley, but he wasn't here. I went all the way around the church—after making sure Jody was alive—but I couldn't find Mr. Sibley."

"Did you see anyone leaving?"

"A dark car with its lights off. It was headed toward Lee's Crossroads. A sports car."

"You're sure, Savvy?"

"Daddy, I know sports cars."

"Did it pull out of the parking lot?"

She thought about that. "I would've heard the gravel spit, wouldn't I?"

"Probably."

"But it *was* pulling out. The car swerved, then left rubber." She glanced at her mother, who was smoking a cigarette in the graveyard. "I'm not the fool Mother thinks I am."

"Well, I don't think you helped your cause tonight."

"She's not being fair."

"Savannah, what else did you see?"

"Jody lying on the ground moaning. You know, when Jody talks to me, he doesn't stutter."

"You're closer to his age."

"His daddy makes him stutter?"

"His daddy intimidates him."

"But you raised me to be independent, didn't you?"

"That's right."

"And now it's turned around and bitten you on the butt?"

Adams couldn't help but laugh. His wife thought that was her cue to return. When she did, she looked from her husband to her daughter and back to Adams again.

"Everything all settled?" She dropped her cigarette to the ground and snubbed it out.

"I'm not grounded, Mother."

"Wheeler, what are you saying? She needs to be punished for sneaking out."

"Mother, remember the deal you and Daddy made?"

"What do you mean?" Rose Mary shook her head. "No, no, this is much too important for that."

"You agreed you wouldn't ground me at the Springs. That was Daddy's job and he hasn't said anything about me being grounded."

Both women looked at Adams.

"Savannah, I didn't say anything because I thought you'd want to extend your stay, you know, taking up Nell's slack." Adams gestured at the burned out building. "She has a lot of work ahead of her as senior steward."

"Daddy, really, I don't think—"

"Didn't you say Nell's been teaching you how to cook? Well, Roosevelt and I still need to eat."

"Well . . . I guess I could help out. Some." Savannah saw the Chicks heading for their station wagon. "Can I go say good-bye to Jody?"

"Just stay out of the way of the firemen."

"Wheeler," started his wife, "don't you think we should—"

"Can it wait until we get home, Rose?"

"Okay, okay, but we are going to talk about this."

"I'm sure we will."

Rose Mary sneered at him before sliding into the cab and placing her cigarettes and lighter on the dashboard. She was using a cell phone to talk with her newsroom when Adams borrowed a light from Bobbie Lee and walked around the far side of the former fire. The volunteers had grim looks on their faces as they hosed down the area; these men weren't about to leave until every last gallon of the 750 gallons had been put on the fire.

Dale Posey saw Adams skirt the far side of the building and followed him, going down the opposite side of the crime scene to join him at the rear. Adams was working the flashlight around the picnic area when Posey arrived.

"Now what are you doing?"

"Just looking."

"You're going to disturb the crime scene."

"That's already been done and the GBI's used to it. You've phoned this into Toby Bryant?"

"Of course I did, but some kids done it. Might be halfway to Florida by now. Saw the building wasn't burned all the way down and decided to finish the job."

"That include knocking Jody Chick over the back of the head?"

Posey followed Adams as he worked the light around the grassy area behind the picnic benches. "No matter how you cut it, your daughter's going to have to answer some questions."

The light stopped as Adams looked up. "And why is that?"

"She was raised on horseback. She's certainly

strong enough to hit someone over the head."

Adams stared at Posey for a long time, then continued working the light over the grass between the picnic benches and the rise.

"And she rode a bike over here," went on the sheriff. "Maybe she didn't want anyone to hear her coming. Jody would've heard a horse."

Adams stopped again. "Are you serious, Dale?"

"I'm just warning you that your family better be ready to cooperate when the GBI arrives. They're not going to put up with your high-handed manner."

"As far as I'm concerned, Dale, you're the one who's got some explaining to do."

"Now what's that supposed to mean?"

The light began to move again, searching the ground beyond the picnic tables. "You're the one who met with the Klan. That'll mean more to the GBI than anything you think my daughter might've done." The light stopped.

"You see, that's just what . . ." Posey's voice trailed off when he saw what lay at Adams' feet. A rifle. He reached for it.

"I wouldn't touch that if I were you."

"I'm only grabbing it by the barrel."

"And where the arsonist might've gripped the rifle to fling it away."

Chapter Nine

Rose Mary and Savannah were waiting when Adams returned to the pickup. His wife asked him what'd been going on back there, behind the church.

"The sheriff found Jody's rifle, that's all."

His wife arched an eyebrow as her husband turned over the engine. "The sheriff, you say?" As he backed out of the parking lot his wife had another question. "Wheeler, why don't we drive into Lee's Crossroads and have breakfast?"

Adams stopped and looked at her.

His wife shrugged. "I'm not in the mood to cook."

"You cook, Mother?"

"Savannah, I'm talking with your father."

"But, Mother, you never cook!"

"That's not the issue."

"Then what is it?" Adams was bone tired and

ached so badly he thought he might have to die to feel better. And his headache had returned with a vengeance.

"We're all wide awake," said his wife. "We couldn't go back to sleep if we wanted to."

Adams only stared at the woman.

"We could grab some breakfast, then go home, turn off the phones, and go to bed for the rest of the day."

"That's no way to celebrate the Fourth, Mother."

"If you want to stay up, my dear, that's fine."

"What about Judge Bennefield's party?"

Adams said, "I never have liked that party."

"But, Daddy, you said we should always show the Bennefields we're not afraid of them."

To that her father said nothing. He was watching the sheriff return Jody Chick's rifle.

"Wheeler, we have to make an appearance."

Adams sighed.

"An appearance, Wheeler, after a nap."

"Mother, I like the Bennefields' party. It's always fun. Besides, Annabelle's going to be there."

"And plenty of boys," said her father rather sourly.

Savannah sniffed. "You'd think the Adamses and Bennefields could put aside their differences at least for one afternoon."

"Wheeler," Rose Mary said, "I do believe our little girl is growing up."

"Mother, please! I'm almost eighteen."

At the other end of the parking lot Adams' most distant relative suffered no such dilemma. After throwing his son's dirt bike in the rear of the family station wagon, Heywood climbed in and roared off, leaving the fire, the church, and all those bothersome colored people behind.

Adams asked, "So what are we doing?"

"Going to Mickey D's," said his wife.

So the Adamses followed the Chicks into town, and from what they could see from the elevated seat in the pickup, Heywood was giving his son one hell of a talking to.

"He hits him, too, Daddy."

"If Jody wants to move out," said her mother, "he can. He's of age."

"Jody *had* to move back in the house, Mother."

"Had to?"

"That's right."

"So why don't you enlighten us, my dear?"

"I might if you weren't so condescending toward my friends."

"It might help, young lady, if you weren't so sarcastic."

Adams thumped his hands on the steering wheel. *"Ladies, please!"*

Both women glared at him as Heywood turned his station wagon off the highway onto a dirt road that lead to one of the few wooded areas remaining in Chick County.

Rose watched the wagon kick up dust as it lumbered down the road. "That doesn't look good."

Savannah gripped the dashboard, raised up in her seat, and watched the station wagon go down the dirt road. "He's going to give him a whipping—I just know it!" She turned to her father. "Isn't there something we can do?"

"Savannah, that is none of our business."

"But he'll whip him, Daddy. He's done it before."

"That doesn't make it our concern."

"But—"

"You didn't like it when the sheriff told your mother and me how to raise you, did you?"

"No, but that's different."

"How?"

"He was wrong."

"He was?" Adams glanced at her. "A seventeen-year-old girl should be out after midnight?"

"Daddy, I don't want to have this discussion again."

"Then say something that makes sense."

Savannah plopped down between the adults. Ahead of them the state highway was dark and silent. This being Sunday nothing much would move until it was time for church.

"Mr. Chick beats his wife, too, though I don't know why I have to call him 'Mr. Chick.'"

"Because he's senior to you, Savannah."

"It still doesn't make sense."

"You'd rather lower your standards to his?"

"Well, it's true."

"Says who?" asked her mother.

"Says Jody. That's why he moved back home. Jody's the only one who can keep peace in the family."

"His mother should move into a shelter."

"I don't think they have a women's shelter in Chick County, Mother."

Rose Mary scanned the darkness out her window.

"That's not all they're missing."

Going down Main Street they passed Sibley's Laundry and Dry Cleaning and saw Norwood and his eleven-year-old son trying to fit a piece of plywood over a broken-out window. The boy was having trouble with his end of the board so Adams stopped to give them a hand. Sunrise was an hour away, so the Sibleys worked under street lights. A toolbox sat in the middle of the sidewalk and a cord supplied power for a saw that had been used to give the plywood the proper shape. Young Sibley reluctantly gave up his end to Adams, and when Rose Mary and Savannah stepped down from the pickup, even spoke to him, the boy didn't return their greeting.

"What happened, Norwood?" asked Adams, taking the other end of the sheet of plywood.

"More Klan, I guess. They knocked out the window so I'd have to leave the church."

The two men fitted the plywood into the frame.

"Maybe Jody Chick ain't as dumb as he looks."

"Mr. Sibley, after you left, Jody was hit over the head and knocked out."

Holding his end in place, the black man looked at the white girl's father. "That right?"

Adams nodded.

"And his daddy's gonna whip him but good."

"'Going to,'" said her mother through her teeth.

"Dr. Nance had to stitch him up."

Sibley fitted a screw into the bit of his drill, then forced the metal pin through the plywood and into the wooden frame. Rummaging around in the toolbox for more screws, he asked, "Was the boy hurt bad?"

"Couple of stitches, that's all," Adams said.

"But he could've been killed."

Sibley didn't respond, only filled his mouth with more screws, then sent them into the frame. Finished, he and Adams stepped back.

"After I seen the damage I called Abe and woke him up. He said he'd bring down a piece of plywood left from enclosing his garage this spring, but he took forever gittin' here. When I called his house I found out why." Sibley faced Adams. "It's all gone now?"

Adams nodded. Rose Mary said something about nothing ever changing in Chick County while Savannah tried to engage Sibley's son in conversation. The boy, however, was listening to his father.

"You set fire to a church, then go back a second time and finish the job? That's gots to be some real mean folks." Sibley looked at the patched up window. "I reckon it should be okay 'til they can bring over a plate from Macon. I'll call 'em first thing tomorrow morning."

"Go home and get some rest, Norwood. You've been up half the night."

" 'Fore I do, I think I'll run out to the church and take a look."

"Don't," said Adams, shaking his head, "not if you want to be able to get to sleep."

The "eal" in the name "Deal" had been knocked off years ago by a truck making a delivery at Mickey D's. So the sign read "Mickey D" and another generation of Chick County youngsters had grown up calling the place "Mickey D's." The name stuck and Mickey had never gotten around to having the sign replaced. Even Savannah didn't know Mickey's last name was "Deal," something her father had tried to explain on more than one occasion.

"As if anyone cares, Daddy."

"'Those who cannot remember the past are condemned to repeat it.' George Santayana."

"'History is bunk!'" retorted the girl. "Henry Ford."

A woman with big hair greeted the Adamses as they came through the door. On the counter sat a cash register, a box of after dinner mints, and an empty, commercial-sized mayonnaise jar. The woman was writing on a piece of notebook paper with a black magic marker. Behind her stood a row of gum ball machines, and behind that, a counter and stools running the width of the room. Between the counter and the booths along the window at the front were tables and chairs with heavily lacquered finishes.

The Adamses took a seat in a booth: Adams on one side, the two women across from him. Savannah looked longingly at the gum ball machines while her mother examined a menu in a plastic protector. Adams stared out the window, wondering just how much one of these things was going to cost Norwood Sibley. In the kitchen you could hear the rattle of pots and pans. Mickey D was back there. Quick, able, and silent, letting his cooking do all the talking. Mickey's wife knew better and that's why she had greeted them at the door. In the darkness a patrol car passed with Johnny Temple at the wheel, then the cruiser was gone and it was a long time before another vehicle came down the street. Adams became aware of the waitress taking Savannah's order. His legs had stiffened up, his back was sore, and the damn headache wouldn't go away. His daughter wanted a chocolate shake.

"Not for breakfast, Savannah."

"I haven't been to bed yet, Mother."

"That's not my fault."

The girl glanced at the waitress who looked perky and ready for another day. The waitress smiled. She had children of her own.

"I've had them before, Mother."

"Not when you're with me, you haven't." Rose Mary gave her husband an accusatory look. "And certainly not with breakfast."

Adams was busy ordering eggs, bacon, toast, grits, and he wanted a short stack after finishing with his primary order. He hadn't eaten since yesterday dinner, and dinner was the midday meal in the South. "And four or five aspirins, if you have them," he added.

As their food began to arrive they saw Uncle Ingram hoof his way down Main Street, then cross over in front of the shoe repair shop before striding into the restaurant. Seeing his relatives in the booth, the elderly man walked over and slid in beside his nephew.

"You walked all the way from the hospital?" asked Rose Mary. "You had my car—why didn't you use it?"

Ingram glanced at the teenager sitting across from him. As the girl moved her straw around inside her milkshake it made a snorting sound.

"Had to give the keys to the preacher last night. He had car trouble."

"Car trouble?" asked Rose Mary.

Adams looked at his wife, then glanced at their daughter.

"And I ain't gonna eat at no hospital. Never know what them institutions put in their food. They're in tight with the government."

"Ingram, you don't honestly believe—"

"They take their money, don't they?"

"And Nell?" asked Adams.

"She's with Minny."

"And Mrs. Plummer?"

Ingram glanced at the teenager again. The sound from the cup was louder now. Savannah was approaching the bottom. Adams held his head in his hands. The aspirin the waitress had given him were taking their own sweet time working.

"Lelia's hanging in there," explained Ingram. "Nell ran me out so they could give Minny a bath. She stunk."

"I hope you didn't tell her that."

"It were the truth, Rose. Folks who have a hard time with the truth usually have a hard time with most everything in life."

"And you're the judge of what's true?"

Adams let go of his head and looked up. "Could we have this discussion another time?"

Ingram asked, "Can you give me a ride back to the Springs?"

"We're going to see Mrs. Jackson and Mrs. Plummer," explained Rose Mary.

"They'll be asleep. Nance came in before I left and said he was giving Minny something."

Savannah stopped slurping her milkshake. "Preacher Charley didn't show up at the second fire, did he, Daddy?"

Her father shook his head, then grimaced. Maybe he should just shoot himself and put himself out of his misery.

"Second fire?" asked Ingram, looking from one adult to the other.

Adams let Rose Mary fill him in.

"Man oh man, but those people need to start carrying some protection."

Rose Mary glanced at Adams but said nothing. Ingram, however, didn't need Rose Mary to wind his stem on that particular issue. He said black folks better get their act together before the government got around to taking everybody's guns. Then what would black folks do when there was trouble?

The waitress returned and took Ingram's order. While the elderly man waited for his meal the sun appeared on the horizon and agents of the Georgia Bureau of Investigation stumbled into the diner. The sheriff brought them in along with his deputies. Johnny Temple wasn't with them, neither was Robbie Simpson. One of the deputies had a cut over his eye and quite a shiner. Well, it *had* been Saturday night last night.

Waitresses spilled out of the kitchen and hustled around, splashing coffee into cups and taking orders. Law enforcement personnel usually tipped pretty well as Mickey D only charged them half price. One of the agents from the GBI was female. Bringing her coffee along, she left the young man traveling with her and ambled over to the booth where the Adamses sat.

Toby Bryant was a solidly built woman who wore a pantsuit and half boots. Her white blouse had a dark streak and her boots and the hem of her slacks were covered with soot. In her late thirties, Bryant cut her hair short; her only jewelry was earrings and a slender watch. Her eyes were brown and hard, as were her hands. After attending Georgia Southern, she had battled her way up through the male-dominated ranks of the GBI, working the family farm on her days off. Bryant lived with her wheelchair-bound mother; her father was deceased. A tractor had fallen on the old man while he'd been working in the fields. Bryant told her mother her father hadn't suffered, when in truth, the old man had laid under the tractor until his heart finally gave out. As far as Wheeler Adams was concerned, if there was any law in Chick County, it was Toby Bryant.

He and Ingram were sliding out of the booth to stand when Bryant waved them back into their seats. She gave Ingram a cursory glance but took more time studying Adams' wife and daughter. Savannah looked away, but Rose Mary met the woman eye to eye. Adams introduced his family and Bryant shook hands with everyone, including Savannah who was now openly staring at the woman, especially after shaking those leathery palms.

"Thought I might talk with you, Wheeler, if you have a minute? Save me a trip out to the Springs."

Adams glanced at the table where the sheriff and his deputies were reading various sections of the morning paper. Toby Bryant's young assistant, however, watched them closely. "As long as it's just you and me."

"That's what I had in mind."

Ingram had been about to hook a chair with one of his legs and drag it over for the woman to join them. Now the elderly man slipped out of the booth and made way for Adams.

"Wheeler, don't forget we have to stop by the hospital."

"'Preciate this," said Bryant, smiling at Rose Mary.

The young man with Bryant watched Adams and his boss take their coffee over to another booth. The agent sat on the edge of his seat, one hand on the back of his chair, the other on the table. Bryant shook her head and the young man settled back into his chair, but Dale Posey continued to stare as if Adams was in cahoots with the devil. He just might be. The GBI was famous for lording it over the locals.

After taking a seat, Bryant asked, "Tell me what you know, Wheeler."

Adams told her about the two fires, what his daughter had seen at the second one, and about finding Jody Chick's rifle.

Bryant glanced at the sheriff. "As if a case of arson isn't hard enough to solve."

"Savannah says the car might've been parked alongside the road, headed in the direction of town."

"I'll have someone check. Did you tell Posey this?"

"No."

"Good," she said with a nod. "The tracks might still be there." After sipping from her coffee, Bryant asked, "What you think, Wheeler?"

"The first fire had to be set by some kid."

"Have any suspects?"

Adams shrugged. "Just about any white boy in Chick County."

"Or someone passing through."

"That's the sheriff's theory."

"Uh-huh. Then maybe we should look in other directions. What's this about Jody Chick standing guard after the first fire?"

Adams shrugged.

"A guilty conscience?"

"If so he got a sore head and several stitches for his trouble."

"Well, I'm going to talk with his father. I'll talk with the son, too."

"What are you going to ask them?"

Bryant thought for a moment, then nodded. "I see what you mean. I'd have to ask Heywood which member of his organization would've hit his son over the head so he could go about the militia's dirty work. Hmmm. Maybe they want us to think someone else did it?"

"The Klan wants us to think a black man finished burning down the church?"

A helpless smile crossed the agent's face. "Wheeler, don't be so hard on me. I haven't been up as long as you have."

"Then start looking for a white kid."

"Jody Chick?"

Adams nodded, then took a drink from his coffee mug.

"What would be his motive?"

"His father's respect, I'd imagine. His old man is pretty tough on him."

"Any candidates for the second fire?"

"As strange as it seems—yes. Dean Meckler."

"Tell me about him."

"Meckler sells industrial life insurance. He may have white customers, but I don't know who they'd be. A year ago he was caught embezzling from the church. He was the treasurer."

"Why didn't I hear about that?"

"Charley went over and talked it out with him and his wife. Dean had gotten into the lottery fairly seriously. Borrowed on his car, anything else he could get his hands on."

"House?"

"No. The house is in his wife's name."

"Well," said Bryant with a slight smile, "I guess the woman knew what she was getting into when she married the man. How did Morton get Meckler to pay back the money? Addicts are notorious for not having any spare cash."

"Dean's wife took out a second mortgage and had the insurance company start direct depositing her husband's paycheck into her checking account. Dean's also required to turn in his collections daily to his supervisor."

"Well, that oughta slow him down."

"And make him hard to live with. From what I've seen of Dean lately he alternates between being a whiner and a jackass."

"How are they keeping him in line?"

"His wife makes him attend Gamblers Anonymous.

A chapter meets Thursday nights at the church. It was organized by Charley Morton."

"Gosh," said Bryant, with another smile, "but that's ironic and gives him a motive."

"And Dean hasn't been to church since resigning from the board of elders."

Bryant glanced at the table where the sheriff and his deputies sat. "Dale said you contaminated the crime scene. What's that all about, Wheeler?"

"Posey's lucky I didn't contaminate the crime scene with his ass. He accused Savannah of having something to do with the fire."

"And?"

"I set him straight."

Bryant leaned back into her booth and studied the man across the table from her. To many people Adams came across as high-handed, but as Bryant was from a similar background, she recognized it as an attempt to be self-sufficient. "It's going to get out of hand one day, Wheeler."

Adams said nothing.

"All it takes is one man with a gun."

"That's been tried."

Bryant sat up. "And this is the first time you've spoken about the incident—to me, that is."

"It's my business, not the state's."

"You should've reported the shooting, Wheeler."

Adams leaned forward himself. "And what would you've done, Toby? A sniper isn't any easier to find than an arsonist."

"Wheeler, at least you've got to—"

"Toby, Nell will want to know what you're doing

about the arson. A lot of black people will want to know what the GBI's doing about this."

Bryant sat back in her seat. "I've got a dog coming over from Macon to sniff out the place, but I can tell you what they'll find. Someone poured gasoline on the doors—it pooled up on the stoop—then lit it with a rolled-up piece of newspaper. A stub was left. *The Telegraph.*"

"And the second fire?"

"That's going to be tougher. The roof of the Sunday School room collapsed on top of the fire. I don't think we'll find anything. What's this about Jimmy Carter being in town? At the jail is what I hear."

Adams nodded.

Bryant sighed. "The number of racial incidents is up since you returned to the Springs."

"I don't have anything to do with that, Toby."

"Sure you do. You just won't admit it. Cavaliering around South Georgia . . ." She watched as Adams slid out of the booth and got to his feet.

"Will there be anything else, Toby?"

"Are you going to the party this afternoon?"

"Savannah wants to; Rose, too—she just won't admit it."

"And you?"

"I never did like that party."

Bryant smiled. "Just promise me you won't get into another fight."

"Is that all, Toby?"

"Well, I'm kind of curious as to why Charley Morton was a no-show for the second fire. At least that's what the sheriff told me."

"I have no idea."

"Drunk again?"

"Don't know, Toby."

"What else you got for me, Wheeler?"

Now it was Adams turn to smile. "You mean, what other part of your job do you want me to do for you?"

"Hey, you're the big shot around these parts. I'm just a lowly government employee."

"Not all that lowly, Toby. You're always invited to the judge's Fourth of July party."

"Wheeler, not only am I invited, but the judge calls and asks me personally."

Uncle Ingram caught a ride with a fellow gun nut who got up early each morning ready to defend the Republic from all enemies, foreign and domestic, real or imagined. The Adamses left him hunched over a table, developing the most complicated theory about the destruction of the black church; something to do with black people burning down their church to draw the federal government into meddling in the internal affairs of Chick County or the other way around, with white liberals as the perpetrators. Adams couldn't sort it all out. He was too damned tired and his head still hurt. What he wanted to do was go home to bed, but he needed to run by the hospital first. In the pickup was an extra set of clothing and overnight bag Roosevelt had placed there last night.

Adams dropped a twenty into the empty mayonnaise jar on the glass countertop. A piece of notebook paper taped to the inside asked for donations to the burned-out church. Savannah watched the bill go, all the encouragement she needed to ask for money for the gum ball machines.

"You don't want to make a donation of your own?"

"Daddy, I didn't bring any money."

Her father gave her all his change.

After the teenager had headed for the gum ball machines, Mrs. Deal said she'd sent some food over to the hospital for Nell and the Plummer boy. "Nobody should have to eat hospital food, especially the day after your church has been burned down."

While the Adamses were waiting for their daughter, an elderly couple came through the door. Arthur Vickery once worked for the Georgia Railroad Bank and Trust, and as bank president, he had been involved in one charity event after another. Vickery was so successful that people would cross to the other side of the street to avoid his outstretched hand. Now retired, Vickery still raised money for his causes. Why not? His wife, Dee, didn't want him underfoot all day. These days Vickery's office was a desk in a corner of his former bank, the only restriction being that Arthur couldn't ask anyone for a contribution. But if someone was foolish enough to step over to Vickery's desk, the customer was on his own. This morning the former bank president wore a white, long-sleeved shirt under a seersucker suit. His tie and his matching suspenders were red. Mrs. Vickery wore a floral print.

"Wheeler, just the man I wanted to see."

"Er—good morning, Arthur. Mrs. Vickery."

The wives greeted each other, then Vickery said, "Wheeler, we need to get organized."

"Organized? For what?"

"It's never too early to get organized. I taught you

that when you were a kid cutting my grass."

Adams appeared to be bumfuzzled, so his wife cut to the chase and asked what Vickery was talking about.

"The church, Ms. Bingham, the church burning last night. Wheeler, I've called people about coming in here as soon as the holiday's over."

Adams gestured at the GBI agents who'd just been served their breakfast. "You need to run that by Toby Bryant."

At her table Bryant watched those at the register as she stirred butter into her grits. The sheriff and his deputies were busy reading an Atlanta paper that said nothing of any fire, but everyone knew tomorrow's edition would carry the full story and an editorial along the vein of: "Haven't we been here, done that?" by Rose Mary Bingham. Bingham didn't have her husband's reputation for meddling in Chick County affairs, but she came close.

"Wheeler," Vickery said, "the bulldozers are free tomorrow because Mac Thrower is giving his men Monday off for the Fourth. Mac and his boys are going to bring them over after they finish with their family doings. And I've talked to George Moore at the lumberyard. He's willing to sell the lumber at cost. Same with Jack Tinsley at the hardware store, for the nails and what-have-you."

Rose Mary gestured at a pink horizon outside. "Mr. Vickery, how do you know about the fire? It's barely morning."

"Oh, Ms. Bingham," gushed Dee Vickery, "Arthur's been up most the night—soon as he heard about the fire."

"The first or second one?"

"What second one?" the couple asked in unison.

"The church was burned a second time—to the ground."

"My Lord!" Mrs. Vickery glanced at her husband. "We hadn't heard."

Vickery shook his head. "Haven't those fools learned we're all Chick County people now?"

"Do they know who did it," asked Mrs. Vickery, "this second time?"

"Not even the first time."

Vickery glanced at the lawmen at the table. "Well, they've certainly got enough people here to find out."

Savannah returned from the gum ball machines and they could see something purple in her mouth when she opened it to say, "Mrs. Jackson and Mrs. Plummer were inside when the church caught fire. My daddy went inside and pulled them out."

"Good for you, Wheeler."

"How are they doing?" asked Dee Vickery.

Rose Mary repeated what Ingram had told them.

Mrs. Vickery pressed her hand to her throat. "My God! I can't believe . . . and in this day and age. Arthur, we'll have to stop by and see them, find out if anything needs to be done."

"They've got Mrs. Plummer hooked up to a machine," added Savannah. "A tube goes down her throat."

"Savannah, please close your mouth," said her mother.

"Jody Chick was standing guard at the church."

"Heywood's boy?"

"Yes, ma'am."

Mrs. Vickery tsk-tsked. "Well, I hope they catch whoever did it. It's not right burning down the Lord's house. Arthur and I are going to pray the sheriff finds who did it."

Adams glanced at Dale Posey stuffing eggs and bacon into his mouth. "I think that'd be a good idea."

"The preacher's going to let me speak to our congregation, Wheeler. He's offered our church for the Shiloh congregation to use until theirs is rebuilt. I called Charley Morton but got no answer. I'll keep trying. The preacher wants Charley to preach at our service this morning. One of us needs to reach him."

"I found him," said Savannah, proudly.

Mrs. Vickery smiled tolerantly. "Found who, my dear? Preacher Charley?"

"Jody—he'd been knocked out."

"Knocked out?" Mrs. Vickery looked at the girl's parents.

Her mother explained. "Evidently, whoever set fire to the church—the second time—hit Jody over the head."

"Why that's terrible," Arthur Vickery said.

His wife smiled. "I'm sure your parents are very proud of you, Savannah."

"No, ma'am. They're upset because I rode my bike over there."

"Savannah," said her mother, ushering the teenager out the door of the restaurant, "I'm sure the Vickerys don't have time for this. Mr. Vickery needs to talk with Toby Bryant."

Climbing into the pickup behind her daughter, Rose Mary asked, "Do you think everyone in this county needs to know our business, Savannah?"

Adams closed the door behind his wife, then went around to the driver's side. While opening his door he saw a patrol car headed in their direction, light flashing.

"You should show some restraint," he heard his wife say from inside the cab. "You represent our family."

"Our family? Our family doesn't even share the same last name. Do you know how embarrassing that is?"

"We've been over this before, Savannah. I made my name professionally and would like to keep it."

"But, Mother, when we meet people you always tell them your name is 'Bingham' and they don't even know if you have a job." As Adams slid into the cab his daughter turned to him. "Daddy, would it be okay if I changed my name?"

"To what this time?" Adams was watching the patrol car pull into the parking lot. The flashing light had been turned off.

"No, no, Daddy, I don't mean about me being named for a city."

"You weren't named for a city," said her mother from behind her. "You were named for a great aunt."

"Who was named for a city," said Adams.

"Wheeler, you're just stirring the pot."

Savannah whipped around. "That's country, Mother! You talked country. I heard you. 'Stirring the pot . . .'" The girl stopped as the patrol car pulled in alongside them.

Adams slipped the key into the ignition, turned the power on, and lowered the window on the passenger side.

"Wheeler, it's much too breezy to have . . . ."

Rose Mary's voice trailed off as she saw Johnny Temple. The Chick County deputy continued toward the restaurant without looking in their direction. Still, they heard what he had to say.

"Jean Chick found her husband on their back porch when she came home from work. Heywood had been shot in the back of the head."

Chapter Ten

Adams knew the back roads of Chick County better than most. He beat everyone to Heywood Chick's house and had five minutes alone with the new widow before the sheriff arrived. On the way over Adams had a word of prayer with his family.

"Nobody goes inside but me."

Rose Mary argued that she was a reporter. Savannah's story was that she knew the Chick boy.

"Nobody goes in with me, understand?"

Adams was able to get that out while his wife and daughter were holding on for dear life as he made a turn taking them out of town and into the county. People turned and stared. One even wrote down the pickup's license plate number.

"What if Jody's mom's upset, Daddy?"

"We know she's upset, Savvy. That's why the sheriff wants to talk with her."

"What do you mean, Daddy?"

"The usual suspect in a case such as this would be the surviving spouse." He glanced at her. "Haven't you learned anything from all that TV you watch?"

Another sharp turn pressed the women against him. When Savannah could sit upright, she asked, "Daddy, why are we even going there?"

"Your father has to, Savannah."

"Why?"

"He thinks he's Sam Spade."

"Who?"

"Remember the movie *The Maltese Falcon*?"

"Yes."

"That's Sam Spade."

"I thought that was Humphrey Bogart."

With one hand on the overhead rung, the other around her daughter's waist, Rose Mary scanned the interior of the cab. "There has to be a gun in here somewhere. I just need time to find it."

"Daddy, do you have a gun in the pickup?"

A final turn and they headed down a county road toward the Chick house.

"Is everyone clear on what they're going to do?"

When no one answered, Adams repeated the question—with considerable heat.

"We understand, Wheeler. We'll stay in the pickup."

Heywood Chick's house was one of several ranch homes that lined both sides of a road outside the city limits. Most were covered with slate or aluminum siding; all had a stand-alone shelter serving as a one-car garage, and the lots were deep enough for a garden.

The Chicks grew a bit of everything: corn, beans, okra, spinach, and always tomatoes. There aren't many Southerners who can pass up a vine-ripened tomato. Just snap it off the vine and bite right in. Tastier than any apple.

Heywood's station wagon was parked in the gravel driveway in front of the stand-alone shelter with his wife's Ford Escort behind it. Jean sat on the front porch in a white, straight-backed chair. At the end of the porch hung a swing. A row of stunted azaleas grew in front of the porch and the grass appeared to have been cut with a grooming mower. The windows of the house were still open from taking advantage of a cool front that had passed through during the night. As there was no curb or sidewalk, Adams pulled onto the grass, stepped down from the pickup, and quickly crossed the fifty or so feet of new-mowed lawn to the porch.

He asked, "May I sit with you, Jean?" The woman still wore her nurse whites.

She looked up from the handkerchief in her hands. "What are you doing here, Wheeler?"

"Heywood and I were related—remember?"

"But how did you know he . . . he was . . . ?"

"Heard about it at Mickey D's."

She nodded. "Then sit."

Adams took the chair beside her. "Is there anything I can do for you?"

"No, but thanks for asking." She glanced at the lower part of Adams' body. "How are your legs?"

"I need to have them checked. I'm sorry you won't be there to do it."

Jean nodded again. "I've been up all night."

"Me, too. The church was burned for a second time."

"Heard about that. I don't know what's getting into people these days. Must be all the TV they watch."

"Your son was injured standing guard."

"And Heywood tongue-lashed him something fierce for doing it. Said that wasn't any of our business, and knowing how his daddy felt about the colored, the boy was just setting himself up for a fall."

"Heywood brought Jody by the hospital to see you?"

"Didn't want me worrying in case I heard Jody had been hurt. Hospital grapevines are the worst. He showed me the stitches Nance put in while I was taking care of Ozzie Tucker. They looked fine; better than most." Jean shook her head. "If there's a bigger whiner in the whole county I wouldn't know who it is. Garland Kelly brought Ozzie in, and once Ozzie was patched up, he got into it something fierce with Heywood. I told Jody to pull his bike out of his daddy's wagon and go on home."

"Where did Heywood go before he brought Jody to the hospital?"

"Where'd he go? What you mean?"

"After leaving the second fire Heywood turned off at Buck's Road. That dead-ends in the woods."

Jean looked into her lap. "Maybe to have that talk with Jody."

"He seemed to be having a pretty good talk with him going down the road."

"Wheeler, what is it you want? Like I've said, my

husband means well." A tear ran down her cheek and she quickly brushed it away. "At least he did."

"Just want to know if we can help out. Savannah found Jody unconscious behind the church. Another reason why we're here. She wanted to know if he's okay."

Jean glanced at the pickup. "That's nice of her, but Jody didn't need to be hanging around any Negro church and I'm sure . . . Heywood would have . . . told him that."

"My wife wants to know if you need anyone to stay with you."

Jean shook her head, then dabbed at her eyes with the handkerchief. "Mama's on her way."

Both of them heard sirens and glanced toward town.

"Jean, do you have any idea who might've done this?"

She shook her head, then twisted the handkerchief in her lap.

"May I see the body?"

"But why?"

"Because the sheriff is going to be handling the investigation into your husband's death."

"I suppose he will. That's his job."

"Then you're comfortable with Dale Posey learning the identity of your husband's killer?"

She glanced in the direction of the approaching sirens.

"Jean, just how much clout do you think you have in this county now that your husband's dead?"

"Clout? What do you mean?"

"There's a reason why your husband was chosen to be the Den leader. Remember what you said at the elevator—how if it wasn't for Heywood, the Klan would be riding at night?"

Jean considered the idea for what seemed to Adams to be an awfully long time. From the sound of the sirens the patrol cars had turned onto the county road and were headed in their direction.

"Jean?"

She dabbed more tears away. "So I'm reduced to one of those you look after, like the colored."

"Jean, we don't have much time."

"You don't think the sheriff'll find out who murdered Heywood?"

"On the contrary, Jean. It'll be the very first person he can pin it on—like your son."

The woman stood up so quickly it took Adams by surprise. He scrambled to his feet, then stepped out of the way so Jean could pass him on the narrow porch. At the door Adams opened it for the woman.

It was cool inside. A little sticky but still comfortable, helped by an attic fan that vented air from the entire house. To the right was a living room filled with furniture hand-me-downs; a worn area rug covered most of the floor. To the left was the family room where a couch, chairs, and a recliner faced a big-screen TV. The hallway was decorated with school photographs. All the kids were there.

"Where's Jody?"

Jean stopped and leaned against the wall but didn't look back at Adams. Beyond her a storm door led to a back porch where Adams could see the tops of some rusty furniture and a greasy barbecue grill.

"Wheeler, don't blame him for running. He said folks would think he'd shot his daddy."

"And why's that?"

She continued down the hall. "Because Heywood tried to give him some spine."

"I heard Jody wasn't the only one Heywood beat."

Now she turned and faced him. "Who told you that?"

Adams shrugged. "I hear things."

"Well, you heard wrong. Heywood never hit me. Sure he used the belt on the boy, but Jody doesn't know what's good for him. He's not stupid, but he sure is foolish sometimes and Heywood had to set him right."

Outside the house sirens wound down as the patrol cars pulled off the blacktop and onto the grass.

"Watch what you say to the sheriff, Jean."

"Why's that?"

"They won't be just looking at Jody for this."

"Me? Why on God's good earth would I kill my own husband?"

At the door Rose Mary put a hand to her forehead to peer through the screen. "Anything I can do for you, Jean?"

"No, no, Rose Mary. I'm—I'm fine." She uttered a sick little laugh. "Considering the circumstances." And without warning her legs collapsed from under her.

Adams grabbed Jean by the arm to keep her from falling. Jean's eyes fluttered. In the yard car doors slammed. Rose Mary opened the screened door and hurried down the hall.

"I'm . . . I'm all right." Jean's face was white.

"Wheeler," asked his wife, "have you examined the body?"

"Not yet."

"Where's Jody?"

"Took off on his dirt bike, I suppose."

"Then find him—Heywood, I mean." Rose Mary took Jean's arm and helped the widow into the kitchen. "Come in here and sit down, Jean. You need a drink or something."

"Don't drink . . . Baptist. He's outside, Wheeler, but it wasn't Jody who done this." And she burst into tears as Rose Mary helped her into a chair at the kitchen table.

Someone knocked at the front of the house as Adams went out the back door. The porch was an unfinished concrete slab, twenty by thirty, and had never been screened in. Anyone who works in a garage all day doesn't care to sit outside in the heat when he comes home. In the middle of the slab, lying on his chest, was his cousin with a bloody hole in the back of his head. Adams saw no weapon on the slab, just the rusty furniture and the greasy barbecue grill. Blood had pooled up around Heywood's head and the blood contrasted sharply with the dull gray of the unfinished concrete. Heywood wore the same clothes he'd had on at the fire; there was soot on his boots and tracks led across the slab from the concrete stairs to the porch.

There were no houses behind the Chicks, only a sparse tree line where Herefords grazed on the other side of a barbed-wire fence. Next door a family was leaving for church. They looked at Adams, then the patrol cars in their neighbor's front yard. The family caused Adams to have a thought of his own: where had Charley Morton been last night? Hopefully home dead drunk.

Another rap at the front door and Rose Mary called out, "In the kitchen. Come on back."

Feet tromped down the hallway. When they reached the kitchen the sheriff wanted to know what Rose Mary was doing here and where was her husband. Adams heard all this through the kitchen windows over the back porch as he knelt down to study the crime scene.

There were no shrubs or bushes around the porch; the yard was grass all the way to the garden and the cars parked in the driveway along the house. The only decent hiding place would've been under the house where a wooden door was latched from the outside.

Would Charley Morton have been allowed to get that close? Would any black man be allowed that close to the Klan leader, much less be invited into the house? Because that was the direction Heywood had been headed when he'd been shot from behind. And where had Jody Chick been while all this was going on? If he'd been home he would've heard something.

There were two sets of footprints across the gray slab, faint, but Wheeler could make them out because the shoes that made them were covered in soot. One set went all the way to the steps leading up to the back door. The other stopped halfway up and retreated down the stairs in the direction of the gravel driveway.

Jean had said that Ozzie Tucker and Garland Kelly had been at the hospital when Heywood had shown up with his injured son. Could one of them be the killer? Or both? Or, if pressed on the subject, would Ozzie Tucker remember an incident that would make Wheeler Adams a prime suspect in his cousin's murder?

Heywood had come out to the Springs while Adams was up on a ladder repairing one of the six columns across the veranda of the Big House. Roosevelt was in town, running his garbage route. Nell was inside, showing some young black girls what to clean next. Thomas Traylor was planting corn on the far side of the gravel turnaround and thinking about writing his brother about coming home to Georgia. He couldn't handle all this himself, especially at planting time. That meant the last time Heywood had been out to the Springs had been Good Friday of last year. Traylor's kids, playing on the veranda, saw the station wagon circle the turnaround and looked at Adams.

From the ladder, Adams said, "You kids go help your daddy. It's about time you did some work."

The kids didn't move. The station wagon had stopped between the veranda and their father in the field.

"March right out there," ordered Adams from the ladder, "and I don't want to see any running."

The children stared at Heywood Chick and his passenger. Then the oldest of the three swallowed her fear and took the hands of her two brothers and marched down the steps, across the turnaround, and past the station wagon. Ozzie Tucker and Heywood Chick watched the children go—Tucker snorted—then they turned their attention to the man on the ladder. Heywood stood behind his car door, leaning on it. Tucker closed the one on his side.

"Hello, in the house," said Heywood.

Ozzie Tucker didn't wait to be acknowledged but simply ambled over. Heywood followed him, closing the door of the station wagon behind him. When Tucker reached the porch he put a foot on the first step. Heywood kept both feet firmly planted on the ground. To the left and right of the veranda, magnolias stirred in a spring breeze.

"Wheeler, we need to talk."

Tucker's boot remained on the step and Adams continued his caulking.

"We have a problem," his cousin said.

"You're including me in your problem?" asked Adams.

Tucker took his foot off the step. "You gonna be a hard-ass, Adams? Heywood said we come here to talk."

"Wheeler, it's in our mutual interest to talk. The judge said so."

"In Judge Bennefield's best interest, I would imagine."

"Adams, don't be giving us none of your shit," Tucker said. "You're either gonna come down here and talk like a man or I'm gonna knock that ladder out from under you."

Adams continued his caulking. "What are you here to tell me, Heywood? How you want to form a militia?"

Heywood glanced at Tucker. "How—how'd you know?"

Tucker turned on his leader. "I told you, Heywood, we've got a spy in the organization, but you wouldn't let me run no lie detector tests. It's on your head."

Actually, Adams had learned about the proposed militia from his gardener, and Roosevelt had learned about the idea while running his garbage route. White people never think their black employees hear anything; many consider them part of the furniture.

Heywood gestured at the rockers lining the veranda. "Mind if we set a spell?"

"Go ahead."

After the two visitors took seats in rockers Adams climbed down from the ladder and took a seat, too, leaving an open chair between him and his visitors. From where they sat they could see Thomas Traylor hustling to get his seed in the ground. After all, it was Good Friday.

"Wheeler, the government has overstepped its bounds and people have to be prepared—"

"Yeah," said Tucker with sarcasm, "people are getting above their raising."

Looking Tucker in the eye, Adams said he had noticed some of that himself.

"Now, listen to me, Adams—"

"Ozzie," cut in Heywood, "you said you weren't going to cause any trouble if I let you come along. Now let me and Wheeler work this out."

Tucker craned his neck to look around what part of the Springs he could see. "What kind of man lives with niggers, Adams? What kind of white man would do something like that?"

Adams stood up. "You weren't invited here, Ozzie.

Now I'm asking you to leave."

Tucker laughed. "Aw, now don't go getting your bowels in an uproar. I ain't said nothing but what's the God's honest truth and you know it."

Adams towered over him.

"Look here," Tucker went on, "we want you to deed over part of the Dark Corner. You know, where we used to take girls and screw them before some asshole put up a fence. Do you take that high yellow over there? Is that why it's called the Dark Corner?" Tucker turned to share his laugh with Heywood. "I heard your daddy didn't mind a little dark meat—"

The scrawny man went sailing out over the turn-around where he landed in the gravel on his shoulder and face.

Heywood stood up. "Wheeler, now there's no cause—"

Adams turned on his cousin. "Sit!" Then to Tucker, "Ozzie, I'm not going to stand here and let you insult the people of Chick Springs."

Tucker brushed dirt off as he got to his feet. "Adams, Ole Billy Ray would've been ashamed of you, taking sides against your own kind."

"Ozzie," Heywood said from his rocker, "I told you this was gonna happen if you came on Wheeler's property and started mouthing off."

"Then I reckon I'll have to wait until he leaves."

Adams leaped down from the veranda and advanced on Tucker. "Ozzie, you and I are going to settle this once and for all. And you can keep that little switchblade knife of yours in your pants, too."

The knife Adams mentioned came out and Tucker

smiled. His feet slid apart and he went into a crouch. "The sheriff won't have no cause to bother if I slice you up in self-defense."

"Then you'd better get started because I'm going to kick your ass all the way down to the blacktop." Adams gestured at Traylor and his kids watching from the other side of the turnaround. "And they'll see it done."

When Tucker glanced in the Traylor family's direction Adams kicked the switchblade out of Tucker's hand. The scrawny man yelped, grabbed his hand, and stumbled back, stopping near the door of the station wagon. He reached through the window for Heywood's shotgun. As he did Nell pushed her way through a pair of double screened doors and stepped on the veranda. In her hands was a pump action shotgun. The weapon was almost as large as the woman, but she held it well enough to sight in on the man standing beside the station wagon.

"Step away from the car, Mr. Tucker."

Tucker froze, hand still inside the wagon. "You ain't gonna shoot no white man, nigger."

Nell worked the action of the shotgun. She didn't do it one-handed like in movies, but she did load a shell. Tucker's eyes expanded, at least to the size of a shotgun shell. Slowly, he drew his hand out of the station wagon.

"Adams, you hiding behind this nigger's skirts?"

But Adams was already returning to the veranda, careful to keep out of the line of fire.

From his seat, Heywood said, "Get in the car, Ozzie, and shut your mouth."

"No, sir, Mr. Chick," said Nell, without taking her eyes off Tucker, "your friend is leaving and he's leaving right now."

Heywood rose up in his chair. "Now I don't know about that—"

Adams hoisted himself up on the veranda between his housekeeper and his cousin. "Ozzie wouldn't be the first white man Nell's taken a shot at."

From the station wagon Tucker shook his fist. "You knock the Klan, Adams, but truth be known, Billy Ray ran with them. And you're allowing niggers to live here on the Springs."

"Black people were here long before Billy Ray arrived. They might not've liked how they got here, but they were still here."

"But they don't have to be living here now, do they?" Tucker gestured at where Traylor's children hid behind their father. "And none of them was here before you come back."

"Mr. Tucker," asked Nell, "would you leave us be?"

Tucker stared at the old woman who continued to sight in on him with the shotgun. "I'm not forgetting this." He cursed them all again, then turned on his heel, crossed the turnaround, and walked between the cedars leading down to blacktop. Satisfied the white man was leaving, Nell returned inside with the shotgun. However, it wasn't until Tucker's foot actually hit the blacktop that Thomas Traylor returned to his planting and he had little trouble encouraging his kids to pitch in.

"Ozzie's got a point, Wheeler. You hiding behind some woman's skirts and a colored gal at that?"

"Everyone has his cross to bear."

Heywood watched Tucker hoofing his way down between the cedars. "He can't control himself. I don't know what I'm gonna do with him."

"He's going to be the destruction of you all."

"That might be, but Tucker has friends in high places."

"Meaning Judge Bennefield."

"Bennefield's brother-in-law is Ozzie's brother, but I don't think it pleases him none. Matter-of-fact I think the relationship's been strained a good number of years."

"What'd you come to see me about, Heywood? You know my family's policy of never selling our land."

"In this case you just might want to rent it some. Come on, Wheeler, sit down. I won't bite."

Adams only stared at him.

"Okay, okay, I won't call them 'niggers.'" After Adams finally sat down, he added, "Really, Wheeler, I don't think I've ever called them 'niggers.'"

"What you want, Heywood? I'd like to get back to work."

His cousin glanced at the ladder Adams had climbed down from, then watched Thomas Traylor and his kids working on the other side of the turn-around. "I don't understand why you have to lift a hand around this place." Heywood waved off Adams' protest. "No, no, I'm not going chasing that rabbit. Wheeler, we want to build a rifle range over in the Dark Corner. You're not using that part of the Springs, hardly ever go—"

"I ride over there. My family rides over there."

"But not that often. You have to load the horses

and take them around by way of the bridge. Look, we want to teach firearm safety to the young people of Chick County. The NRA has a program. You ain't saving it for some endangered species, are you?"

As a matter-of-fact Georgia Pacific listed the Dark Corner as part of their old growth program. The Dark Corner hadn't been logged in more than a hundred years.

"And your colored friends want a farmers' market built across the road from it, don't they?"

"Is that why the Klan's been busting up the stands, softening them up for this?"

"The judge said the rifle range would be good insurance for the stands your people put up over there."

"They aren't my people, Heywood."

"Okay, okay. We'll build the whole range, won't cost you a dime."

"I'm sure you have something in mind."

Heywood leaned forward in his rocker. "There's this little berm that'd make a good backstop. I crossed the fence to check. I hope you don't mind, but I wanted to have an idea of what was over there when we talked. Anyway, we could build it up some—if you'd let a tractor in. Billy Gilbert at the gravel pit said he'd supply all the gravel."

And that's how the Klan ended up using the Springs for their weapons training. Once or twice the farmers' market was shot up, but after Adams locked the gate allowing access to the Dark Corner, people finally got the message and the produce stands were left pretty much alone.

"Left pretty much alone" is a relative phrase. Nell

and Rose Mary gave Adams hell, saying he'd allowed a cancer inside the Springs. There was little Adams could say to that. They were right. Still, he did wrangle a concession out of Heywood, that the black citizens of Chick County would be able to take *their* children over to the range Thursday nights and teach *their* kids how to shoot.

"The coloreds have guns, Wheeler?"

"Wouldn't you if you lived in Chick County?"

Adams was hunched down, studying the crime scene when Toby Bryant pushed her way through the storm door at the rear of Heywood Chick's house.

"Wheeler, what are you doing here?" In the woman's hand was a biscuit with a slab of ham tucked inside. A couple of bites were missing.

"Came to see Jean."

"You related to her?"

"Heywood."

Bryant let the door close behind her. "Well, you know the rules. We can't have you back here."

"And I shouldn't've come," Adams said, standing up, "but I couldn't believe it."

"Believe what?"

"The leader of the Klan assassinated."

"Assassinated?"

The sheriff and his deputies, followed by the young GBI agent, came out of the house and trooped down the steps. "Adams, what in the devil you doing here?" One by one, including Johnny Temple, the sheriff and his deputies took up a position around the body.

Adams told Posey the same thing he'd told Bryant.

"Well, you're disturbing the crime scene and I want you out of here."

"I'll go be with Jean until her mother arrives."

"Yeah. Why don't you do that? I might have some questions for you."

"Ask them now, Dale, not in front of Jean."

Standing beside the sheriff, Johnny Temple winced.

Posey glanced at him, then asked, "First one would be: How come you're here in the first place?"

"Heard about the shooting."

"Who told you?"

"Heard it over the two-way in Temple's cruiser when he went into the diner."

The sheriff looked at Temple, who had absolutely no expression on his face.

Bryant, who had been squatting down beside the body, stood up. "If you don't need me, Sheriff, I've got another crime scene to investigate and I don't want the FBI stomping all over it before I get there." She nodded at the circle of men. "Sheriff. Wheeler. Deputies." Going up the steps, she asked her fellow agent, "Did you reach the preacher?"

"No answer."

"The preacher?" asked the sheriff.

Bryant turned around on the stairs. "Yes—with the leader of the Klan murdered he's an obvious suspect."

"Toby, I didn't ask for your help."

"That's right, you didn't." And she disappeared into the house with her biscuit and the other agent. Adams followed her.

"Where's Heywood's kid?" was the last thing Adams heard the sheriff ask as he entered the house.

In the kitchen the two women sat in chairs at a dinette set with Rose Mary holding an arm around Jean. Savannah stood in a corner, and when her father came through the door, she grabbed him, pulled him close, and cried softly against his chest. The kitchen needed a new coat of linoleum, and corners of the dinette chairs had stuffing sticking through cracks. A small black-and-white TV sat on the counter and the wall phone hung beside it. The phone book was tucked between several cookbooks.

Jean wiped at her eyes. "I told him this might happen, Wheeler. I told him to stay out of the Klan."

Rose Mary pulled away from the woman. "You think someone with the Klan shot him?"

Adams frowned, his arm around his daughter who still clutched him. Rose Mary ignored her husband's frown, passed Jean a tissue, and repeated the question.

Jean dabbed at her eyes. "You don't know what Heywood was going through, holding down those boys. They wanted to go back to night riding, but Heywood got them into paint ball instead. Still, it wasn't enough. You couldn't keep them busy, especially on Saturday nights. The ones who'd lost their jobs when the Big Mill closed, they were the worst, and Heywood couldn't leave work every time one of them got into trouble."

"Did your husband mention anyone in particular he was having a problem with?"

Jean shook her head. "Not in this house, he wouldn't."

"What do you mean?"

"I never . . . I never let him talk about the Klan in this house."

They heard the storm door open. Dale Posey and Johnny Temple joined them in the kitchen. The deputy didn't come into the room but stood in the hallway.

"That preacher friend of yours, Adams, I'm sending someone over to pick him up."

Savannah gasped and clutched her father tighter. Adams teared up. His breath came in shallow gasps.

"Why's that?" asked Rose Mary.

"Same reason I want to know where Wheeler was after the fight on the state highway."

"He was with me."

"Mrs. Adams, everybody knows you don't live at the Springs."

"That doesn't mean I don't visit."

The sheriff shook his head. "Sorry—that won't do."

"My daddy was there," Savannah said. "Mama was there, too."

"I think I'd rather have an independent witness."

Savannah looked at her father. "What about Roosevelt?"

Again the sheriff shook his head. Behind him Johnny Temple's face was impassive.

"Why not?" asked Savannah. "Roosevelt saw us."

"This is silly," Rose Mary said. "What reason would my husband have for killing Heywood?"

"Bad blood between relations."

Rose Mary laughed. "Wheeler's related to more

people in this county than anybody. Does that make him a suspect for every murder that comes along?"

"This isn't any murder, Mrs. Adams. It looks more like an assassination."

"Then it only makes sense to look into the Klan."

"Mrs. Adams, I can understand you wanting to stick up for your husband, but you weren't there to see him throw down on Heywood."

Jean gasped and gripped the table. "Wheeler, I never would've thought . . . ."

"Now that really is a stretch," Rose Mary said.

"There are those who say it happened that way, Mrs. Adams."

"Jean, don't listen to this. And the name's 'Bingham,' Sheriff, as I've told you before."

"Yes. I never did understand that."

"I'm not surprised."

He turned to the woman's husband. "Was this some kind of a feud between you and Heywood? Is that why you backed the colored—because you couldn't have the Klan?"

There was a knock at the front door, and when Jean tried to get to her feet, Rose Mary gently pushed her back into her chair. "I'll get that, Jean."

"Thank you . . . Rose Mary. And thank you, Wheeler, for everything you've done."

"What'd he do?" asked the sheriff.

"Oh, he wanted to . . . Wheeler just wanted to help out . . . ."

Posey put his thumbs in his belt and rocked back and forth on his heels. "Adams, it's time you were moving along."

"I was waiting to get that word from Jean."

"I'm giving it to you now."

The Chick County coroner stopped at the kitchen door long enough to ask where the body was. The sheriff told him and the coroner went out the back door and down the steps. Johnny Temple went with him, looking pleased to leave.

Adams said, "Maybe I should go over and ask Charley Morton to turn himself in."

"Or run for it—like the Chick boy done? That'd make you an accessory. Which I'm not sure you aren't already."

"Charley's not going to come along peacefully. He remembers what happened the last time he was in your jail. I'll bring him in. With a lawyer."

"You'll do nothing of the sort. You stay away from that preacher. And this house."

"What about Jody?"

"I'll have my men keep an eye out for him."

"No APB."

"What business is that of yours?"

"Dale, I'd like to keep it casual, so the boy, who is also my relative, won't be afraid to turn himself in."

Rose Mary returned from the front of the house with a gray-haired woman who hurried into the kitchen. She and Jean met in the middle of the kitchen, Jean falling into the older woman's arms and bursting into tears. Savannah started crying again, so Adams decided it was time to get his family out of there. Going out the front door, he pulled a jacket off a clothes rack and brought it along.

Chapter Eleven

A person can be arrested in Chick County for loitering or parking in a tow-away zone, and that is how streets are quickly zoned when drug pushers or gangbangers move in. Or for cussing in the presence of children—any child under the age of twelve. And the elders of the Shiloh Church backed each and every one of these measures. They all reduced crime, but there was a downside. It co-opted the leadership of the black community and led the bishop to select a rather pushy preacher for a congregation that had become docile under the reign of a bunch of white people.

After that lineman fell across his knee Morton lost his scholarship; worse, he was at a loss as how to make it on his own. Like most athletes Morton had been cut slack other students could only dream about. Charley ended up driving a truck because his knee disqualified him from going overseas; then he lost that job to someone who also had bad knees but was a Vietnam veteran—and a white man. Finally Charley found a job as a janitor in a building where a good number of the children of the affluent worked: lawyers, brokers, salesmen, and the like. Upon learning one of the janitors sold coke on the side, Charley set up the white man for a fall and took over his territory. Pretty soon Charley wasn't janitoring any longer.

However, the white man had played his cards close to the vest, stashing his money away for an early retirement. Charley was young and wanted to party and be the center of attention as he had been in school. Nobody gets the girls like football players, not even musicians. When Charlie was caught selling dope to his former college teammates, the coach gave him one hell of a scolding; when caught in downtown Atlanta, he was sent to prison where the Black Movement taught him how to really hate. If it hadn't been for his mother's influence, Charley might've even changed his name to something Islamic.

Clara Morton's last request was for her son, when released from prison, to go to church for a full year. If he missed a Sunday, he'd have to start all over again. That's all she asked and her soul would rest in peace. Charley did it. Well, he finally did but only after being packed off to prison one more time. Back on the streets Charley swore he'd do anything not to return to prison, even sit through church a whole damn year.

In church Charley learned of the sacrifices made by his Lord and Savior—and hated every minute of it. And because he was one of the few bachelors, the married ladies tried to fix him up. What these well-intended ladies didn't know was during the week this bachelor was drunk more than he was sober. Charley couldn't walk the walk and talk the talk with that damn sermon ringing in his ears, another looming over the horizon. Without knowing it Clara Morton had cast her son into a new kind of purgatory. Or perhaps that's just what she had in mind. Someone, or something, was wrestling for this young man's soul. Charley's salvation was the persistence of the good women of the church. They fixed him up with a widow woman who turned his life around, and while finishing his mother's final request, Charley fell in love.

When asked if his being an ex-con was a problem, the widow replied, "It would if it happened again."

Mattie Powell took her time falling in love with Charley Morton. Widowed by a war where so many black families watched their sons go off and die in a land where the locals considered even white people second-raters, Mattie Powell wasn't in any hurry to marry a man at war with himself. But the day Charley went forward to accept Jesus Christ as his Lord and Savior and was baptized into the church, the date was set. After the honeymoon Charley enrolled in seminary.

During Charley's first posting Mattie became pregnant and had a child, Charley, Junior, but when the boy was five-years-old he ran out into the street and was run over by a car. Charley took to drink again and lost his posting. It was Mattie who held the family together. Mattie finally became pregnant again, but during one of her checkups she was diagnosed with breast cancer, which spread to her liver. Mattie died, the baby miscarried, and Charley fell off the wagon and lost his posting again. Then he was assigned to the Shiloh Church—over the objections of the elders. And the bishop was a bit perturbed when the board didn't agree with his selection. Not only had Charley Morton agreed to attend AA meetings, but the Shiloh Church had gone a full year without a proper preacher, many more years without a backbone.

With the posting came a shotgun house, named because one blast through the front door would pass out the back one. Shotgun houses consisted of three rooms in a row: a parlor, a bedroom, and a kitchen where fireplaces might still be used for cooking. Sometimes another series of rooms was built alongside the original and that was called a "double shotgun"; and sometimes, if the owners had money, they might add rooms to the rear, giving the house a T-effect. It was creativity at the very bottom of the economic ladder.

When Wheeler Adams pulled to a stop beside his wife's sports car in front of Charley Morton's house, a boy of eleven or twelve left the house across the street and raced across to greet the white man. Patrick Hampton wore his Sunday best and he had played on a Pop Warner football team Adams had once coached. Neighbors stood on their porches and stared at the goings-on in the street.

"Mr. Adams! Mr. Adams!"

"How you doing, Patrick?" Adams knelt down, putting himself eye-to-eye with the boy.

"Mr. Adams, Mama says to tell you the preacher's got a gun in there. So you be careful, my mama says."

Adams glanced at the house with the screened-in porch. Below the screened door, and on the first step, sat a Pepsi bottle with fresh daises sticking out its mouth. "How's your mother know that, Patrick?"

"'Cause he woke up the whole neighborhood last night. Least that's what my mama told me. I didn't hear it. I was asleep. The bullet hit our house. Mama's gonna let me have it if I can dig it out."

Adams squeezed the boy's shoulder as he stood up. "Thanks, Patrick. I guess you'd better get on home now."

"I was hoping to go with you, Mr. Adams."

"I don't think that's such a good idea."

"I promise I won't get in the way."

"I'm sure you wouldn't, but your mother probably thinks you've already done enough."

"Sure I can't go?"

"I'm sure, Patrick."

"Well, okay . . ." And the boy's shoulders slumped as he recrossed the street.

Rose Mary called from the pickup, "Wheeler, I've got a gun in my glove compartment."

"I don't think so."

"Daddy, maybe you'd better take it." Savannah was chewing her nails again.

Adams shook his head as he crossed the dirt yard of Morton's house. Coming out the door of the screened porch was Elder Reynolds and his wife. Selma Reynolds wore a pink dress; her husband, a gray business suit. Mr. Reynolds might be the elder, but his wife usually did all the talking.

"We ain't got time for this, Wheeler. The white preacher been calling all morning, inviting us over to their church for services, contacting the elders when he got no answer here. But the elders won't go if Charley's not there and neither will I." When Mrs. Reynolds reached the bottom of the steps, she looked into the house. "If the preacher's so big on colored folks having rights, then why ain't he exercising them, 'cause worshipping the Lord is a God-given one."

"He's passed out in there," explained Mr. Reynolds, holding the screened door open for Adams.

"We got problems aplenty," said his wife, "and this is how he handles it. Why don't he just use that pistol on himself and put all of us out of his misery?"

Adams looked through the front door and saw Morton sleeping on a couch with a bedcover over it. A pistol lay on the man's huge chest, which rose and fell with his breathing. Empty liquor bottles stood in a row at the foot of the couch; one of them had fallen over.

"Mrs. Reynolds, you knew something like this could happen. Charley's not all that well put together these days and the fire had to take its toll."

Selma Reynolds set her jaw. "Wheeler Adams, I done buried two children, one dead from gangbangers, the other from TB, some disease ain't 'posed to be 'round here no more. And Clarence is my second husband, not my first. The first I threw out because of his drinking, so I think I know what I'm talking about when it comes to drinking."

And with a jerk of the head the old woman was gone, striding across the dirt yard. Her husband gave Adams a wan smile, then followed her into a street filling up with black people all dressed up with nowhere to go. In the pickup Savannah chewed on another nail; her mother had the window down, puffing away on a cigarette. They all watched Adams enter the house.

The preacher wore the same clothes as the night before—pajama tops and jeans—and he reeked of smoke. His shoes lay across the room in front of a console TV. His snores filled the room, rattling loose glass in windows.

The first thing Adams did was take the gun off Morton's chest and check the chamber, where he found the expended round Patrick Hampton had told him about; then Adams jammed the weapon into his jeans. Uncle Ingram had a model like this, the same one he hadn't been allowed to bring into the hospital. Was it possible . . . ?

Next Adams went to the kitchen, passing through a room with an unmade bed, clothes lying in piles, and a dresser covered with Bibles, paperwork, and personal items. In one corner a closet had been turned into what had to be a claustrophobic bathroom for a man with the broad shoulders of Charley Morton. Clothing hung on a rack nailed to the wall.

In the kitchen Adams found what he was looking for: an empty pot. The pot didn't have to be clean, and it wasn't, just empty. Adams filled it with water, carried it into the living room, and dumped the contents on the preacher. Morton came up sputtering.

"Wh—what?" He wiped water off his face and squinted at Adams. Swinging his feet off the sofa, he knocked over a couple of empty liquor bottles. "Wheeler?"

Adams put down the pot.

"What you doing here?" Morton looked around;

then he saw the daylight and the crowd in the street. "Why are you here?"

Adams tapped the pistol in his lap. "Because nobody wanted to get their ass shot off."

Morton stared at the weapon, then ran his hands over his head. He rubbed his face with his hands, wiped them on his trousers, and looked around. Most of the liquor bottles were empty, but there was one with some brown liquid remaining. Adams saw Morton calculating how much effort it would require to reach the bottle, making the calculations with probably a head to rival the one Adams had from the night before. Mind made up, Morton reached for the bottle. When he did Adams whipped the pistol out of his lap and threw a shot at it.

The bottle exploded, spraying the preacher with glass and liquor. Morton jerked back and stared at Adams. Outside someone screamed. But Adams was already through the front door and headed for the porch. There he opened the screened door and broke open the pistol, letting bullets and shells fall from the cylinder. Finished, he tossed the gun away. That stopped the crowd from moving toward the house, but not from milling around. Patrick Hampton stuck his head out the door across the street, then his mother jerked him back inside. Rose Mary shoved her daughter into the pickup, told her to stay put, and shut the door; then she pushed her way through the crowd and over to her Z-car. She was digging around in her glove compartment when her husband disappeared inside Morton's house again.

Adams returned to the living room where Morton was wiping his face on the bedcover. The coverlet was soiled and dirty and it had been that way long before Morton returned from the fire last night.

"That was pretty damned close, Wheeler." When Adams didn't reply, Morton said, "God but I've got a headache."

"Join the crowd."

The black man studied him for a moment, then lurched to his feet and limped into the rear of the house. He returned with a couple of Coca-Colas and a bottle of aspirin. He tossed a can to Adams who fielded it.

"No coffee?" asked Adams.

Morton took a seat on the dry end of the sofa, then downed several aspirin with his soft drink. "No coffee in this house." He tossed the aspirin bottle to Adams. "Not much of anything in this house anymore. Just some ghosts."

"I didn't come over here for a pity party, Charley."

The black man's eyes iced over. "You don't know anything about my problems, Wheeler."

"I know more than you think. The sheriff is sending someone over to pick you up for the murder of Heywood Chick."

"Heywood . . . your cousin is dead?"

"Shot in the back of the head as he walked into his house last night. Shot with a gun like that .38 I just threw into the yard. Put a good-sized hole in his head."

"They think I did it?"

"You know the sheriff. He's looking for someone and he always finds him—whether the fellow did it or not. Where'd you get the pistol?"

"From Uncle Ingram."

Adams shook his head and returned to his seat in the recliner. He opened the Coca-Cola and drank from the can. Down went several aspirin.

"Wheeler, what you saying—you don't think a black man should be armed in Chick County?"

"Charley, it was damned foolish of you to leave that pistol out where members of the congregation could see it and have to testify to what they saw."

"Black folks are a lot tighter than white ones. You should know that by now."

"Everyone has enemies, Charley, especially alcoholic preachers jammed down a congregation's throat. If the sheriff can pin Heywood's murder on you, and the church burning on Tucker, it'd solve a lot of problems for the judge."

"I thought Tucker was related to Bennefield."

"Blood counts for nothing, if you're a problem. That's the judge's number one rule." Adams took a swallow from his Coke.

"You think Tucker killed your cousin."

"I don't know, Charley, but I may have to find out."

"Oh, so *I* won't have to go to prison?"

"I'd be doing it for me."

"They think you killed him?"

Adams let out a long sigh. "I don't know how many times I have to tell you, but anytime I'm thrown in the Chick County jail, it has nothing to do with race or politics."

The preacher looked through the door at the crowd in the street.

"Charley, what's this about burglars trying to break into your house last night?"

"What? I don't remember . . . burglars, you say?"

"Patrick Hampton's mother says that's what you told her after putting a bullet into the side of her house."

Morton's faced twisted up in irritation. "That woman's too damn nosy."

"Or cares too much." Adams gestured at the empty whiskey bottles, the condition of Morton's clothes, and the preacher's unshaven face. "This isn't going to impress anyone, especially the sheriff."

"I'm not going back to prison again, Wheeler."

"Toby Bryant is here investigating the fire. I want you to turn yourself into her."

"Why? I didn't do anything."

"Better the Macon City jail than the Chick County lockup."

"If they're looking for suspects, the GBI will test your hands like they'll test mine, especially after the brawl out on the state highway." Morton took a swig from his soda, then glanced at the remains of the whiskey bottle Adams had blown away. "I don't deserve this from you, Wheeler."

"I'm doing it for Nell. Her life revolved around that church."

"Like she let me be a part of it."

"And she and others would like to know why you weren't at the fire last night?"

"I was. Remember, I dragged your ass out."

"The second fire, Charley."

"The second . . . fire?" Morton had to rest his soft drink on the cushion next to him. "There was a second fire?"

"Someone came back, knocked Jody Chick over the head and burned what remained of the church to the ground."

Morton looked stricken. "It's all gone?"

Adams nodded.

"The Sunday School and choir building?"

Again Adams nodded.

Morton looked through the door at the growing crowd. "But that's where we were planning on having services this morning." He looked back at Adams. "Jody Chick—what was he doing there?"

"I think he was trying to make amends."

"And Norwood Sibley?"

"Lured away by a break-in at his place."

"And Dean Meckler?"

"Showed up later."

Again the preacher stared through the door at a patrol car that had pulled in beside Adams' pickup. "Then there's nothing left, nothing at all?"

"Nothing, Charley."

Morton sat there, saying nothing, just staring out the door. Every once in a while he shook his head. Finally, he put down the soft drink can and fumbled to his feet where he towered over the man in the recliner. To tell the truth it made Adams nervous.

"Wheeler, I'm sorry, but all this is my fault."

"Charley, before you go crawling up on that cross, remember your congregation needs the wood for their new church."

Morton stuck out a hand that Adams reluctantly shook. "Wheeler, I want to thank you for everything you've tried to do. I'm sorry it didn't work out."

Adams got to his feet. "What in the world are you

talking about, Charley?"

Morton didn't answer but limped through the front door and out onto the porch, down the steps to where the pistol lay in the dirt of the front yard. Adams followed him. He had no idea what Morton was up to, but if the preacher wanted to kill himself, he'd have to find a bullet, and with his bum leg, that was going to be quite a chore. After picking up the pistol Morton started toward the street in that limping gait of his. Johnny Temple stood behind the open door of his cruiser, arm resting on the door frame and talking with Rose Mary, waiting for her husband to bring the preacher out.

Among those in the crowd were Edward Nance and his teenage son. The Nances had hustled down the street after hearing the pistol shot. Now Edward Nance had his son videotaping the impending confrontation in front of the preacher's house. The camera dipped when the preacher picked up the pistol; then young Nance righted the camera as Charley Morton charged the patrol car, shouting he'd never go back to prison.

Johnny Temple turned and stared at the huge man lumbering toward him. The preacher was no more than twenty feet away when Temple held up a hand and shouted for Morton to stop, his other hand reaching for his weapon. Then, when all the deputy could see was a load of black man bearing down on him, he knelt down behind the open window of the patrol car and put four bullets into Morton's chest. That didn't stop him. The preacher slammed into the door, knocking the deputy backwards and flinging him and his gun out into the street.

Chapter Twelve

*A*dams stood on the porch, stunned. But there was no time for that. The crowd was closing in on his daughter, who had leaped out of the pickup and rushed over to where the preacher lay. Johnny Temple sat on the blacktop, dazed, not aware his pistol had gone missing. Edward Nance dropped to his knees beside Morton, and the crowd shuffled into a reluctant circle around their downed leader. Pushing and shoving his way through the crowd, Adams found Savannah kneeling beside Morton and cradling the huge man's head in her arms. Tears ran down the girl's cheeks.

"Preacher Charley . . . ."

He smiled up at her. "Savannah . . . you take care . . . of yourself . . . girl." Morton coughed blood, then looked up at the people peering down at him. "Please forgive me . . . but it had to be done." Then he closed his eyes and was gone.

Savannah gripped the man's huge shoulder and buried her face in his chest. Edward Nance pulled the girl away and handed her off to her father. Savannah came away with Morton's blood in her hair. It stained her father's shirt when she buried her face in his chest.

"Why, Daddy? Why'd he do it?"

Nance checked for a pulse, and not finding one, shook his head at Rose Mary who held a cell phone. Rose Mary stared at Nance, glanced at Charley Morton, and then remembered she was the one with the open line to EMS. Around them people mumbled, some saying the Lord's Prayer, others the Twenty-third Psalm, a few begging the Lord for mercy. Children cried as they leaned against their parents. Johnny Temple found he couldn't breathe sitting up and lay down on the blacktop. Putting away the cell phone, Rose Mary took her daughter by the arm and pulled her into the pickup, the locks thumping into position behind them.

"What happened in there, Wheeler?" asked Nance, standing up.

"I really don't know . . . I asked Charley to turn himself in to Toby Bryant and he suddenly got up and ran out of the house."

"Turn himself in—for what?"

"Heywood Chick was shot last night and Charley's one of . . . was one of the suspects."

"Your cousin's dead?"

Adams nodded.

A mumble ran through the crowd. Someone said "Good riddance." Another reprimanded the man, reminding him which day of the week it was. Eddie Nance continued to videotape. No one seemed to notice, least of all his father. In the truck Savannah wailed. Many of the black children joined her and clutched their parents. Adams wanted to get his family out of here but there was the injured deputy to consider.

He went over to where Temple lay. "You okay, Johnny?"

"I think . . . I have . . . some cracked ribs . . . ." He looked around. "My gun's . . . around here . . . somewhere."

Adams scanned the asphalt but only saw dress shoes, the cuffs of pants, high heels, hose, and flats. The light on the patrol car continued to flash as the doctor called for something to cover the preacher's body. A young woman broke away from the crowd and headed for her house. As she did more people began to wail. Others muttered under their breath, several asking what right did some cracker cop have to come into their part of town and shoot their preacher; then someone broke into a song about the River Jordan. Many joined in. Nance knelt down and checked Temple's pulse, then loosened the deputy's belt and tie. Someone nudged Adams out of the way. It was Nance's nurse.

Getting to his feet, Adams saw Johnny Temple's pistol under the cruiser. Before he could grab it a kid beat him to it. The boy stood up and turned the pistol over, examining it. A finger slipped through the trigger guard, trying the weapon on for size. Adams held his breath.

Patrick Hampton looked up from the weapon. "I don't have nobody to take me out to the firing range and teach me how to shoot." He held out the pistol to the white man.

Adams let out his breath, took the weapon, and put the safety on. "I'll talk with your mother about it."

The boy's eyes brightened. "You will?"

Adams glanced at the body of Charley Morton. "Give it a few days, Patrick." He reached inside the patrol car and snapped off the flashing light. Over the two-way came the voice of the dispatcher, wanting to know if Temple had picked up the colored preacher yet.

Hattie Williams returned with a blanket and a young man in tow. She hurried over to the preacher, knelt down quickly, then tenderly covered the dead man. Tears ran down her cheeks. She was pulled to her feet by her friend. The boyfriend looked as if he'd just woken up and had no plans for attending church. He was barefoot and wore jeans and a tee shirt saying: It's A Black Thing. Adams slid the pistol back into Temple's holster, snapping the strap across the butt.

Nance saw this. "Wheeler, you're getting your fingerprints all over everything."

"Yes. It appears that I am."

Selma Reynolds was waiting for him when Adams got to his feet. "Wheeler, what happened in that house? The preacher was passed out when Clarence and I were there. What'd you say to him?"

"I told him the church had been burned again, that

this time there was nothing left, and that Jody Chick had been clubbed over the head by someone—probably the person who lured Norwood Sibley away."

"That's right," said Sibley's brother-in-law. "That's how it was done." He looked around at the crowd. "And Norwood would be here, but he's been up all night."

More muttering from the crowd. Three young men had grouped behind Hattie Williams and her boyfriend.

"But what was that shot?" asked the elder's wife.

"Charley was reaching for a bottle, Mrs. Reynolds, about to take a drink."

That stopped the woman. Evidently she'd never consider such drastic action when it came to her first husband's drinking problem.

"But, Wheeler," Thomas Traylor said, "Charley shooting your cousin? It don't make no sense."

"It would if Heywood threatened him," Mrs. Reynolds said. "And don't tell me I didn't hear it, Wheeler. Your voices carried across the highway."

"Mrs. Reynolds, Charley didn't kill my cousin."

"It's okay with me if he did," said a voice from behind Adams.

"That's right," said another young man behind Adams. "We ain't got no friends among the Klan."

"Black folks got no white friends at all," said Hattie Williams' boyfriend. "How long's it gonna take you people to figure that out?"

Adams faced the young man in the tee shirt. "You're not from around here, are you?"

The young man was built like the runner, Michael

Johnson, and had an aristocratic, rectangular head. Tall enough to meet Adams eye to eye, he did. "What's the problem, Mister, can't tell us apart?"

"Darnell," Mr. Reynolds said, "you got no right talking to Mr. Adams like that."

The young man looked around at the crowd. "You folks are really whipped down, taking this off some white man."

"Taking what?" asked Edward Nance, standing up. "You kids take offense at everything said by some white person, you're going to have a long and miserable life."

"At least I'm no Tom."

"Watch your tongue, kid," Adams said.

"Oh, you think I'm gonna take any shit off you, Mister Charlie?"

Hattie squeezed the young man's arm. "Watch your language, Darnell."

"What you doing in that house anyway, Mister? You take a shot at the preacher—that why he's running for his life?"

"Wheeler threw the gun out," said Elder Reynolds. "Charley come out and picked it up. We all saw that."

"Yeah," said Darnell, looking Adams over, "but if 'n we searched him, I'll bet we'd find another gun—the one he used to run the preacher out of the house."

"Darnell, you can't be sure—"

"Looks like some sort of a setup, that's what it looks like. This one runs the preacher into the street and the other honky shoots him."

Temple coughed. "No . . . it wasn't that way . . . ."

Edward Nance snorted. "Then next time you need

a better plan, Wheeler. Temple's got a couple of broken ribs for sure."

"Darnell," Adams said, "I'd watch what you say. You're in the country now and people are liable to take offense."

"You gonna do something about it?" The young man looked around. "Why, we got quite a crowd here. You'd better learn *your* place where black people gather."

Over the two-way in the patrol car the dispatcher demanded that Johnny Temple answer him.

Hearing this, Adams turned to Nance. "Edward, can Johnny drive or do I need to—"

Darnell took Adams by the shoulder and turned him around. "Don't you turn your back on me—when I'm talking with you."

Adams glanced at the hand on his shoulder. "Like I said, kid, you're in the country now and someone's liable to take offense. Now take that hand off me."

Darnell grinned as he tightened the grip. "That'll be the day when some cracker tells me what to do."

The window of the pickup slid down and Rose Mary stuck a pistol in Darnell's ear. When she pulled back the hammer, Darnell froze, and his eyes got real big. "Listen here, kid, there's not a prejudiced bone in my body, but that's the father of my child you're threatening. Now turn loose."

Still the hand remained on Adams' shoulder as the young man searched faces in the crowd. "You people gonna let them do this to me?"

"Don't whine, Darnell," Nance said, "your mouth got you into this."

Darnell scanned the crowd, ever conscious of that

barrel at his ear. "Are you all Toms here?"

"Darnell," Rose Mary said, "I'm going to count to three, then Hattie's going to have to find another boyfriend. Hattie, move out of the way."

"Darnell, please . . . ."

The hand slipped off Adams' shoulder and the pistol was drawn back inside the cab. This time the window went up, but only halfway.

Now this gave the young man from Atlanta the chance to really examine the crowd. "What you got out here 'posed to be so special, niggers? The Klan burned down your church and what you doing about it?" Darnell gestured at Williams. "Hattie asked me to come down here and meet her family; I go to Morehouse, she goes to Spelman. We don't go to no white school where you have to act *incognegro*. So I come down here with an open mind, not stuck-up like you people thought I'd be and I'm ashamed of being in the same race. Like I said, what's so special about living in the country?" Darnell looked around again. "All the Toms you got?"

The young people listened closely, but the older ones only stared at the ground. Black people in Chick County certainly had their problems, but this rabble-rouser could decamp for Atlanta at a moment's notice, leaving them in a county that hadn't changed much since the first black man insisted on his civil rights. That man had voted in every election until being killed during a hunting accident.

"Hattie," asked Edward Nance, "why don't you take Darnell in the house before he says something he'll later regret?"

But when Hattie tried to take his hand, Darnell shook her off and pulled at his tee shirt. "You see here, niggers, I'm not dressed to go to church because there's no church to go to. It was burned down by somebody like this white man. In the city we don't take shit off white people, and we sure as hell don't let them come into our part of town."

"Darnell," said Edward Nance, "you don't know enough about us to be running your mouth."

The young man snorted. "I know a Tom when I see one."

"Darnell, you shut your mouth before I shut it for you."

Darnell laughed and looked around again. "No Tom's going to tell me what to—"

The punch shut him up. Something else Darnell of Atlanta didn't know. Edward Nance had boxed light heavyweight in the navy. The young man stumbled back, lost his balance, and sat down hard. Hattie gasped, then knelt down beside him. It appeared that Darnell's eyes had trouble focusing.

Nance rubbed his hand. "And read *Uncle Tom's Cabin*. Tom was more like Dr. King, not some 'step-and-fetch-it' like you young people make him out to be these days." The doctor faced the crowd. "Sorry, people, but I'm sick and tired of . . ." He saw his son videotaping the going-ons. "Put that thing away, Eddie."

"You're doing great, Daddy, just great." With his free hand the boy made a circular motion. "Keep going. I'm gonna sell this to Channel Two. Maybe win an award."

"I said put it away, boy."

Eddie brought down the camera, but held it where he could film Darnell on the ground and his daddy standing to one side. His father was not taken in by the maneuver.

He held out his hand. "Give me the camera, Eddie."

The teenager pulled the camera against his body. "Daddy, you know I got this camera for Christmas."

"Eddie, we don't need this on tape."

"But, Daddy, you don't understand—"

In one step Nance reached his son and knocked the camera from his son's hand. When it hit the street its lens broke off and rolled away. The back of the camera popped opened and the tape fell out. As he passed by Nance put a foot on the cartridge, crushing it as his horrified son looked on.

"Daddy . . . ."

But his father had stalked away, through the crowd that was making way for him, toward his house at the end of the street.

Two of the young Turks who bore marks from the fight on the state highway hauled Darnell to his feet. "This ain't over, Mr. Adams," said one of the young men.

"You're right and tomorrow I'll be here to pick up you and your friends. You've got some work to do."

"What you talking about?" asked one of the two. Between them Darnell sagged.

"Junior Bobo's house was firebombed last night and you're going over there and fix it up, paint it up if necessary."

The boys glanced at each other, then at a third kid behind them. "We don't know nuthing about that."

"Doesn't matter. It'll be a gesture of good faith, like Jody Chick made last night. I want everyone on the corner at eight sharp. And don't make me come looking for you."

"Mr. Adams, you can't tell us what to do."

Another said, "He only got what he deserved anyway."

Selma Reynolds had been taking all this in, hardly able to believe what she was hearing. "Are you fools telling me you tried to burn out Junior Bennefield last night?"

"We didn't do nuthing!" all three said in unison.

Another woman pushed her way through the crowd to stand next to Mrs. Reynolds. "J.R., is what Mr. Adams sez true? Did you do this thing?"

"No, ma'am, I did not!"

"Boy, are you telling me the truth?" She looked from one young man to the other.

"We didn't do nuthing."

"Are you telling me the truth, J.R.?"

"You calling me a liar?" Her son stuck out his chin.

His mother slapped that chin. "Don't take that tone with me, boy."

J.R. glanced at his companions. "You got no reason doing that, Mama."

"If 'n you did what Mr. Adams said you could end up in jail or dead. You want that? You want to break my heart like your father did when he was killed in Desert Storm?" She gestured at the other two teenagers. "You all hang out together, but not one of you knows what it means to take care of a house, even your own room. But you're going to learn. Wheeler, just tell me where you want J.R. and he'll be there."

"And Stanley. My boy will be there," said another woman, coming out of the crowd and gesturing at the third one who'd said nothing. "We shore don't need no trouble with the judge."

"Tommy, were you part of this?" asked an elderly woman. She was referring to the other teenager who held Darnell on his feet. "I raised you better than that."

"Grandma, I wasn't even with these guys last night.

J.R. and Stanley glared at him.

Tommy cleared his throat. "I'll be there, Mr. Adams. Eight o'clock, you say?"

"Stanley, let go of that boy. If'n he can't stand on his own two feet, he's not man enough for you to be associating with."

"Mama—"

"Don't you 'mama' me. You let go of that boy and do it now."

When they did Darnell sunk to his knees. Hattie had to grab him or Darnell would've fallen on his face. The boys were pulled away by mothers or grandmothers and told they were going to church this morning. Somewhere. Anywhere. Maybe even down King County way. It was left to Adams to haul Darnell of Atlanta to his feet and walk him over to the Williams' house. Behind him the crowd buzzed with the news of the attack on Junior Bennefield's house. Down the street came a cruiser with the sheriff at the wheel.

Rose Mary slid out of the pickup. "Mr. Reynolds, there's another gun around here: the preacher's."

The crowd started moving around and searching the ground. No one saw the missing gun so the three teenagers were quickly returned for more questioning. When they denied having the gun, their mothers frisked them. Not finding any weapons on the boys, the women said, "Well, you can still help us look."

In the cruiser down the street, the sheriff saw all these black people walking around and looking at the ground. He glanced at Robbie Simpson who sat beside him. Simpson shrugged. You never knew what the colored would be up to next.

Adams came down the steps of Hattie Williams' house and saw everyone milling around. "What's everyone looking for?"

"A gun," said more than one. "The preacher's."

"We don't need any more guns in Creekside," said another.

Adams searched the crowd with his eyes, especially the children. "Where's Patrick Hampton?"

"I sent him home," said his mother. "Patrick don't need to see any more of this." She glanced at the dead man under the yellow blanket. A red circle marked where Johnny Temple's bullets had hit home.

"Ask Patrick if he's seen the preacher's pistol."

"I don't think . . ." A flash of recognition crossed Mrs. Hampton's face and she turned on her heel and stalked across the street toward her house. "Why that little rat. I'll tan his hide."

Over the two-way the black people could hear the

sheriff calling for backup. They stopped looking for the missing pistol and clumped together between the cruiser and their dead preacher. Behind the crowd Adams took Johnny Temple by the hands and pulled him to his feet. The deputy gasped as he came up. His face turned white.

"I don't think he should be moved," said Nance's nurse, standing up beside the unsteady deputy.

Adams gestured down the street. "It's best Johnny be found sitting up."

The nurse saw the patrol car and helped Adams maneuver Temple onto the front seat of the squad car where they sat the deputy with his feet in the road. Temple groaned. Sweat broke out across his forehead. Places on his uniform had changed color from all the sweat. Over the radio the dispatcher told Johnny he'd better answer if he knew what was good for him.

"Your pistol's in your holster, Johnny."

Temple nodded, then gasped as he turned to reach for the mike. Seeing the deputy in such pain, Adams leaned inside and picked up the microphone, keying it and holding it to Temple's mouth. Temple told the dispatcher the sheriff was here and to get off his case, then nodded to Adams who hung up the mike.

When the sheriff got out of his patrol car he unlocked the shotgun and brought it along. Walking over, with the weapon in the crook of his arm, he glanced at the body covered with the blanket. Robbie Simpson followed Posey, keeping an eye on the crowd and a hand on the butt of his pistol.

"What's going on here?" The sheriff used the shotgun to gesture at the body. "Who's that?"

"Charley Morton," said someone.

"The preacher?"

"Yes."

Posey looked around. "Who done it?"

"I did . . . sir." Temple tried to pull himself to his feet by pushing off the steering wheel but fell back across the seat. Tears ran down his cheeks. He gasped for breath. More sweat soaked his uniform.

Posey stepped over to the patrol car. "What happened to you, Johnny? You hit? Need a doctor?"

"He . . . he came at me, sir. I didn't mean . . . mean to do it."

"Then why you lying there? You sick at your stomach?"

"He has a couple of cracked ribs from where the preacher ran into him," Adams said.

Posey nodded. "No wonder he had to shoot him. And I'm not surprised to find you here, Adams, since I distinctly told you to stay away." He walked over to the body. "Pull back that blanket."

"Sheriff," protested Adams, "there are children here."

"No better way to keep them in line."

Savannah stumbled out of the cab and into her father's arms. She buried her face in his chest again. "Daddy, Preacher Charley never did hurt anybody."

The crowd murmured as the blanket was pulled back, revealing the four wounds in the preacher's chest.

"Good shooting, Johnny. Looks like you got Heywood Chick's killer before we could put an APB out for him."

"Sheriff, I don't think—"

"Shut up, Adams."

The crowd grumbled as Posey returned to his deputy across the front seat of the cruiser. "You gonna be able to drive or you need some help?"

Temple pulled himself into a sitting position by holding onto the steering wheel. "I'll . . . make it."

"Good. Go by and get your chest x-rayed. Looks like I'm going to need every deputy I've got." He glanced around. "It's always that way when a deputy shoots a black man. We never seem to have that much trouble when white people get shot."

"Probably because your deputies shy away from shooting their friends."

The sheriff gestured with the shotgun. "Move away from your family, Adams."

The hair on the back of Adams' neck stood up. "Why, if I may ask?"

"I'm tired of your lip and you're going to jail."

"I don't think so."

The shotgun was aimed at a place where the blast would rip Adams in half. "Just move away from the pickup. No reason for your family to be involved."

Savannah hiccuped, caught her breath, and stepped between them, tears running down her face. "He's—he's not going anywhere with you, Sheriff. I'm—I'm not going to let you kill my daddy."

"Young lady, if you don't step aside, I'll take you and your daddy downtown. Remember what I told you about kids I found out late at night."

Rose Mary pushed her keys into her husband's hands, and then pushed him and her daughter away.

"Wheeler, would you mind putting Savannah in my car." She took the sheriff by the arm and led him away. Robbie Simpson backed up against Adams' pickup and loosened the strap on his holster.

When Adams opened the door to the sports car, Savannah slid inside, taking the keys with her. He was closing the door when Patrick Hampton's mother crossed the street behind him. In the woman's hand was the missing pistol.

"Here you are, Wheeler." Hampton held it by the butt with two fingers. "Now what's this 'bout you taking Patrick out to the firing range? Don't you think we've had enough of guns for a while?"

"I agree."

"I told Patrick he was going nowhere."

"Thank you."

"Wheeler, you can't go putting crazy ideas in these boys' heads. They can't be growing up to be like you."

"I agree," said his wife, joining them. "You're free to go, Wheeler." Rose Mary saw the gun. "After turning in that pistol to the sheriff, of course."

"Thanks for finding the pistol, Mrs. Hampton."

"And you won't be talking to my boy 'bout no guns?"

"I'll tell Patrick you forbid it."

The black woman nodded. "And I do."

To his wife, Adams said, "I'll follow you and Savannah out of here."

Their daughter leaned out of the window. "Mama, what'd you say to the sheriff?"

"Oh, I reminded him that I was looking forward to attending Judge Bennefield's party later today, but if the noise level stayed so high, I'd have to call in more reporters so I could enjoy myself."

Leaving Creekside, the Adamses saw a young man pounding a For Sale sign in the lawn in front of a brick house. The yard was neatly trimmed, flower pots lined the porch, and a black sports car was parked in the driveway. The young man was Gary Plummer.

> *August 8, 1867—After a supper prepared by Belle, who a week ago delivered twin Boys & is causing James to strut around something fierce, I met again with Miss Sherwood in my Study. Mrs. C. led our discussion.*
>
> *Wife said she had been telling Miss Sherwood something of life at the Sprgs. & that I would have to forgive the things previously said by our guest. I looked at the woman. Miss Sherwood sat on the settee & did not appear contrite. And I was giving this Woman free Room & Board? Mrs. C. went on to explain that Miss Sherwood understood she had arrived too early to school anyone, black or white, that there were Crops to be considered & the people living at the Sprgs. dependent on those Crops. Mrs. C. informed Miss Sherwood that the children would be available after those Crops were harvested & that would be closer to the end of October than the first of September. I allowed that I was pleased to hear this.*

Miss Sherwood interrupted to say this left two months free & reminded me what Mr. Benjamin Franklin, late of Philadelphia, had said about Idle Hands. Mrs. C. spoke up—they were working in tandem, as any fool could see—& suggested how to employ the Yankee Woman's time. Sherwood had offered to teach our house nigger how to thoroughly clean a house. Since Mrs. C. did not take offense, I sat there & listened as Miss Sherwood said she had no idea how the Big House was kept before the War, but she had to tell me it was lacking in the most rudimentary values of cleaning. As she spoke, I scanned the study. There was a layer of dust on everything, but that was normal. No one closed any windows during a South Georgia summer. Still, I had no idea why these Women were bothering me with this. I had nut grass to contend with & no time for trifles. Already 300 acres had been overgrown by the pernicious weed & if I did not make significant inroads, I might lose much of the bottomland. Miss Sherwood went on to address the differences between city & country standards & said that Mrs. C. had a complete knowledge of how to give a party, but the work of the former slaves must be brought up to city standards. I grew weary of all this talk & asked what it had to do with me.

I was astounded to learn Wife wanted to

*pay this Yankee Woman for supervising the
house niggers. When I pointed out Miss S.
lived here at no charge, Wife said something
irrelevant, as women are oft to do. For the
first time since meeting this woman, she
looked at the floor when she spoke.
The dusty floor, I might add. She told me she
had spent her last dollar to reach her post &
had no idea the federal government would
be so tardy in wiring her wages. When she
looked up, she said her father's business
had failed during the War & she could
expect no assistance from that quarter.*

*Now that was news to me. I did not
know of any Yankee who had lost money on
the War. In the field, the Blue Bellies and our
own men had the same Complaint: clothes &
boots that fell apart before the end of any
Campaign. Crooked dealers on both sides
had retired rich after the War. I asked Mrs.
C. how much had she promised Miss S. for
these two months that Miss S. would work
for the Sprgs. & was further astounded to
learn I was to pay this School Teacher the
same as I paid James to work in the Fields.
Now Mrs. C. looked at the floor as the
Yankee Woman proposed an arrangement:
Judge her work for one week, then make my
decision.*

*And that was the bargain we struck & I
have to say I have never seen a White
Woman work as hard as this Yankee. Even*

Belle & the Children complained, but not Wife who pitched in & scrubbed & washed & did all manner of cleaning, that, in the past, had only been done by slaves. Finally, I had to admit that I would pay the woman a dollar a day for such work but not Sundays. That did not bother the Woman. She worked on the Lord's Day as if it were any other. Yankees. I do not think I will ever understand them.

Chapter Thirteen

*I*n an empty hospital room down the hall from where Minny Jackson lay, Nell received the bad news. Nell had heard of the second fire, but at the news of the death of the preacher, the elderly woman just had to sit down.

"This is so crazy, Wheeler . . . What's gitting into folks' heads these days?" Lordy, did she hope there'd be a better life on the other side, and she wasn't so sure if it might not be time to give in and make that journey herself. The old woman stared at the yellowing linoleum floor as Adams put an arm around her.

"Any news on Mrs. Plummer?" he asked.

"It's bad, Wheeler, real bad. She could go any minute. And we ain't gots no preacher to say the funeral over her."

"Would you like me to call the bishop?"

"Would you, Wheeler? The board would shore 'preciate it." None of the elders wanted to make that call, not after they'd complained when the bishop had rammed Charley Morton down their collective throats.

"Anything you need for yourself or Minny?"

"Them clothes Aurelia picked out is jest fine. Dr. Nance is coming . . . well, it were 'posed to be before church. I guess he gots held up in Creekside. Minny's brother come by. Said he had to work today or he'd be here. He's serving drinks at the jedge's party. Imagine, drinking on the Lord's Day."

"That's where I'm supposed to be, but I think I'll pass."

"Wheeler, you can'ts let the jedge think he's got a leg up on us."

Adams took his arm from around her. "I don't know, Nell . . . with Charley's death it doesn't seem right."

"And the preacher jest run out the door and let that deputy shoot him down?"

"Made Johnny Temple kill him."

"But why would the preacher do something like that?"

"I don't know, Nell, but Charley Morton was determined to die."

"You really think so, Wheeler?"

"He as much as told me good-bye before going out the door."

"He told you . . . good-bye?"

Adams nodded.

"I guess it was too much . . . his child, his wife, and now the church." She stared at the yellowing floor again.

And so they sat there, deep into their own

thoughts. It was quite awhile before they were ready to return to Minny Jackson's room.

Outside Jackson's room stood a line of people who'd come to check on Minny as visitors weren't allowed in intensive care. None of them had heard of the preacher's death and Adams didn't raise the issue. The elderly black people said they hoped Wheeler could do something about their church.

Kate Grant said asking some white man to solve black folks' problems wasn't the answer. Kate Grant was a large woman who wore box braids and continually lobbied for Nell to move her family down to King County. Kate Grant considered King County to be the Promised Land.

"Sorry, Wheeler, but one white man can'ts make a difference, and certainly no black ones."

Adams said he thought he might go check on Lelia Plummer.

"That woman ain't gonna make it," added Grant. "I'm here to tell you."

"We're praying for her," said a woman in line.

"It's gonna take more than prayer. Lelia was a smoker."

The crash cart beat Adams there.

At a window Gary Plummer watched a nurse and the resident work on his grandmother. A tube ran down the old woman's throat. Tears streamed down the young man's face.

"She's not going to make it, I just know it."

Adams put an arm around the boy's shoulders. Plummer wore his Sunday best, tie askew.

"They said she'd have to have a double lung transplant, but she's too old and it'd be too much of a strain on her heart."

The teenager slapped a hand against the window separating him from his grandmother. The nurse looked up. The resident stayed bent over his charge.

"That damn church killed her, Mr. Adams. She loved it too much to leave."

"And that's why you went back and burned it to the ground, isn't it, Gary?"

The young man shuddered. "Jody . . . ?" He wiped tears away. "What was he doing there?"

On the other side of the glass the doctor stuck paddles to the old woman's chest and yelled "clear." The woman's thin frame lifted off the bed and the thump could be heard all the way into the hallway. Her grandson sobbed, but he couldn't pull his attention from the glass. "Clear" was yelled several more times, the paddles stuck to the woman's flat, brown chest.

A flat line ran across the monitor along with that awful whine that tells you the patient isn't going to make it. The resident glanced at a clock, said something to the nurse, then pulled the sheet up over the old woman's face.

Plummer bolted from Adams' grasp. "Maw-Maw," he screamed, running around the glass wall and throwing himself across the dead woman.

The resident patted Plummer on the back, said something Adams didn't hear, and left the room. Seeing Adams outside the door, he stopped.

"Mr. Adams, isn't it?"

Adams nodded.

The resident glanced at Adams' legs. "You should be home resting."

"Later, I guess."

"Someone said you were related to Heywood Chick, the husband of the nurse working in the ER last night."

"That's right."

"Now he's dead? Murdered?"

Adams nodded again.

The nurse wheeled the crash cart out of the room and parked it in front of the nursing station. Gary Plummer still lay across his grandmother, begging her not to leave him, asking for her forgiveness.

"You're the one who dragged the other woman out of the fire, aren't you?"

"I had some help. What's Mrs. Jackson's prognosis?"

"We're sending her over to the burn unit in Augusta later this afternoon."

"And her feet?"

The resident shook his head. "I'm sorry."

Adams bit his lip, unable to forget how he'd labored to reach the unconscious woman. If he'd only pushed himself a little harder . . . .

"I'm sure you did everything possible." When Adams didn't reply, the resident added, "Well, this has certainly been an experience. You don't usually find this many people interested in the condition of some old black woman."

"Lelia Plummer wasn't some old black woman. She taught my daughter in Sunday School."

"I didn't mean—"

"I know what you meant, Doctor."

The young man flushed. "What's being done about the church?"

"It'll be rebuilt, and the whole community will pitch in."

"It . . . they will?"

A phone buzzed at the station. After hanging up, the nurse told the doctor he was needed in the ER, that a sheriff's deputy had just come in from a shoot-out in Creekside, the colored community.

"I'll be right there. Well, Mr. Adams, I wish you luck." And the young man hurried off down the hall.

The nurse looked at Plummer lying across his grandmother, then at Wheeler Adams.

Adams went inside the room and pried the boy off his grandmother. Tears streamed down the young man's face as he allowed Adams to walk him out of intensive care, across the hallway, and into the chapel. At the altar Plummer shook off the white man's hands and knelt in front of a wooden cross. Adams waited for him in a chair in the front row. When Plummer finished praying, he took a seat, leaving a chair between them, and for the first time, a home-boy attitude appeared on his face.

"What you doing, bringing me in here—to confess?"

"Gary, I'm not the law in Chick County."

"You sure act like it." He examined the small room. "You know what your problem is, you want everybody to like you. That's why none of the white folks like you. But you can't make black people like you either. I hear what they say behind your back."

When Adams said nothing, Plummer went on, "I'll tell you what they say. They say you oughta give black folks part of the Springs. Ever think of giving some of that land to people who deserve it?"

"Who deserves it, Gary?"

"Why black people, of course."

"All black people?"

"Yeah. That'd do." He nodded a few more times. "Yeah. That'd be 'bout right."

"Who's to say I haven't done that already?"

"I don't means sharecropping. What I means is why don'ts you give away some of that land—free? You got plenty."

"Buy friendship—is that what you're saying?"

Plummer leaned forward. "Mr. Adams, there ain't no two ways about it, you owe black people big time. Chick Springs is only there 'cause of what my people done for yours."

"Funny. That's what Nell told me when I returned to live at the Springs."

"Well, I don't see you doing nuthing. Oh, yeah, I see you stepping between us and The Man so you can be a big shot, but what you oughta be doing is giving away that land."

"Gary, I'm only going to say this once: No one sharecrops the Springs."

"What you mean? There must be up to fifty families working out there?"

Adams didn't answer.

Plummer sat up. "They don't pay no fees?"

"Those farming the bottomland do. I have taxes to pay like anyone else."

"And the others?"

"A dollar a year so the land remains part of the Springs."

Plummer snorted. "You oughta give it to them outright. You've got plenty."

"I can't."

"You can't?" The young man laughed. "Who's telling *you* what to do?"

"It's in Billy Ray's will."

Plummer laughed again. "That's a load of crap if I ever heard some. You used to be a big-time lawyer. You could find some way 'round that if you really wanted to."

"But not the intent."

"You're full of it, Mr. Adams. Why you need all that land?"

"To pick and choose my neighbors?"

"Or act like some big shot."

"Gary, you talk like a man who's leaving town."

"I am. Jest as soon as I sell Maw-Maw's house." He laughed. "Want to buy it?"

Adams shook his head. "I own too much of Creekside as it is."

Plummer pushed back in his chair. "You own . . . where we live?"

"Only the houses people wanted me to buy."

"Why'd they sell to you?"

"I didn't ask. It wasn't any of my business."

Plummer shook his head. "You're like some vulture, waiting to take advantage of folks."

Adams remained silent.

"All those acres going to waste . . . You oughta be

doing something with 'em."

"I guess not too many folks want to be farmers these days."

"Can you blame them?" Plummer gestured at himself. "Now take me, I've got plans. I'm gitting out of here. The Braves are talking to me."

"So your next stop is Atlanta?"

"One of their farm teams for sure."

Adams waited for him to go on.

"Well, actually, I needs to work on my hitting. There ain't nobody can pitch much around these parts, some over at Georgia Southern, but I don't get to play them too much."

Adams only stared at the young man.

"The church—you gonna tell?"

"Like I said, Gary, I'm not the law in Chick County." He pulled out his wallet and gave Plummer Toby Bryant's business card. "But if you decide to turn yourself in make sure it's to this lady."

Plummer read the card, stared at the white man for a moment, then stood up. "Well, I needs to be seeing about my grandmother."

"Gary, I know how you feel."

Plummer laughed. "I knew we'd get around to that sooner or later. You're gonna tell me how you can feel my pain."

"What I meant was: When I was your age I couldn't wait to leave Chick Springs. Problem was Chick Springs never left me."

"Not me," said the teenager, puffing out his chest. "When I knock the dirt of this county off my spikes I'll never look back."

"So staying here all these years was only for your grandmother, it had nothing to do with your spiritual geography?"

"Spiritual *whaaat?*"

"A sense of where you belong."

"Nah. It weren't that." Plummer cleared his throat. "Well, I needs to see to my grandma."

"Gary, let the stewards help. They'll want to be involved. Nell and your grandmother went to Sunday School in that church when they were children."

The young man nodded, then left. Adams did, too, but only after saying a prayer of his own. Now he was ready to face Nell. Or so he thought.

When he told her about Mrs. Plummer crossing over, Nell looked like she might faint. He and Kate Grant had to grab an arm to keep the elderly woman on her feet. Several people outside Jackson's room moaned. A prayer circle quickly formed. White people in the hall stared at them.

"Nell, is there anyone you want me to call?"

"We'll be taking care of this, Wheeler," Grant said.

"Most of Lelia's family moved up north, Wheeler."

"Not all of them," said Grant. "She has a grand-child lives down the street from me."

"In Jackson City?" asked Nell, plainly astonished.

"Nell, we don'ts let all the good ones get away."

Before Grant could launch into her Chamber of Commerce speech about why black folks were better off living separate from whites, Adams thanked her for being there for Nell.

"Where you going, Wheeler?" asked his house-keeper as Adams turned to leave.

"To find Jody Chick."

"You're still going to the jedge's party this afternoon, aren't you?"

"Wheeler Adams," asked Grant, "you're gonna go to that man's party and you say you're a friend of black folks?"

Nell shook loose from Grant's grasp. "Kate, I'd 'preciate it if you'd tend to King County business and leave Chick County business to me and Wheeler."

When Adams called Heywood Chick's home he reached Jean's mother. She told him her daughter had taken a sleeping pill and gone to bed. No. Jody hadn't come home, but the APB was no longer out because the sheriff had caught Heywood's killer.

"And who would that be, ma'am?"

"Why that nigger preacher. The sheriff said they trapped him in his house, and when the sheriff asked him to come out peacefully, the nigger came out shooting. Why, Wheeler, under those circumstances the sheriff just had to shoot him down."

*November 2, 1867—I was in Lee's
Crossroads—not that I get into town often—
when some of my Friends asked me to step
into McKelvey's Boarding House. The rear of
McKelvey's is a Social Club where members
of the Klan hold meetings. I am sure the
Blue Bellies know all about it. When I
entered the bar & saw everyone there, I realized it was not business with the bank that
had called me to town. Everyone from our*

old unit was there but for Johnny Ryan who was down with the flu again, meaning he was drunk. Johnny wasn't much of a drinker before the war; nowadays he's in his cups all the time.

Mark Lee took the lead, as he is likely to do. Lee did not serve but sent a substitute so he could stay behind and play politician. Before the War, Lee was behind the Movement to annex the Island of Cuba & I purchased his land rather cheaply when he moved into Atlanta. Nowadays, it is not unusual for Lee's children to be found on their former land, trapping & fishing for food. Lee did not take his family into town & we men knew why. What was astounding was that Lee's Crossroads was named for a good friend of my grandfather's & a great leader in the war against the Creek Indians. It is amazing that Mark Lee could be descended from such an extraordinary man.

The Scalawag got right to the point. He told me they knew there was a Yankee School teacher living at the Sprgs. I told them their information was correct, that the woman was teaching my children to read & write. While Lee questioned me, those who had served in my troop stared at the floor & held their hats in their hands. I could have offered any of these men's children the opportunity to attend Classes at the Sprgs. & Lord knows some of them deserved it *because of their devotion to the Cause, but I leave all that selling talk to those who must make their living that way. Lee added they also understood the Yankee woman was teaching my former slaves to read & write. I allowed that he was correct in this matter. Lee wanted to know if I didn't see anything wrong with that arrangement. I said I did. When I agreed, everyone looked up from the floor. One of my former comrades asked why did I do such a thing if I knew it to be wrong. I asked if I had to explain myself to Friends. The Question did not sit well with my So-called Friends. Boots scuffed the floor & there was a good deal of mumbling. It shamed me to explain my predicament, but I told them I had tried to be released from the Obligation but was not allowed. The Military Governor—you remember the last time he was here? I asked these So-called Friends of Mine. Most grumbled that they did. Several wanted to ambush the Governor, but I told them my Yankee killing days were over. Which was not exactly true. I would sorely love to kill the woman living in my House.*

The day I had tried to be released from my Obligation, Gen. Pope had sat across from me on the same settee the Yankee woman used when she & Wife confronted me. God! How Yankee men can tolerate such forwardness! The Gen. said he was there to inquire as to why I had refused to allow the freedmen employed at Chick Sprgs. to be educated by Miss Sherwood. Many of my former slaves had returned from Atlanta after running through the Gold I had given them for the 40 acres Congress granted them—of my land! Now there were twenty-one former slaves working the Sprgs. & the Yankee woman had sent the General a letter, complaining of my noncompliance.

Two weeks later, Pope & a troop of horse soldiers showed up on my property. He asked if I was aware that Georgia was still under Military Rule & that I could be jailed for Insubordination. Pope's aides had their hands on their side arms. They did not know I had given up riding with the Klan, but when Gen. Nat said enough was enough, I bowed out & allowed Mark Lee to take the reins of an organization which had become a refuge for ruffians, bullyboys, & scoundrels.

I asked Gen. Pope if I didn't do as this Woman demanded, would he have me arrested? Pope opened his mouth to tell me just that, but I cut him off. I asked if he was telling me he would have me thrown in a military prison & I would not be able to bring in my Crops & my family could starve to death come Winter. The Gen. leaned back on the settee & regarded me. A smile crossed his face. He said that was exactly what he had come to tell me & addressed me by my former military title. Then he looked at the

Schoolteacher & told the Woman he did not
want to hear of any more squabbles
between Us & asked the Woman if she
understood. The Woman outrageously asked
Pope why he was not asking Me the same
question. The Gen. reminded her that I was
an Officer & a Gentleman.

This was not what the woman wished to
hear. She stormed out of our presence without asking permission, muttering something
about all men being the same. I do not know
about all men, but it appears all Officers
share a common bond. And this was what I
told my So-called Friends at McKelvey's
Boarding House who had tricked me into
attending their Meeting. However, Mark Lee
would not turn loose of the issue. He questioned me about my building a Church for
the niggers. When I asked Lee if he had
some problem with the negroes having a
place to worship, he glanced at his audience
& said it appeared I went out of my way to
accommodate them. Now, I want to be per-
fectly clear as to what was said between
Lee & myself & I have transcribed our conversation as I best remember.

"Mark, how can a man who has never-
darkened the doorway of any Church understand why another would build a church for
anyone?"

"You're saying the freedmen are equal to
the White Man?"

"Mark, where did I say that?"

"I thought—"

"Give everyone some Peace & do not think so much."

"Billy Ray, I'm not some soldier you can order around."

"That is correct. You were never any kind of soldier."

My former Sergeant, Jared Bennefield, had to separate us. After the room was quiet again, I made what I think was the second speech of my whole life; the first being the time I recruited these same Men to ride off to defend Georgia.

"Friends, the Yankees cannot stay here forever. Someday they will have to leave & we can handle our own affairs once again."

"But they're changing the laws," said someone, "giving the slaves the right to vote."

When I had the floor again, I said, "The negroes cannot vote in the state of Michigan or several other Northern States. If we bide our time, after the Yankees leave, we can change the Laws to suit Ourselves."

Most nodded in agreement, but Lee made a motion that the Klan should ride anyway. I squashed that by saying it would only encourage the Blue Bellies to stay even longer.

"What about our Honor?" asked Lee.

I gave him a sharp look before saying to those who had served with me, "Listen to

*what I have to say, men. You want to dis-
courage the freedmen their Schooling but not
allow them to share Crops on your Land.
Why do you think the negroes have time to
attend this School? I say: Put them to work,
take that idle time away & your families will
eat better next Winter."*

*That ended that & the following Spring
more black hands were put to work tending
the fields of Chick County & things began to
somewhat resemble what they had before
the War, except I still had that Damned
Woman living in the Big House with me.*

Chapter Fourteen

When Roosevelt pulled into the farmers' market across the highway from the Dark Corner, he said he was there to pick up some barbecue for the folks at Chick Springs. That wasn't true. Adams and his family had already headed over to the Bennefields' annual Fourth of July party, and Nell was helping Gary Plummer with his grandmother's funeral arrangements. Be that as it may, more than one person gave Roosevelt a hard time about the car he drove.

"Roosevelt," said the man cooking the pig, "what's that car you're driving there?"

The gardener ran a hand across the lime green Z-car before walking over to where Michael Weston and Clarence Benton sat. The two black men wore overalls and work boots but were bareheaded. Michael Weston's head was as slick as a baby's bottom;

Clarence Benton still had most of his hair, but like Roosevelt's, that hair had turned white many years ago. The two black men sat in the shade of a tarp running from the side of Weston's pickup to Benton's and away from the smoker. It was hot as blazes out here, over ninety degrees and an equal measure of humidity. To the left and right of the smoker black folks sold a variety of items, mostly produce. One even sold boiled peanuts, but that was for any white people who might come along.

"You didn't buy that car with that money you're making hauling all that garbage?" asked Benton, smiling at Weston.

"Nigger, you know I don'ts make 'nuff money hauling garbage to make payments on a car as fine as this."

Michael Weston let out a hoot and slapped a knee. "Then what's that red Cadillac doing parked behind the barn at Chick Springs? Got its own shelter and you're the nigger keeps it shiny-new."

"Aw," said Roosevelt, walking over to the smoker, "you know that Cadillac got to belong to Mister Wheeler Adams. How's a nigger with a trash route gonna have 'nuff money to afford a Cadillac?"

"Then," Clarence Benton said, giving Weston a knowing smile, "when we see you racing down the highway in that Cadillac, that's just Wheeler Adams letting you blow the carbon out."

Roosevelt smiled. "And I'm doing the same thing with his wife's car today."

It took a few minutes, but Roosevelt finally got around to asking the question he'd been asking all over Chick County, at least to black folks. Leaving the farmers' market, he fussed at the sports car. "You tempted me like some kind of she-devil. I could've learned what I wants to know on my first stop, but no, I gots to run into town, race around, and show you off."

The Bennefields' Fourth of July party is something to see, sprawling over several acres, with a bluegrass band and more than half a dozen hogs on spits. There are sack races and other games for the kids, an Olympic-size swimming pool that's always packed, and a dunking machine guests try to talk the judge into taking a turn in. It's considered bad form to be a no-show, and many a sleepless night has been spent by wives who thought their husbands might have offended the judge.

You could sit on blankets and broil in the sun or lounge under canopies borrowed from funeral homes in three counties. Each tent had a fan going and plenty of folding chairs. The tents encircled a pit where a couple of pigs had been cooking since yesterday. A black man in a chef's white uniform sliced off pork and served it; people stood in a line stretching fifty feet long, using paper plates as fans.

About 4 PM the Adamses arrived at a party with more than its share of drunks, two fist fights, and a woman who claimed she'd been raped. A staccato of firecrackers went off on the far side of the property and a wisp of smoke began to rise in that general direction. When the pickup stopped in the grassy area serving as the parking lot, Uncle Ingram climbed out of the bed, rambled across the field, and disappeared into the crowd, saying there were people he needed to see.

Rose Mary watched the old man go. "For someone who lives in a cabin along the river, Ingram certainly has plenty of people he always needs to see."

On his way down the hill Ingram nodded to a bear of a man headed in the opposite direction, drinks in both hands. With the man was a chubby teenage girl with peroxide-blond hair. Someone at the gate had used a walkie-talkie to announced the Adamses' arrival to Bennefield and his daughter.

Heading toward the Bennefields, Rose Mary said, "You know, Wheeler, I didn't see my car at the Springs."

"I think Roosevelt borrowed it."

"For what?"

"Said he had some errands to run."

"On the Fourth of July? I'll bet."

"Mother, you let everyone drive your car but me!"

"I'm not sure I want Roosevelt driving it either. He appears too eager."

The Bennefield's house was a two-story affair with four columns across the front and appeared rather imposing—from the road. However, from this side, where the cars were parked you could see the house was nothing more than a New England saltbox with four columns stacked across the front.

Savannah embraced the judge's daughter as Bennefield zeroed in on Adams' wife. As the teenagers disappeared into the crowd, Adams saw that Annabelle Bennefield wasn't wearing enough clothes to be seen in public. For that matter, neither was his daughter. The other thing he noticed was that his daughter appeared to be more pleased to see Annabelle than Annabelle did to see Savannah.

"Wheeler and his Rose," said the judge, leaning into the auburn-haired woman and giving her an armless embrace. He handed Rose Mary a Tom Collins. The beer was for her husband.

"Rather Rose with her Wheeler," Rose Mary said, taking the drink.

Bennefield laughed. "But not here in Chick County."

The judge was a round-faced man with considerable bulk, most of it gut, as tall as Adams and with a full head of gray hair. Growing up in Chick County, Adams and Bennefield had two distinct methods of dealing with their opponents: Adams used fisticuffs, Bennefield worked behind the scene to destroy his opponent. Today, Hizzoner wore a green pullover with a Masters Golf Tournament insignia and a pair of yellow slacks. Cordovan loafers and no socks. Heading toward the tents, Adams' wife and the judge took up where they'd left off last time they'd seen each other.

"Now tell the truth, Rose. You just had to come here today. You were bored out of your mind over at the Springs."

"Actually, things have been rather exciting."

"And you city gals love the fast lane—which runs through *my* property on the Fourth of July."

"Oh, I don't know why you think it's so exciting. It's the same people year after year and never a black face to be seen, except for the help."

"There's always the congressman."

"An Oreo if there ever was one." Rose Mary was

referring to a black man who had been elected to office more than twenty years ago by those favoring a strong federal government and its subsidies. When that base began to erode, the congressman began to vote against federal spending—and against gun control.

"Which only proves people can overcome their upbringing," said the judge.

"Or any sense of integrity."

"My dear, those people over in Creekside would legalize marijuana tomorrow if given the chance. They see it as a white man's law."

"I'm not so sure marijuana shouldn't be legalized. It helps people undergoing chemotherapy."

Bennefield laughed and called for another drink. Very quickly it was brought by a black man in a white uniform serving drinks on a tray. "That's the trouble with you city folks. You don't think there's such a thing as an actual fact. Fact is, a black lady of child-bearing age can hardly find a husband that can support her. Most black men are either in jail, on parole, or out on bond. Those people see the war on drugs as a war on them. Now that's a fact, Rose, not some story out of California about how smoking dope is good for you."

"Selling drugs—to white people—might be the only way they have to keep bread on the table, Your Honor, if there are no jobs."

"My dear, you sound like you admire them."

"Oh, you don't think having a bunch of babies and receiving a mailbox full of welfare checks isn't just a variation on the American Dream?"

"Those days are over, my dear. Everyone has to pull his own weight."

"Then where were the white people last night? You heard about the church fire?"

Bennefield nodded at Adams, trailing along from behind. "And your husband's heroics." The judge steered Rose Mary toward the head of the serving line. "But we're not going to ruin my party by talking about that."

"Which—the fire or my husband's heroics?" Rose Mary pulled Bennefield to a stop several feet from the line. "Your Honor, you're not thinking of putting us at the head of that line, are you?"

"Don't worry, my dear. All these fine folks are back for seconds." He glanced down a line of people who watched him closely. "Isn't that so, friends?"

Many nervous nods from the men, quite a few flashes of anger on the faces of their women, and too many clean plates for folks to be returning for seconds. Rose Mary demurred, saying she wasn't all that hungry, that she needed to see some people.

The judge smiled. "More folks to rile up?"

"If the congressman's here, I want to talk to him about the sewage being dumped into the creek between Lee's Crossroads and Creekside. It'd be advantageous to everyone if it were cleaned up. As the largest taxpayers in Chick County you and Wheeler pay for that at the emergency room."

"I'd rather those people get a job and their own insurance plan."

"And when was the last time you allowed new industry to locate here, Your Honor?"

"I was all for that new prison, but Wheeler wouldn't sell the land."

"I favored an alternate site," her husband said.

The judge laughed. "Always buy, never sell—right, Wheeler? How many jobs did we lose? A hundred and thirty six?"

"Eighty-five by the county council's count. And try as you might, Judge, you couldn't get anyone to bring it before the council. Nobody wants a prison in their backyard."

"*Your* backyard, you mean. That was a good deal for the county. Those were high paying jobs. We had plenty of people who wanted those jobs."

"Of course," Rose Mary said. "Most guards are on the take—bringing in drugs for resale."

Bennefield looked from one Adams to the other and shook his head. "Such smart folks with so few friends." He pointed toward the house. "The congressman's over there, Rose. If he'll speak with you."

"That's his job—to listen to his constituents."

"Oh," asked the judge with a smile, "does that mean you'll be moving back in with Wheeler?"

"Not on your life. I like the peace and quiet of Atlanta."

Another laugh and the judge was gone, leaving Adams to follow his wife over to where the congressman addressed a small crowd. Across the yard Bobbie Lee stood with Ernie Ellis. Both volunteers wore clean clothes, and for the first time they didn't reek of smoke. Lee looked particularly attractive in a green sleeveless blouse and a pair of tan walking shorts, revealing her freckled arms and legs. When Ellis asked Lee if she wanted to speak with Wheeler, pointing to Adams and his wife, Bobbie Lee snapped "no" and turned away. Ellis followed her as she hurried across the yard in the direction of the band. Ellis figured the gal wanted to dance. Women were like that, always changing their minds on the spur of the moment.

Adams could stand this political talk so long as it focused on local issues, but when the discussion turned to a water project outside Chick County, he drifted away, speaking to people he hadn't socialized with since last year. Arthur Vickery came out of the crowd and took Adams by the arm and told him that he had to do something about getting those GBI people away from the church. Mac Thrower and his boys were scheduled to bring over their heavy equipment later today, and Vickery didn't want them put off by a bunch of law-and-order types.

As Adams took a beer from a black man passing through the crowd, he asked, "Have you spoken to Toby Bryant?"

"She won't listen to reason." The Vickerys still wore their church clothes and Mr. Vickery had his seersucker jacket slung across his arm. His wife held a parasol over her head.

"I don't know what I can say to change her mind, but if I see Toby, I'll speak to her about it."

"Oh, thank you, Wheeler," Mrs. Vickery said. "I'm sure you'll get it all worked out. Arthur really wants to get started on this."

"And don't forget to give me a call later tonight so I can tell Mac everything's set."

Adams watched them go, then someone passed by expressing condolences on the death of his cousin. "The terrible things people do these days," said the man who farmed bottomland at the Springs. "And to think it was a preacher." The farmer headed toward a canopy.

Before Adams could catch the man and straighten out the misconception, he was sidetracked by Uncle Ingram lecturing a group of white people about how the black people of Chick County needed to learn to defend themselves. Those listening to him appeared to be too dumbstruck or too drunk to rebut. Among them was Toby Bryant, listening to someone who not only manufactured moonshine but was rumored to have his own machine gun. When she saw Adams, Bryant took his arm and walked him away from the lecture and toward a crowd gathered around the sheriff.

With a smile, she said, "You can do more damage over here, Wheeler."

Ozzie Tucker was part of the crowd and he was bragging about how Dale Posey had successfully brought Charley Morton to justice. Toby Bryant released Adams' arm and stepped away.

"Got him dead to rights," finished Tucker. Next to Tucker stood Garland Kelly, the sharpshooter of Chick County.

Posey noticed Adams' arrival. The blond man cleared his throat. "I know you don't like putting the noose around the neck of one of your nigra friends, Adams, but you sure did it this time."

"A black man killing a white one. When was the last time you remember that happening in Chick County? It's so absurd it makes you wonder who would've profited from my cousin's death."

"Oh, he's your cousin now?" asked Tucker. "First time I remember you claiming Heywood as relations."

The sheriff nodded. "He's got a point, Adams."

"Dale, did you ever consider it might be more important who's going to be the next den leader for the Klan?"

Under his cowboy hat Tucker's eyes narrowed. "What the hell you mean by that?"

The sheriff turned to Tucker. "Don't be swearing on the Lord's Day, Ozzie. Adams, we don't have much Klan around these parts. It's more for show, you know, like those reenactors."

"Then who's going to be the new leader of the militia?"

"The mission of the militia is to keep the government off the back of the white man," stated Tucker.

"And the black man?"

"Shit, Adams! I ain't seen the government doing nothing but raising niggers up above their station. They sure as hell aren't on their backs like white people."

The sheriff warned Tucker to watch his language again.

"You ain't taking up for the colored, are you, Wheeler?" asked Garland Kelly.

"I don't think that's the point."

Tucker looked at the crowd gathered around them. "What the hell you think's the point? You've lived with them so long you think like them."

"Sheriff, we need to learn who killed my cousin and the place to start is with the Klan. Or the militia."

"Yeah, your cousin," Tucker said with a sneer. "I never seen you at any meetings, you nigger lover."

"And what meetings would those be, Ozzie? The ones where the Klan get together, like reenactors?"

Tucker stepped over and squared up in front of Adams. "I'm not gonna stand here and let you slander the Klan, if not for me, then for Billy Ray. Billy Ray was a relation of Heywood's, too."

Adams ignored him. "If the murder of my cousin was racially motivated, as the sheriff suggests, we need to nip this in the bud, don't you think?"

Most everyone agreed. Nobody wanted the government intervening in Chick County again. The Feds hadn't, not since ordering school desegregation, but everyone remembered like it was yesterday.

"Adams, what we don't need," said Garland Kelly, "is your wife writing another article about Chick County."

Everyone agreed with that, some wondering why Adams couldn't keep his wife on a tighter leash.

"The preacher didn't kill my cousin. Besides a black man can't be the leader of the—"

With that Tucker threw himself on Adams, knocking the taller man to the ground. A gasp ran through the crowd as they stepped back and made way. But before Tucker could raise up and draw back to hit him, Adams bashed the scrawny man in the face with the only weapon available: his forehead. Tucker's nose exploded in blood and he rolled away, holding his face. When he stood up, blood ran between his fingers, down his hand, dripping on his shirt. Adams used the tail of his shirt to wipe blood off his face.

"You lousy bastard!"

When Tucker moved toward Adams again Toby Bryant stepped between the two men. "Settle down, boys. This is a party, remember."

Garland Kelly had picked up his friend's cowboy hat. Now he grabbed Tucker's free arm with one of his own. "You ain't gonna hurt him with one hand, Ozzie."

"Adams, somebody's always stopping me from fixing your wagon."

Palms open, Adams asked, "What did I do?"

"You know what you said."

"And that was?"

"Listen, boys . . ." said the sheriff.

But the boys weren't listening.

"You're saying I kilt your cousin."

Adams looked around at the crowd. "Did anyone hear me say that?" People looked at each other, then shook their heads. Adams shook his head. "You're the one with the guilty conscience, Ozzie."

"You sumbitch," shouted Tucker, and he charged again. "I'll kill you for saying that!"

This time Adams sidestepped him, then gave Tucker a small push on the rump which caused the scrawny man to lose his balance and end up on the ground. Tucker slid across the grass as people leaped out of the way. Dale Posey and Toby Bryant rushed over.

"Ozzie," said the sheriff, standing over Tucker, "I don't know what set you off, but if I remember correctly, Adams was talking to me."

When Tucker tried to get to his feet Toby Bryant put a foot on his back, keeping him on the ground. "Stay there, Ozzie! Would someone get this man some ice?"

A woman went to fetch some. When Bryant finally allowed Tucker to sit up, he mumbled that Adams was screwing him again, always screwing him.

"Ozzie, would you please watch your tongue?" asked the sheriff. "There're kids here and you don't want me having to arrest you."

"Ozzie," asked Adams, "do you have something to tell us about my cousin's murder?"

That got Tucker on his feet. Ice cubes scattered across the grass as Tucker lunged for him. Dale Posey and Toby Bryant each grabbed an arm and struggled to control Tucker.

Judge Bennefield came out of the crowd. "Now what've you done, Wheeler, started another fight?"

"Your Honor," said Rose Mary, appearing at the judge's side, "it's been my experience that Wheeler doesn't start fights, he finishes them."

Adams bent down and picked up several ice cubes and wiped them across his forehead, then down the back of his neck. That didn't help. Hitting the ground had reminded his body of the beating he'd taken out on the state highway. It was only last night? Hard to believe. He needed to go home and lie down—for a week.

"What happened here, Dale?" asked Bennefield.

"Don't rightly know, Judge. All of a sudden Adams was on his back and Tucker's nose was bleeding. You know Adams' reputation for being a smart-ass."

Garland Kelly said, "Ozzie was provoked."

Voices from the crowd disagreed, saying the sheriff was right, Ozzie had attacked Adams.

"What's your problem, Ozzie? You know I'll run you off my property. I've done it before."

Tucker held a cloth to his nose and pointed at

Adams. "He accused me of killing his cousin." Pieces of grass littered the front of Tucker's blood-stained pullover.

"Wheeler, that's a pretty serious charge. Do you have any proof?"

"All I said was that black men don't kill white men in Chick County, and that the sheriff should learn who had the most to gain from my cousin's death."

Rose Mary nodded. "Makes sense to me."

"Well, Dale," asked the judge, "are you going to question him—Tucker, that is?"

"Er—yes, sir. But first, I think he needs to get his nose fixed. Ozzie, can you drop by and see me in the morning?"

"In the morning?" asked Rose Mary.

"Mrs. Adams, this ain't the city. Ozzie knows what it means if he don't show up tomorrow."

"But if he's guilty?"

"Mrs. Adams—"

"It's 'Bingham,' Sheriff. Let's show a little respect yourself."

"Okay, okay," said the judge. "I think we know what the score is here. Wheeler, if you're not going to cause any trouble you and Rose are free to stay. Stop by the house and we'll find you a shirt. You can clean up in the downstairs bathroom."

Adams nodded as he ran ice over the back of his neck.

"Judge," said Ozzie Tucker, talking through his nose, "I'm the injured party here and it sounds like you're siding with the nigger lover."

"There's no reason for such language," said Rose.

"Ozzie, you'd better watch your mouth or I'll have you before me for being drunk and disorderly."

With this, Garland Kelly dropped Tucker's hat at the scrawny man's feet and stepped back into the crowd.

Still holding his nose, Tucker said, "But he's the one started it, Judge."

"Don't whine, Ozzie."

"Go home, Ozzie," said the sheriff. "Get yourself cleaned up."

"And you'll stay there if you know what's good for you," added the judge.

Tucker looked from one face to another. "This ain't right and you know it." He looked at his tormentor. "Adams, this ain't over between us." And he stalked away, the crowd making way as the blood-and-grass-covered man headed for the parking area.

Through the hush someone on a PA system called for contestants to gather for the sack races, another string of firecrackers went off, and the judge told the sheriff to move the crowd along. In the field serving as the parking lot, Ozzie Tucker climbed into his truck, cranked the engine, and because he could use only one hand—the other holding his nose—fought with the straight drive as he bumped through the field and down to the driveway.

"Wheeler," Bennefield said, "I don't remember one of my parties where you haven't gotten into a fight."

"I don't go looking for them, Judge."

"Oh, no, you just live over there with a bunch of colored people and thumb your nose at the rest of us. Don't you think those chickens are looking for a place to roost?"

"What would you recommend Wheeler do, Your Honor?"

"Rose Mary, I live in the real world. How many black people visit in your home?"

"There are a few."

"And there'd be a lot more if they acted like white people."

"Oh, you mean like Ozzie Tucker?"

"I think we've seen the last of Ozzie," said the judge, watching Tucker's pickup go through the gate. "You know what I'm talking about, Rose, like the congressman."

"You want them to act white, Your Honor?"

"Yes—like the people who created our civilization."

"If civilization was created by white men, it was built on the backs of the colored races—and women."

"Don't give me that glass ceiling foolishness, Rose. Women can climb as high as they want if they're willing to give up hearth and home. 'Course when you think about it, who'd want to be married to a woman like that. Now, if you don't mind I have other guests to attend to."

As he left, Rose Mary turned on her husband. "Did you hear what he said? He was talking about me."

"Not unless you take it personally."

"Why didn't you speak up?"

Adams brushed grass off his pants. "You, of all people, need a knight in shining armor?"

"You know what I mean."

"Rose Mary, I have to live here." Adams wiped sweat from his forehead and threw it off with a finger. A waiter passed by and he took another beer from the tray.

As they started away, the sheriff said, "I'd appreciate you not accusing people of things you can't prove,
Wheeler. It can come back to haunt you."

"Is that a threat?" asked Rose Mary.

"No, no, Miss Bingham. It's just that sometimes
your husband can't keep his mouth shut."

"Sorry, Sheriff, but Savannah and I don't agree. We
don't think Wheeler talks enough."

The sheriff didn't know what to make of that. "Just
keep in mind what I said, Wheeler." Posey wandered
off to find his wife and kid. It was a downright shame
when one person could ruin a whole party.

"Was he making a threat?" asked Rose Mary.

"No—just trying to communicate."

She pulled a handkerchief from her walking shorts
and dabbed at her forehead. "Wheeler, wouldn't you
rather go home and get out of this heat?"

"What about Savannah?"

"She won't leave." Rose Mary flushed and it wasn't
just from the heat. "And we'd have the house to ourselves."

"You don't want any barbecue?"

His wife stared at the pit and licked her lips. "Well,
maybe, one plate. But only one."

As they walked toward the pit people stopped and
stared. One of the couples was the Vickerys. Another
was Bobbie Lee and Ernie Ellis. Ellis saluted Adams
with his beer. Bobbie Lee said nothing. Both Vickerys
shook their heads.

"Savannah shouldn't even be here, but she looked
so miserable when I tried reasoning with her . . ." Rose
Mary took a beer from a waiter and rolled the bottle

across her forehead. "She should be with a shrink after what she saw."

"Let's not make a big deal out of it and see how it shakes out."

"And how the hell do you do that?"

Adams shook his head. "I don't know, Rose. So far all I've had to deal with is boys calling the house all hours of the night."

Rose Mary brushed grass off her husband's shirt, then put an arm around his side as they walked toward the pit. Adams didn't tell her how much that hurt.

At the pit the cook served them with a smile. Even Red came over and asked how much they liked the pig. The Adamses replied in the most perfunctory manner. They were searching the faces of those participating in the sack races. All the teenagers should be there, tripping and falling, a hodgepodge of legs and arms, boys and girls being more intimate than should be allowed. But the one kid they couldn't find was their own daughter.

Chapter Fifteen

Rose Mary wanted to come into the Bennefield's bathroom and help her husband clean up, but Adams only smiled and said that wasn't such a good idea. His wife flushed and left, saying she'd wait for him on the porch. Leaving the house they were met by the black man who'd been slicing up the pig. He asked Adams if he'd like to have another plateful.

"Wheeler, I thought you were on a diet."

That was enough to send Adams back to the pit, while Rose Mary set her sights on a county commissioner.

Once the black man had Adams alone, he said, "Mr. Adams, I have a message from Roosevelt."

"You do?"

"Yes, sir. Roosevelt said the person you're looking for is over in the Dark Corner."

"The Dark Corner, you say?"

"Yes, sir. I'm sorry, but I don't know where that is."

"Not your problem. Thanks for the information."

"Sorry to hear about the fire. Have any idea who done it?"

"The person over in the Dark Corner."

"Good," said the black man, setting his jaw, "the sheriff will be happy to hear you've found him."

"You're not from around here, are you?"

"No, sir, we're from Atlanta." He looked at the crowd. "Pretty good turnout for this kind of weather."

"It's considered bad form not to be here."

The black man nodded; plainly there was something else on his mind. "Er—Mr. Adams, there's something else I'm supposed to tell you."

"Yes?"

He saw Adams' wife headed toward them. Very quickly he said, "Judge Bennefield's daughter-in-law set fire to her own house, not those boys everyone thinks did it. Minny Jackson's brother—he's pouring drinks because one of our people didn't show—overheard Lizzie tell her friends she'd figured out how to get a new house out of the judge. I don't know why I'm telling you this, but they asked me and you haven't been by the bar."

"What's going on, Wheeler?" asked Rose Mary.

"I was just saying how good this pig is."

"Would you like another plate, Mrs. Adams?" asked the black man with a warm smile.

Rose Mary shook her head. As they walked away, she asked, "What was that all about?"

"I guess Hizzoner thought I couldn't get into another fight with my hands full."

When Rose Mary saw her husband wasn't going to be more forthcoming, she said, "I swear but you can ruin a party with the least little effort."

"Is that why you don't invite me to the parties you have in Atlanta?"

"What do you mean?"

"Savannah says you have more fun when I'm not there."

"That goes without saying."

Adams looked toward the field where the games were being held. The judge had taken a seat in the dunking machine; lots of nervous laughter followed by a quick-forming line. Adams didn't see his daughter there and Savannah had a pretty good arm.

His wife was talking, ". . . have the flashbacks anymore that's why you don't need me, isn't it?"

Adams dropped his half-empty plate into a fifty-gallon drum serving as a trash can. "Rose, would you stay and look for Savannah? There's something I want to take care of."

His wife put her hands on her hips. "Now I know something's up."

"Is that a 'yes' or a 'no'?"

"How will I get home?"

"Give Roosevelt a ring."

"I might call him right now to get him out from behind the wheel of my car."

Adams left the party without thanking the judge for inviting him. It wasn't polite, but Adams preferred to let Bennefield, and every other white man, think he was still there.

At Chick Springs he picked up a long-sleeved shirt and a bloodhound by the name of Elvis. Black and tan, a slow but sure tracker, Elvis belonged to Uncle Ingram. With Roosevelt was a white man by the name of McKelvey who had a son crippled by Junior Bennefield. From time to time McKelvey pulled guard duty around the Springs, as he sure as hell wasn't going to any Fourth of July party given by the judge. Roosevelt and McKelvey had the dog in his box in the bed of the pickup when Adams came out of the house.

"You got something to track with, Mr. Wheeler?"

Adams nodded and tossed a jacket into the cab. "Thanks for all your help, Roosevelt. Mr. McKelvey."

"Don't thank me," McKelvey said, "Roosevelt's the one went down to the river and got the dog."

"Have any trouble with Rose Mary's car?" Adams asked as he climbed into the pickup.

Roosevelt's face split in a huge grin. "That car's a real sweet thing, Mister Wheeler. Handles real good on curves, too."

"And no county mounties on the roads today?"

"No, sirree, I was free as a bird."

Leaving the Springs, Adams let down the windows and pulled out the tail of his shirt. Darkness would come about nine, but it wouldn't be much cooler; however, he expected to be out of the Dark Corner before nightfall. Elvis was one of the best trackers in all South Georgia; the Georgia Department of Corrections often borrowed the dog for tracking escaped convicts.

Across the highway from the entrance to the Dark Corner black people were in their stalls, selling all

manner of produce, including boiled peanuts. Someone had even hauled a smoker out there and was selling barbecue. Several people recognized the pickup
and waved at Adams. Elvis barked, probably for the
barbecue. Elvis didn't care much for boiled peanuts.

The gate to the Dark Corner was open and that
could only mean someone was spending the holiday at
the firing range. As Adams drove down the gravel road
through the pines, he heard the sound of a weapon
being fired on full automatic. Illegal as hell, but anyone can make the adjustment from a semiautomatic
with the right device, and these days more and more
people have the correct device.

The shelter was a long wooden thing with no sides,
elbow-high tables for reloading, and a railing separating each station from one another. The machine gun
let off another clip as Adams took the curve quietly.
The pickup parked in the gravel parking lot of the
shelter was owned by none other than Ozzie Tucker.

Glancing in his rearview mirror, Adams saw
Tucker staring at the pickup as it disappeared into the
forest. "You know, Elvis, I think I'll be taking along my
pistol when we go spelunking."

Elvis yelped. He also cared little for the sound of
machine guns.

Adams drove into the forest, paralleling the river. In
about fifteen minutes he reached a sunken road once
used by oxen and their carts. Over a hundred years
ago the rutted-out road had led down to the river and
a ferry operated by one of Adams' ancestors. Adams
stopped and got down from the truck, noticing where

a dirt bike had made the leap across the sunken path and landed on the other side, causing more of the wall to collapse. Adams cursed. He hated dirt bikes.

After taking a pistol and flashlight from the cab he locked the truck, then let Elvis out, but only after muzzling the animal and strapping on a leash. The boy's odor was here and Elvis matched it to the jacket. Then off they went with Elvis straining on leash.

The most recent tracks went in and out of the woods several times, stopping at the rutted-out road. It was as if the kid didn't seem to know whether he wanted to play hide and seek or go for help. Splashes of light broke through the canopy, casting wavery shadows across the floor as a breeze moved through the trees. Here and there a rabbit broke and ran. Before Adams knew it Elvis had snuck up on four deer who, upon seeing them, bolted deeper into the woods. On the floor of the forest the humidity was thicker and Adams' long-sleeve shirt quickly became soaked with perspiration. Little noise but for the cicadas.

Elvis was pulling him in the direction of a place every boy had to explore, practically a rite of passage for kids in Chick County. White boys, that is. No black kid dared be caught inside a cave when a bunch of white boys came crawling through. The caves were where Billy Ray Chick was supposed to have hidden the gold he'd stolen during the last days of the War Between the States. And, from reading his ancestor's journals, Adams' could tell Billy Ray had been quite pleased with the heist. The wagon contained enough gold to back up six months' pay for Sherman's troops marching through Georgia.

Adams pulled a bandanna from his pocket and stopped long enough to wipe his face and neck. The dog didn't like it. He wanted to get on with business. Adams told Elvis to calm down, that he knew where they were headed and they had plenty of time to get there. Elvis' only answer was to tug on his leash. Minutes later they were along the river where the water appeared almost black and languished under the heat of a summer sun. All sorts of stories were told about these caves, the silliest being how the Creeks had used them for rituals involving kidnapped white women. The Creeks would laugh at the idea—if they could put behind them their own version of the Trail of Tears.

The cave Adams was looking for was set back about twenty feet from the river, an abrupt fifty-foot climb from the water. A wide rock made a pretty good overhang; small trees and bushes grew in dirt pockets on top of the overhang, also inside the mouth of the cave. Sand and leaves littered the place; picnickers had made fires and trash lay here and there. Adams cursed again. He and Savannah would have to come over here and clean up this mess.

The boy's dirt bike was there, parked under the overhang, as was a moped Adams recognized as belonging to Annabelle Bennefield. Hadn't Savannah told him Annabelle and Jody Chick were tight?

Elvis tugged at the leash and whined. He wanted the muzzle off. No way. Jody Chick might have his rifle along and think dogs had been turned loose on him. No reason for him to remember what day of the year it was and that all the deputies were at the Bennefield's

Fourth of July party. Adams hunched down and peered into the cave. When he did automatic weapon fire clattered behind him.

Bullets zinged overhead, ricocheting off the over-hang and thudding into the sand floor. Adams rolled across the mouth, and as he did, released the leash. Elvis took off, racing toward the rear of the cave. Crawling low on elbows and knees, Adams returned to the mouth. From his belt he pulled an army Colt .45.

Sliding down the hill on one heel instead of using the trail came Ozzie Tucker. The wiry man was twenty yards away when Adams threw a shot at him, causing his cowboy hat to fly off. Tucker yelped and leaped behind a tree.

"Damn you, Adams, now I got another reason to kill you. That was my favorite hat."

"Oh, something might change your mind?"

Tucker laughed from behind a tree. "You're right, you bastard, I was going to kill you anyway. How'd you know about me and your cousin?"

"You hang around the sheriff too much. Not everyone's that dense."

"Well, I'd rather be lucky than smart. I couldn't believe you'd fallen into my hands out here in the Dark Corner."

"There are others in this cave, Ozzie."

"Bullshit."

"I'm serious. You're going to have to kill more than one person to bury my cousin. Head on back now and I won't tell the sheriff about this until tomorrow. You'll have plenty of time to clear out."

"You won't live to see tomorrow."

"Don't know about that, Ozzie. You shot at me when I had my back turned, you killed Heywood from behind. How are you face-to-face? And can you kill a kid? Or his girlfriend?"

"What the hell you talking about?"

"Annabelle Bennefield is in here."

"The judge's daughter? Now why would she be in there?"

"Her boyfriend's here, too—Jody Chick, so why don't you leave? We don't have to come out."

"Don't worry, Adams, you'll be coming out. A round can sure bounce around inside those stone walls and I've got plenty. Sooner or later you're going to catch one. That'll make you more than anxious to show yourself."

"Ozzie, do you know how far back this cave goes?"

"About the length of a football field and plenty of low bridges. Shit, Adams, I grew up 'round here. Maybe not in a big house with a bunch of niggers waiting on me hand and foot, but I know my way around."

While chatting, Tucker had been moving around and listening to the position of Adams' voice. Now he let off a few rounds that sailed over Adams' head and ricocheted around inside the cave. One searched out Adams, biting into his side as he hugged the ground.

Shit, thought Adams. He didn't need any more complications. Speaking of complications, Savannah crawled out of the darkness. With her was Annabelle Bennefield, Jody Chick, and Elvis. The dog beamed at his discovery. Jody carried his rifle in the crook of his arms, but the girls were all arms and legs as they scrambled to the cave's mouth. A cut on Annabelle's knee stood out in sharp contrast to her pale skin. She held a flashlight.

"Savannah, what are you doing here?"

His daughter reached to touch his side. "Daddy, you're hurt."

Adams glanced at the wound. It stung as the air got to it. "Don't worry, we're not going to be here long enough to worry about it."

"Take off your shirt. I want to take a look."

"Savannah, get your butt back inside the cave. Tucker might fire again."

"Ozzie Tucker?"

"Yes."

"What's Mr. Tucker doing here? And why would he want to shoot you?"

"Because I found out he killed Jody's father."

Behind her the boy gulped. Jody tried to speak but could only sputter.

"When we got here Jody was about to kill himself," Savannah said, unbuttoning her father's shirt as Adams' lay on his side. "He figured everyone blamed him for his daddy's death."

Jody stared at the floor and said nothing. He looked like he was about to cry. Annabelle put an arm around him and pulled him close. "Now you can get on home to your mama."

Adams grimaced as Savannah wrapped the shirt around his waist and tightened it. "But that's not why you want to kill yourself, is it, Jody?" asked Adams.

"What are you talking about, Daddy?"

"I'll leave that to Jody to explain. Let me see if I can negotiate us a way out of here."

No such luck. Tucker let off another burst and he'd

changed positions again. Hmmm. They receive a lot better training in the militia than in the Klan. With bullets ricocheting around in the mouth, the girls and Elvis yelped. Jody groaned. The boy had taken one in the chest. He collapsed to the floor and the rifle fell from his hands. Both girls screamed, then hustled over to the boy.

"Ozzie, can you hear me?"

"What's your problem, Adams? You hit? Some of the others hurting—your make-believe friends?" Another laugh.

"Annabelle Bennefield is in here and you've already scared the bejesus out of her. Why don't you stop this before it gets out of hand?"

"You're bullshitting me."

"If you weren't so stupid you'd've checked the cave and seen that her moped is parked there."

"I don't think I'll be doing that. I've already seen what kind of shot you are with a handgun."

"The judge isn't going to be happy with this."

"The judge and I are quits and you know it. He sided with you at the party and Garland's set to be the next den leader. Besides, what would the Bennefield girl be doing here?"

"Trying to talk Jody Chick out of killing himself." Adams turned to the girls and lowered his voice. "Move Jody into the rear. I'll stay here and make sure Mr. Tucker doesn't fire into the mouth again."

"Daddy, Jody's coughing up blood. The bullet must've hit a lung."

Adams saw that was true. The teenager was drooling bloody fluid onto his shirt.

"Can you help her, Annabelle?"

The pale girl's mouth trembled.

"Daddy, we've got to get Jody out of here."

"Savannah, do as I ask."

"Your daddy's right," Annabelle said. "We've got to get in the back where the bullets can't hit us."

"Ricochets can follow us anywhere."

Adams stared at his daughter. How did she know all this?

Another burst of fire and everyone ducked. Elvis yelped and headed for the rear of the cave. The teenagers followed. Savannah put an arm under the wounded boy and helped him stumble into the darkness. Annabelle took along the light.

"Now you've done it, Ozzie. You've hit Annabelle."

"Shit, Adams, I was raised 'round dogs. That was your hound took one. Where'd he take it? In the ass?"

Tucker laughed, then fired a few more rounds, some zinging off the walls and biting into the sand floor. While Tucker was reloading, Adams stood up and shot in his direction.

"Damn, Adams, but you are good. Round took off the side of the tree. I think I'll keep my head down from now on."

Savannah reappeared with Jody's rifle.

"What are you doing, Savvy?"

"You need my help." She was out of breath. "I got Jody . . . settled in back there. Now, I'm going . . . to help you."

"No, you are not."

"Yes, sir, I am."

"Savannah, you are just too much like your mother."

"That's silly, Daddy. I'm too much like you."

"But I don't want you here."

"Get over it, Daddy. What do you want me to do?"

"I want you to get as far back in this cave as you can and stay there."

"Mr. Tucker isn't going to wait much longer. What's the plan?"

Adams stared at her. Jeez, kids could sure pick their moments. "You sure, Savvy? This is going to get real grown up and in a hurry."

"Daddy, I'm almost eighteen."

"Okay, let's try this. Can you push the moped down the hill and into the river if I stand between Mr. Tucker and you, so all he'll see is the moped going down the hill?"

"Daddy, that moped was given to Annabelle for her sixteenth birthday. It's very special to her."

"Savannah, answer my question or get back in the cave with the rest of the kids."

"Yes," said his daughter, frowning. "I can do it." She started to stand, but he pulled her down.

"No! Not until I call for you."

She nodded.

Adams gripped her shoulder. "And if this doesn't work, you've got to make the others move into the Outhouse."

The Outhouse was a room only kids and skinny teens could reach, by crawling under a slab of rock. The room looked like a two-holer where water had worn bowls into another slab you could sit on. You could eat the lunch you'd brought along or tell your girlfriend the batteries were dead in the flashlight and you didn't know if you'd ever get out alive.

"I'll kick Mr. Tucker in the face if he tries to crawl into the Outhouse. I've done it before."

"I don't think I want to hear about that." Adams shouted, "Ozzie, how about Annabelle shows herself, you see that it's her, and then you take off."

"That'd be just like you, Adams, hiding behind some girl's skirts."

"You don't want to see Bennefield's daughter?"

"I'm in here, Mr. Tucker," screamed Savannah, "and if you don't let me go, you'll be in real trouble with my daddy. I can promise you that. Mr. Adams and I are going to show ourselves and you'd better watch it! You've already hurt Jody Chick."

Adams stared at her. All he could get out was, "Don't forget the dog."

"Yes," shouted Savannah, "and the dog!"

"Ozzie, you going to shoot us if we show ourselves?"

No answer from outside.

"Mr. Tucker, what do you say?"

"I'm thinking about it. I'm thinking about it."

"Honey," said Adams, shaking his head, "that's a 'no.'"

For the first time fear crept into the teenager's face. "What—what do we do, Daddy?"

"Well, Pumpkin, I'm going to kill Mr. Tucker and I wish you'd get back into the rear of the cave so you don't have to see it."

"No, no, I can do this." She nodded. "I have to do this."

"Why, for God's sake?"

"Because I'm your daughter."

Adams didn't know what to say to that.

"Show yourselves, Adams, and no guns, you hear?"

"Hell, Ozzie, you've got all the firepower. All we've got in here is a pistol."

"And a .22 rifle—if Jody Chick's in there. Throw them out."

"No way."

"Thought you wanted to give yourself up. Change your mind?"

"Actually, I'd rather you come to your senses. I can toss my keys in the river. That ought to give you plenty of time to get away."

"I'm waiting, Adams."

Adams saw his daughter tremble. "How about crawling back into the rear of the cave with the others, Savvy?"

"No, no." The girl gritted her teeth. "Anyone can push a moped down a hill. There's nothing . . . there's nothing to it."

"Okay, let's do this thing." Adams got to his feet. His side hurt but the headache was gone. First time he'd noticed.

"Daddy, I don't look anything like Annabelle. My hair's the same color as yours—brown."

"Forget it. Just run the moped down the hill. I'll take care of everything else."

Savannah nodded, then shivered. Adams gave her a hug, then he picked up Jody's rifle and the two of them duckwalked to the mouth of the cave.

"Remember, Savvy, wait until I'm blocking Mr. Tucker's view."

"Yes—yes, sir."

"Ozzie, I'm going to throw out the rifle in a gesture of good faith."

"I don't give a shit about any gestures. Just get the girl out here where I can see her."

"I'm coming out first, Ozzie. Right after this rifle." He tossed the .22 to a point where it slid, butt first, down the hill toward the river. He just might need that thing, and down the hill he would go, making Ozzie Tucker concentrate more on who was leaving than who'd been left inside. "Hold your fire."

"I'm waiting, Adams."

Adams jammed the pistol into his jeans, then raised his hands. "I'm coming out, Ozzie, so don't get trigger-happy." Adams moved into the mouth of the cave, in a low voice said, "Your turn, Pumpkin."

Something scuffled in the sand behind him, then he heard the sound of the kickstand being put up. Tires crunched on the sandy floor. Ten yards away Tucker stepped out from behind a pine tree almost a foot in circumference. The M-16 was pointed in Adams' direction and Adams had no doubt it was on automatic.

"I don't see no girl, Adams."

"She's scared, Ozzie, but she's coming."

"Ready, Daddy," said his daughter.

"Well, do it!" he snapped, glancing over his shoulder.

When Adams looked again, Tucker was bringing up his rifle. Adams' hand went to his belt, and at the same time the moped flew out over the hill and down the embankment. Tucker's rifle followed it.

"Get back inside, Savannah! Now!"

Tucker cut loose at the moped as the machine crashed through the underbrush, then realized it was the wrong play. The barrel of the automatic weapon swung back to the mouth of the cave and opened up.

Most folks use a two-handed grip and spread their feet to steady themselves, but Adams was a snap shooter. Concentrating on a target almost guarantees he'll miss. Adams jerked the pistol out of his jeans and threw a shot at Tucker, then hit the ground. Looking up, he saw his daughter standing in the mouth and staring in the direction of the automatic rifle's fire.

Chapter Sixteen

A week later Nell and Wheeler were sitting on the veranda of the Big House, watching the sun go down. A light flashed off in the distance. A thunderstorm moving in from the direction of Lee's Crossroads. At the site of the former church, the remains of the burned-out building had been shoved to one side by Mac Thrower and his boys and a new foundation laid. Even Jimmy Carter and Rosalynn showed up for the groundbreaking. This time the church would be built of brick and a sprinkler system installed; next week the congregation would raise the walls. Then more members could become involved, if they could find a place to work. White people were coming out of the woodwork to prove Chick County wasn't a hotbed of racism as it had been portrayed by the news media. Something Judge Bennefield and the county commissioners took great pains to explain at a hastily called press conference.

But before the news conference could begin the commissioners realized they had no colored folks on the dais. A call went out to Edward Nance for the good doctor to hustle down to City Hall. Nance said he'd be there, but first he had to go by and pay a traffic fine. The judge said not to worry about it, just get down there and fast. He'd fix the ticket.

At the press conference an auburn-haired reporter from Atlanta stood up and asked, "Does this mean something is going to be done about the Creekside sewer line that runs at full or near capacity even in dry weather?"

Bennefield tried to cut off the woman but to no avail.

"I've heard, Your Honor, that manhole covers pop like fireworks during heavy rainstorms."

Bennefield said he was looking into that, but this press conference was to answer questions about the church burning—under investigation by both the Georgia Bureau of Investigation and the FBI.

"We are here to tell you that Bibles and hymnals have been sent from Billy Graham Ministries, Georgia-Pacific will supply all the wood for the new church, and Home Depot is donating any tools and fasteners needed. As we meet today," added the judge, "the largest brick manufacturer in the Southeast has a truck on the road heading for Lee's Crossroads. And tomorrow the congregation will join the members of the First Baptist Church for services."

The white preacher on the dais nodded vigorously.

He'd been upset when no one from the Shiloh congregation had shown up at his church the morning after the fire. Figuring they were too scared to come without encouragement, he'd gone into Creekside—something his wife said he was damn crazy to do, especially the day after those people's church had been burned down. The white preacher soon learned it wasn't only the burned-out church they had on their mind. Many had seen their preacher shot down in cold blood.

After that, the preachers of all the white churches got together and agreed a different church would take in the Shiloh congregation each Sunday until their own church was rebuilt. This was done to the grumbles of a few, mostly folks who didn't regularly attend services. As it turned out, the Shiloh choir elevated the quality of the singing in those white congregations.

Gary Plummer was one of the hardest working and most devoted to the rebuilding. No one had arrested him, but Gary said he planned to turn himself in once the church was rebuilt. And he'd turn himself in to the church elders, not to the sheriff or the GBI. He figured there might be more a young man could do for the church by being on the payroll of a major league ball club. Gary was talking of following in the footsteps of Charley Morton, too. If other athletes could play ball and preach, why not him?

The proceeds from the sale of Lelia Plummer's house were passed along to the congregation over the objections of several members of the Plummer family. Edward Nance had to be called in to mediate, and he said it got pretty ugly until Gary took the floor and asked: What do you think Maw-Maw would want done with this money? After the funeral most of those relatives dropped out of sight, but only after being asked to sign a release—and break a sweat in the raising of the new church.

At the conclusion of the press conference, Rose Mary Bingham returned to the city, but her daughter stayed behind—at the bedside of Jody Chick. Jody had already confessed to his mom what he'd done and she'd told him he'd have to turn himself in. His father agreed. Unfortunately, that particular conversation had been overheard by Ozzie Tucker. Outraged at Heywood's advice to his son, Tucker followed Heywood home, where he tried to convince the Klan leader of the wonderful thing his son had done. Then seeing he was getting nowhere, Tucker had pulled out a pistol and shot Heywood in the back of the head.

The shot woke up Jody, who, upon finding his father dead, fled on his dirt bike and hid out in the caves along the river. Later he slipped out to the highway and called Annabelle from a pay phone. Annabelle promised to meet him but said she couldn't get away until later. Annabelle was miffed at having to miss the party, but Savannah said they'd best go check on Jody.

Upon regaining consciousness in the hospital, Jody begged them to let him die, but the girls would have none of that. They sang and danced and read to the boy and prodded Jody to stay with them. Slowly but surely Jody came around. Now only one stone remained unturned—if you already knew that Lizzie Bennefield had set fire to her carport in hopes of acquiring a new house. The last Adams heard, the sheriff was still looking for the arsonist.

From deep in her rocker, covered with a quilt despite the warm July night, Nell said, "I jest don't understand why Charley Morton would make that deputy kill him. Shoot him down in cold blood like that. It don't make no sense." Nell's skin had an ashen look to it and when she spoke her voice was hoarse. "Wheeler, why you think he'd act that way?"

"I don't think it was the first time Charley had contemplated suicide."

Nell looked at him hard. "What you mean, boy?"

"I think the bullet that lodged in the Hampton's house across the street might've been the first try."

"It's hard to believe . . . a preacher? Why, it goes against everything in the Good Book."

"Charley had Dean Meckler change the beneficiary of his life insurance the week after he was locked up in the Chick County jail. Charley figured he'd end up there again."

"The church is gonna collect on the preacher's insurance then?"

"Yes, ma'am, it is."

Nell stared into the darkness. Even Thomas Traylor and his brother had gone home for the day, but not before the brother had asked Adams if he could have forty acres of his own to farm.

"I think I've got the hang of this thing, Wheeler," said the young black man with a grin. "I'm ready to give it a try."

"No reason to return to Detroit?"

"Nah. I didn't lose anything up there."

"You know the rules?"

"Yes, sir, I do. One fourth of the land has to be planted in rotation so the soil will be ready for the next time 'round; I can't plant any tobacco"—the black man grinned—" and I'm to complain to high heaven about the shares to anyone who'll listen."

"You got any particular place picked out?"

"If you don't mind, I think I'd like the parcel next to my brother so he and I can work together. We've got our eye on a used tractor down in King County." He grinned. "You know, Wheeler, one day I might make a pretty good farmer."

"James Oglethorpe said the soil in Georgia was so rich you didn't even have to add manure."

Traylor's brother had laughed. "Well, if we had more of that talk we shore wouldn't need much manure."

"Wheeler," asked Nell, as she watched the approaching storm, "why wouldn't our insurance pay for the fire? The church had insurance, didn't it?"

"Charley let it lapse." The Shiloh church, hard up even in good times, had been hit even harder by Dean Meckler's embezzling, and its preacher had been unwilling to take another handout from the local squire. Worse, Charley knew his alcoholism had split the congregation, limiting donations.

"The devil had that man by the throat, didn't he?"

Adams could only sit and watch Nell suffer. Nell believed in monsters who could leap out of the darkness, seize your life, and never turn loose. Why shouldn't she? She was a black woman, and Adams hadn't met too many of those with smiles on their faces.

Nell waved at a bug. "I don'ts know what they means 'bout cold weather 'posed to kill all these bugs. We had a rough winter last year and still them bugs is out."

They sat there watching the thunderstorm approach the Springs. After a while, Nell said, "Wheeler, I'm thinking of moving down to King County. It'd be for jest awhile."

Adams looked at her, but the old woman continued to stare over the turnaround and into the darkness.

"Kate Grant wants me to come down and bring Aurelia and Rebekah. I don'ts think anybody will miss us."

"Perhaps I will."

"Aw, Wheeler, you knows you've been wanting to git rid of me for the longest."

"And since I couldn't, you're lending me a hand."

Canting around in her chair, she said, "I'll tell you one thing, boy, you'd better watch your tongue 'round folks, especially that daughter of yours. Savannah's gitting to be too much like you."

Now it was Adams' turn to look off in the distance, remembering what his daughter had said after he'd pulled her down beside him in the cave during the shoot-out.

"Everyone says what a good shot you are, Daddy, but I've never even seen you shoot. I just had to see."

A quick look at the remains of Ozzie Tucker's skull on their way out of the woods and Savannah was puking her guts out. Her father had held her around the waist so she could lean forward and not mess on her new running shoes.

*March 17, 1868—After the Yankee Woman
finished her first year with us she came to
me in the study without Mrs. C. present. And
the Woman shut the door behind her. She
appeared nervous & addressed me by my
former military title, something I don't care
for but appears to be important to women,
children & those who did not go off to War.
Miss S. did not sit down but stood in front of
my desk. She said she wanted to ask a
favor, and after glancing at the door, she
said she would like our conversation to be in
strictest Confidence.*

*I did not know what to make of this.
Before the War, no Single Woman would be
alone with a Man, but Public Morals have
broken down considerably with the Federal
Army responsible for Law & Order in
Georgia. Trying to regain control of the situation, I asked what was the problem. When
she said it was a personal problem, I about
bolted from the room. Then she confirmed
my worst suspicions by telling me it was a
family problem.*

*I had heard enough. I asked Miss S. if she
would please ask Mrs. C. to step in here
with us. The Woman flushed & said she
would prefer to keep This between us until I
had come to a decision. I remember clearing
my throat & it seemed to take a very long
time to do so. I asked her what decision she
was referring to & Miss. S. reminded me she
had told me, upon her posting here at the*

Sprgs., that she had no family but for a married sister. I think I remember that, but, as I have mentioned before, I am having trouble with my memory. That makes a journal that much more important.

The crux of Miss S.'s dilemma was she had received a letter informing her that her sister & her sister's husband had been killed in a trolley car accident last month in Boston. I returned to my seat, having to remember exactly what a trolley car was. I told Miss S. I was sorry to hear of her loss & assumed she would be returning North. The woman shook her head & stared at the floor. She had no money for such Frivolities. And unfortunately her brother-in-law had left several unpaid bills & collectors were already pestering her mother. She looked up from the floor & said she was at my mercy. She said that is why she had come to see me in Confidence, to ask a Favor for her nephew's sake.

Miss S. said the boy had no one with which to live & he could not live with Miss Sherwood's parents. They were much too old & her father's memory was worse than mine. He did not even remember his wife. He is quite addled, added the Woman. Miss S. stepped closer to my desk & said that her mother knew of her situation at Chick Sprgs. & wished the boy to have a fresh start & not be remembered as the son of a debtor.

As I had told my friends, the Yankees

cannot stay forever. Sooner or later, they must return home. But that was not to be. This woman had another proposition. She said we had had our Differences in the Past & we certainly came from different Ways of Life, but she would not like to leave the South with her Work undone. She said that was why she had brought her Proposition to me. After all, as General Pope had pointed out, I was an Honorable Man.

I told Miss S. if she needed money to return home, that I would be willing to advance her a sum without interest— because I would be happy to see her go. To tell the truth, I did not know what to think of this woman. We had many Disagreements & it went without saying she was not the example I preferred have set for my daugh- ters with her outspokenness & strange ideas. Still, I had to admit she was quite intelligent for a woman & worked like the Devil & had warmed, somewhat, to our Way of Life. Her proposal was to send for her nephew to live with us so that he might have a Proper Education. This way, Miss S. could continue her work & the Springs would have an extra set of hands.

"My nephew is the same age as your Billy & from what I have been told, he stands almost six feet tall & spends his mornings shoveling coal at a Notions Store before the Owner arrives. That is how he earns his

Keep, Col. Chick. He must be quite
Trustworthy to be given a key to the store &
I believe he could learn a great deal from a
Gentleman such as yourself."

Billy Ray Chick was a Gentleman? I, a
man who worked from dawn to dusk—with
his hands!—was a gentleman? No. The days
of the Cavalier dashing around Georgia were
gone forever.

"If you decide against my Proposal, Sir,"
went on the woman, "would you be so kind
as to tell me in confidence." And then she
thanked me & started for the door.

I was so stunned, I did not know how to
conclude our Discussion. And the Woman
was leaving without being dismissed. "Er—
what is the boy's name?" It was all I could
think to ask.

At the door, the Woman turned and faced
Me. "His name is John, Colonel, but we call-
him 'Johnny.' Johnny Adams."

Introducing

the Prequel to Black Fire

BLACK FUNK

Chapter One

In the South

In the South it's considered impolite to talk about murder before breakfast, but that's just what the young lady wanted to do, and she found someone with a similar interest working in the garden behind the Big House.

The Big House is a fifteen thousand square foot antebellum monster situated on a low hill in the middle of ten thousand acres along the river. When Wheeler Adams returned to Chick Springs, he thought he'd put all those years living in Atlanta behind him, but sometimes the city searches you out, even raises its dead.

A mist hovered near the ground when the young woman came out of the Big House, actually the mud room, then down the steps to cross a gravel area between the house and a garden. To the woman's right was a pickup in front of a new barn and the smokehouse that had been there since before the Civil War. Beyond the garden were a couple of Yuppie log homes, then acres and acres of untilled land until you reached a tree line as you approached the river.

Anna Graham Sanders had coal black hair to her shoulders, a puffiness in her face, as if she'd been crying, and on her petite frame, a yellow sundress looking as if it'd been slept in. Good shoulders—white shoulders—nice breasts, and long, slender legs. Green eyes, lips a little larger than should go with such a narrow face, and a pallidness having nothing to do with anyone's emotional temperament.

Working in the garden was an elderly black man and a white man about to become middle-aged. Sanders made straight for the white man. In her hands was a mug of coffee and a bottle of Coca-Cola. Wheeler Adams was well over six feet, tanned, with brown hair and eyes. Still, there was plenty of muscle on his lean frame. His jeans and tee shirt were wet with sweat though the sun was hardly up.

Adams didn't remember her. Sanders could see that in his face. He was staring at her, trying to place her, then Sanders realized that was all wrong. The hoe fell from Adams' hand, thumping to the ground after bouncing off a stalk of corn. Now the black man was at Adams' side, gripping the white man's arm.

"Mister Wheeler—you all right?" The old black man wore overalls and a Braves baseball cap.

Sanders didn't know what to do, didn't know what to say. She had no idea she'd have such an effect. How could she have such an effect? The last time she'd seen Wheeler . . . she didn't remember and she had certainly been a child.

Sanders cleared her throat. "Wheeler, I'm Anna Graham Sanders."

"Megan's . . . kid sister."

She extended the hand with the Coca-Cola in it. "After all these years I'm surprised you remembered."

Adams shook loose of the old man and took the bottle of Coke. "I remember."

Sanders gestured at the garden: a full acre and watered by sprinklers. "Can you take a minute from your work?" When Adams continued to stare at her, Sanders gestured at the house. "Nell said it wasn't too early for you and Roosevelt to take a break." She smiled. "A short one, that is." Nell Douglass was Adams' housekeeper, a small black woman who ruled Chick Springs with an iron hand and very little velvet glove.

"Mister Wheeler," said the elderly black man, "it's okay."

Adams looked at him as if seeing the Chick Springs gardener for the first time.

Roosevelt smiled. "These weeds—they ain't going nowhere."

"Thank you, Roosevelt. I'll be on the veranda if you need me."

"Yessuh."

The veranda had six white columns, a long row of rocking chairs, and overlooked a gravel turnaround. A dirt road led through two rows of cedars to the county highway. Sanders took a seat in one of the chairs and patted down her sundress. Adams took another, swinging the rocker around to face her, a third rocker in-between. With a bandanna from his back pocket, he went to work on his arms, neck, and face, especially his face.

"It's been a long time, Anna Graham. I see you grew up to be a fine-looking young lady."

"Thank you, Wheeler. I really didn't think you'd remember. I doubt I've seen you more than twice since my family's troubles."

The troubles Sanders spoke of included her father blowing his brains out after being caught embezzling from the Georgia Railroad Bank; her brother, Troy, wrapping his fancy sports car and himself around a telephone pole on Peachtree Street; and only last month, sister Megan dying in a murder-suicide in King County.

Sanders looked over the north forty or so acres, little more than scrub pine and weeds with kudzu moving in. Kudzu takes over when you don't do your planting: cotton, beans, corn, whatever, and there wasn't much planting or planning being done around Chick Springs. That smacked too much of city life.

"I heard you were living out here. That you'd—"

"Retired."

Another nervous smile. "I guess 'retired's' as good a word as any, even for someone your age." She sat up. "I'm in the advertising business now, Wheeler, Pepper Martin's Agency, and we advertising people— the flaky ones for sure—hang around the Warehouse Theater and that's where I ran into Rose Mary. Rose saw me moping around and tried to cheer me up. When that didn't work, she brought me out here. I slept in the guest room. I hope that's okay. Rose Mary told me how territorial you can be about the Springs."

"Well," said Adams, forcing a smile of his own, "you're certainly up early for someone visiting the Springs."

"Didn't get much sleep last night. Don't know the last time I did."

"What's the problem?"

"Not my problem. Megan's."

"Megan's?"

"And if I don't do something about it, I think I'll go crazy. You heard how they found her in King County?"

"Yes—I'm sorry I didn't make the funeral. I was out of town." Hiding out at the Springs is what his wife had said.

Sanders waved off the apology. "It was a small service." The young woman leaned forward, coal black hair falling down around her pallid face and green eyes. The gesture caused Adams to shudder, striking a nerve from some long ago past.

"Pardon me for saying this, Wheeler, but Megan wouldn't be caught dead with someone as trashy as that Grady Candler." Meaning he wasn't one of the Coca-Cola Candlers.

After clearing his throat, Adams was able to get out, "If I remember correctly the papers said Candler picked her up after the races down at Riverside, that she'd been seen down there often."

"But it's not right. Megan wouldn't've done such a thing."

"Anna Graham, are you saying Megan was found dead with some man she didn't know? Then why in the world would he kill her?"

"I know, I know, and that's what keeps me up nights. I don't think I slept two hours and it wasn't because of the accommodations. Rose Mary made me feel right at home."

"What did the King County sheriff say?"

"Murder-suicide. Lovers' quarrel. Just because I couldn't see my sister running with someone as ordinary as Candler wasn't reason enough to reopen the case. Besides, King County's all black, and he's a black sheriff. Why should he get all worked up over a couple of white people dying? Nobody gets all that excited about black couples found in similar circumstances in Atlanta. But I can't let it go, Wheeler. I owe Megan for everything I've accomplished. You remember how my father . . . died?"

Adams nodded.

"At the time I really didn't understand what was happening. Only later did I realize it was our family that had lost our home. We were the ones who had to move in with those two old maid aunts. But, still, compared to Megan's life, mine's been a piece of cake. After Mama died Megan took me away from those hateful aunts, put me through school, and then got me my start in business. So there I am in my new corner office and I can't tell her all her sacrifices paid off. Megan attended all my PTA meetings, made sure I kept my grades up, piano lessons, too. When Pepper promoted me to vice-president Megan was out of town—a meeting at the home office—then we misconnected after she returned, playing telephone tag, and the next thing I know the King County sheriff's calling, saying my sister's been killed. Murdered, for God's sake, in a cabin out behind some honky-tonk. I couldn't believe it. Not my sister. Not Megan." She let out a long sigh as she leaned back in her rocker. "So now I've got a reputation as a comer and my sister's buried in Oakland, and the name she made for herself has been buried with her. People no longer think of Megan as that hotshot store manager who worked her way up from counter sales, but some floozy who slept her way to the top."

"Anna Graham, I don't think . . . ."

The woman looked at him hard. "Wheeler, I don't know who killed her, whether it was this Candler fellow or not, but whoever it was stole what Megan worked so hard for: her reputation. Where we used to live, who my family was before my father's death, who our friends were—I don't know anything about all that. I was a baby when my father died. But I can tell you this, if Megan were alive today, she'd be doing something about the way people are talking about her."

About the Author

Steve Brown was born and raised in the South and believes he has a pretty good take on those living there, black or white. Steve hopes he has been diligent in his portrayal of the complexity of personal relationships in the modern South. You can contact Steve through www.ChickSprings.com.